Slow Death
in the
Fast Lane

A Brendan O'Brian Legal Thriller

J.W. Kerwin

"The two enemies of the people are criminals and government, so let us tie the second down with the chains of the Constitution so the second will not become the legalized version of the first."

– Thomas Jefferson

ISBN: 1494305372
ISBN 13: 9781494305376

1

"I'd sure wanna know."

I'll probably never know when my wife stopped loving me, but I'll always remember the day I discovered she wanted me dead.

It was an unusually warm Tuesday in November, a day that felt more like a harbinger of spring than the last gasp of autumn. I had spent the morning reviewing the file for *United States v. Berkowitz*, the criminal trial that was my main focus at the moment. My client, Harvey Berkowitz, was facing a three-count indictment for criminal tax fraud. The government was using a prosecutorial rifle rather than a shotgun, concentrating on three recent and well-documented examples of Harvey's creative accounting while ignoring the hundreds of less obvious irregularities he was guilty of over the years.

The government had solid evidence for the first two counts, making this one of those seemingly "unwinnable" cases that I've built a reputation for somehow managing to win. Harvey's "ultimate chutzpah" tax deduction, which was the subject of the third count of the indictment, was another matter. Uncle Sam had solid evidence for that one as well, but the government's case hinged on whose version of events the jury believed.

When midday rolled around, I munched on a tuna sandwich while looking out the window at my restored 1965

Mustang in the parking lot. I do some of my best thinking staring at my pony car, which looks as good as the day it rolled off the assembly line twenty-three years ago. Actually, I do some of my best thinking staring at cute girls in short skirts looking at my car, but none were available at the moment, so the car itself would have to suffice.

"Brendan." I turned to find Carolyn, my secretary, poking her head around my partially opened office door. "I know you didn't want to be disturbed, but Mr. Rizzo is in the waiting room, insisting he needs to see you right away. He says it's urgent."

Eddie Rizzo is commonly known as Eddie the Skunk, supposedly because of the white streak that bisects his otherwise jet black hair. Having spent countless hours sitting next to him in a courtroom, I tend to think it may have more to do with personal hygiene than hair color. Yet despite his olfactory assaults, Eddie was a good client. He always made it a point to thank me effusively for what I did for him, and he never quibbled about fees. That's more than I can say for some of the country club clients my partners bring in. Although I don't usually see people without an appointment, I made an exception for Eddie. He's the kind of guy you didn't say "no" to. And besides, there was a good chance this visit would result in more business from him or one of his associates.

I first represented Eddie two years ago in a hit and run accident that I suspected was heavy on the "hit" and light on the "accident." My suspicion was based, at least in part, on Eddie's offhand comment that "the best defense is a good offense" and his insistence that the victim "got what he deserved" for hiring someone to mess with one of Eddie's associates. I won an acquittal, thanks to a prosecution witness who fell apart on cross-examination.

My second encounter with Eddie involved another hit and run, and that one I'm sure was no accident. The State of

New Jersey had a better case that time, but I still managed to secure a not guilty verdict, in the process convincing my client that I was, to use his words, "the best damn lawyer in New Jersey."

Eddie's most recent involvement with the law was the result of a fight in a drinking establishment known for its colorful clientele. Eddie's opponent ended up in the emergency room with a broken nose, and Eddie ended up in the county jail awaiting arraignment on a charge of battery. During our first meeting after his arrest, Eddie was extremely agitated, drumming his fingers on the conference room table. "Make this go away fast and I'll owe you one," he said. I discovered later that he had an upcoming "business deal" that couldn't be conducted from behind bars, making even a short stay as a guest of the State of New Jersey problematic.

As it turned out, the victim, whose reputation with the local constabulary was no better than Eddie's, picked a fight with the wrong guy the day after Eddie's arrest and ended up in the morgue instead of on the witness stand. I pointed out to the prosecutor assigned to the case (who owed me a favor) that he no longer had his prime witness, but what he did have was a heavy caseload that could be instantly reduced by dropping the case against my client. He agreed, but only after informing me that I owed him one. The legal system, as you may have gathered, is based on everyone owing someone a favor. This doesn't necessarily result in justice being done, but it does expedite whatever justice we manage to achieve.

Eddie was delighted that the battery charge had disappeared, and so on the Tuesday afternoon in question he sat across from me at my desk, dressed in his customary jeans and white polo shirt, and with a thick gold chain draped around his neck. He leaned back, put his arms over the back of the chair and delivered the favor he said he owed me.

"Someone I know knows someone who says his buddy heard that some guy got a contract to have you whacked." It took me a few seconds to unravel Eddie's syntactic Gordian knot and realize I was receiving something less than firsthand information. He apparently interpreted the ensuing silence as a lack of interest because he asked, "Don't you wanna know who put the contract out on you? I mean, if it was me, I'd sure wanna know." Before I could answer, Eddie supplied the identity of the alleged contractor. "Your old lady," he said. "I don't know what you done to piss her off, but she wants you dead."

"D-E-A-D," he added for emphasis, displaying what I suspect is the full range of his spelling abilities.

2

"Time to play ringmaster."

Because of Eddie the Skunk's revelation, dinner that evening could have been a bit stressful if, in fact, it had actually taken place. But as is frequently the case in the O'Brian household, Aimee was off at a meeting of the local Art Alliance, an organization that apparently exists to badger rich people for money so "starving artists" can spend other people's money instead of making their own.

So in lieu of an actual meal, I made myself a tuna sandwich, poured a generous glass of Jameson's, and settled into my favorite chair by the fireplace in the living room. After finishing his dinner on the back porch, Buddy the cat joined me, landing on my outstretched legs in one graceful leap.

Buddy was mine, to the extent a cat can be said to belong to anyone, before I married Aimee. He showed up outside my bedroom window one rainy night while I was in law school. Wet and bedraggled, and looking as though he hadn't eaten in a week, he silently sat by the window looking in until I felt guilty enough to open the window and let him jump inside. It was supposed to be a temporary stay, just long enough for him to dry off, but he's been with me ever since, an affable companion who in recent years provides more affection than Aimee. Buddy and Aimee took an instant dislike to each other. Aimee hates the cat with a passion, supposedly because he peed on her coat. The cat refuses to say why he hates Aimee.

I waited while Buddy did his airplane-circling-to-land routine, which concluded with him curled up on my stomach, his paws kneading my chest and his purring machine in full throttle. Then I opened the Berkowitz file.

My client, Harvey Berkowitz, the owner of an auto salvage yard, half a dozen small businesses, and more real estate than he can keep track of, was both a sinner and a saint. He played fast and loose with the tax laws every chance he got, yet despite his creative accounting, paid more than his fair share to the government. He donated huge sums to charity, lavished his family with love, and was kind even to people who didn't deserve his kindness. He would never be my best friend, but it was impossible to dislike him.

Harvey's creative accounting had grown more brazen over the years. I suspect it had become a game with him, a battle of wits between him and the organization he referred to as the Infernal Revenue Service to see just how much he could get away with. One of his more outlandish tax deductions, which I termed "the ultimate chutzpah" when I first learned about it, caught the attention of the IRS Criminal Investigation Division, which promptly arranged for Harvey to be charged with criminal, not civil, tax fraud, putting both his freedom and his bank account in jeopardy.

When Criminal Investigation agents get you in their crosshairs, you've got a really big problem. The Criminal Investigation Division or CID is more ruthless than the CIA. They may not kill you, but by the time they're finished, you might very well wish they had. CI agents investigate thousands of ordinary taxpayers every year, getting indictments in ninety-nine percent of those cases. Uncle Sam wins over ninety percent of the resulting trials, extracting fines, penalties, and interest that are often triple the amount of tax owed, and sending otherwise upstanding citizens to prison for a longer period than that typically served by the perpetrator of a violent crime.

Harvey Berkowitz was facing a formidable opponent with resources we couldn't hope to match. Criminal Investigation agents can interview, threaten, intimidate, and browbeat everyone from your boss to your brother-in-law to get the evidence needed to put you in prison. They're assisted by a small army of analysts, forensic accountants, and other specialists. The Department of Justice or DOJ, which prosecutes cases of tax fraud, has an even bigger army backing up its attorneys. In addition to almost unlimited resources, the IRS and DOJ both have a win-at-all-costs mentality that makes them dangerous to anyone they target.

Assuming the case was an easy win, the Feds assigned a newly hired attorney named Lionel Newton to prosecute Mr. Berkowitz, hoping to boost the newcomer's confidence with an early victory.

Government attorneys come in three varieties. The first are the Ivy League wunderkinds like Mr. Newton. These people invariably think that having a law degree from a prestigious school makes them the smartest person in the room. Some of them are, but most aren't. Lionel Newton was a definite "aren't." The first time I met the inestimable Mr. Newton he informed me that his name wasn't "Lionel Newton," it was "Lionel Newton the third." Apparently there were two previous versions of Mr. Newton, both of whom graduated from the same Ivy League law school and both of whom were no doubt as pompous as the current incarnation.

The second type of government attorney is someone whose family is politically connected. It doesn't matter what law school they attended since stuffing a sufficient amount of money in the right politician's campaign coffers can overcome even the most pedestrian pedigree.

In recent years a third type of government attorney has become all the rage. If you're a black, handicapped, Spanish-speaking, transgender lesbian whose family came to this country illegally, you're an automatic hire as far as Uncle Sam is concerned, even if your pet has a higher IQ than you do.

The judge assigned to the Berkowitz case was Shelly Abrams, who didn't graduate from an Ivy League law school, wasn't politically connected, and may or may not have been a lesbian, but who, to the best of my knowledge, had neither a handicap nor parents who came to the country illegally. What she did have was a solid record as a former federal prosecutor and a reputation for unpredictability, allowing defense attorneys far more latitude than many judges, only to shut them down unexpectedly. As one of my colleagues who had appeared before her many times put it, "You never know where you stand with her until it's too late." The biggest obstacle to successfully implementing my trial strategy would be to gauge just how far I could push her.

Judge Abrams had overseen jury selection with an iron fist, repeatedly blocking my attempts to help prospective jurors understand why the only logical outcome to the case was a not guilty verdict. After innumerable skirmishes, I gave up and announced that any of the prospective jurors would be acceptable to the defense since it was obvious the government had no legitimate case against Mr. Berkowitz. It was a risky move, but as I later explained to my client, it was consistent with my overall strategy. We eventually seated a jury of twelve people who would be called upon to decide if Harvey should spend years in a federal penitentiary for violating a law they couldn't begin to comprehend.

I must have dozed off while reviewing the Berkowitz file because the next thing I knew it was morning and Buddy was nudging my chin like a good little alarm cat. "Time to play ringmaster," I said to Buddy as he jumped off my lap and headed for his food dish on the back porch by the kitchen.

3

"What he said is crap."

The following morning, Harvey Berkowitz and I were back in federal district court in Newark, New Jersey, a once great city that had long since fallen on hard times. For reasons that have everything to do with politics, federal courts always seem to be located in the most undesirable part of the most undesirable cities. Nobody in his right mind goes to Newark, Trenton or Camden if he doesn't have to. Yet that's exactly where the federal courts in New Jersey are located. I guess the politicians realize that without the economic boost the courts provide, those cities would be even more wretched than they are.

The morning's proceedings began with the newbie attorney introducing himself to the jury as "Lionel Newton the third," immediately alienating jurors whose social standing didn't grant them use of a number after their name. Then, failing to heed Shakespeare's admonition that brevity is the soul of wit, the enumerated Mr. Newton delivered a long-winded opening statement packed with mind-numbing references to the Tax Code. As frequently happens in those situations, my mind began to wander.

I thought about how Aimee and I had met. We were both students at a small, but prestigious New England college. She was there because every member of her family, going back more generations than anyone could remember, had gone to that college. I was there because that was the school that gave me the biggest scholarship. Aimee had money and a family history that traced back to colonial times. I had brains and a family whose most prominent member was arrested for making homemade gin during Prohibition.

Aimee and I were part of an outdoor team building exercise that consisted of a bunch of suburban kids making their way home from the middle of nowhere. Ten of us were dropped off in a forest with one map, one compass, and ten bottles of water. We were apparently supposed to share the map and the compass, but not the water. As it turned out, nobody shared anything. While everyone in the group knew how to drink water, I was the only one who knew how to use a map and a compass. As a former Boy Scout, I was also the only one who could tell poison ivy from a harmless plant or how to spot a ground hornet nest before someone stepped on it. Consequently, I became group leader, keeper of the compass, head navigator and Aimee's personal savior from all the evils of the great outdoors. We began dating when we got back to campus, and the rest, as they say, is history.

"Would you care to make your opening statement, Mr. O'Brian?" Judge Abram's question snapped me out of my daydream, and I stood to face the jury.

"What he said," I began, facing the jury and pointing to Lionel Newton, "is crap." Then I sat down and pretended to study my notes, sneaking a peek to see the reactions my statement had generated.

Most of the jurors seemed amused, with two or three openly laughing. The fledgling prosecutor looked mad as hell. And Judge Abrams, initially stunned into silence, finally banged her gavel and ordered "in my chambers," adding "right now" to make it clear she was somewhat less than pleased with my truncated opening statement.

"Are you out of your mind, Brendan?" Harvey whispered as I gathered my notes and headed for the judge's chambers.

"Absolutely," I replied. "That's why you hired me."

My client didn't realize he had just won the opening round in what was destined to become a convoluted war with the government.

4

"I love circuses."

The sign outside our office reads: Santorini, Woodson, Glickman & O'Brian, Attorneys at Law. As the last name on the list, I'm the low man on the seniority totem pole, but that's okay with me because I make good money. I can't spend seniority, but I can spend money, or to be more precise, Aimee can spend money. The reason I make as much as I do is because I put in long hours helping paragons of virtue like Harvey Berkowitz and Eddie the Skunk escape the grasping tentacles of the law.

Our four-man shop is a general practice firm that does pretty much everything from bankruptcies to real estate closings. Because of his political connections, Rick Santorini, who founded the firm in the 1950s, handled the lion's share of land use matters in my hometown of Troy Forge where our office is located. Like many of the towns in northern New Jersey, Troy Forge underwent a transition from rural to suburban starting in the early 1960s, providing an endless supply of lucrative work for guys like Rick who knew how to expedite the necessary development approvals, often in ways that weren't completely by the book. Rick used to say the secret was to know which local officials were straight shooters and which ones weren't. He never really explained what he meant by that, and I never asked.

As Troy Forge became more suburbanized and the last big parcels of open land were developed into shopping centers, office parks, and condominiums, Rick's land use work dropped from a torrent to a trickle. At about the same time, his memory began its sad, slow decline. These days he doesn't usually do much more than make a ceremonial appearance at client meetings and sign documents prepared by Carol, his secretary (or paralegal, as she insists on being called). Carol claims Rick is suffering from Alzheimer's. The rest of us think it's plain old-fashioned senility. Whatever the cause of Rick's problem, the man who hired me, and who I quickly came to consider a friend and mentor, is slowly slipping away, and I miss him. There are moments when the Rick Santorini of old reappears, but those instances are growing fewer and disappearing faster.

Scott Woodson, Rick's first partner, handles bankruptcies and divorce work, a logical combination since an expensive divorce frequently leads to bankruptcy. I've often thought we should offer clients a package deal, something like: "pay full price for the divorce, get the bankruptcy at 50% off." I think that would be a snappy slogan, but Scott doesn't seem to agree with me.

About a year ago, Scott assumed the position of the firm's managing partner. We never took a vote; it just happened. But if we had voted, Scott would have won because he was the logical choice. In addition to being Rick's original partner, he was the sort of reliable, serious minded guy you wanted at the helm. I often thought that if Scott had lived a century earlier, he would have made the perfect Old West sheriff. He not only had the demeanor, he had the look, right down to the chiseled features, graying hair, and leathery skin from too much time spent in the sun.

Avery Glickman, the third member of our firm, is a different type of serious. Avery's the kind of guy whose smile is more like a grimace, as though the mere thought of anything funny is painful. He's a good, though unimaginative attorney, but a great businessman. Avery has never set foot in a courtroom, but he's a whiz with things like contracts and business deals. He can be a nitpicking pain in the ass, but the financial success we've enjoyed is due in large part to his attention to detail.

Scott makes the occasional appearance in Superior Court, at bankruptcy proceedings, and before zoning boards and planning boards, but he and Avery spend most of their time in the office. I, on the other hand, spend virtually all of my time in one court or another. We make it a point to meet at least once a week to update each other on open matters, conduct firm business, and figure out more efficient ways to separate our clients from their money.

"I understand you turned today's federal court proceedings into a circus," Scott said, opening the meeting from his seat at the head of the conference table.

"I love the circus," Rick said from his seat in the corner of the room. Rick used to chair these meetings, but these days he's usually more of an observer than a participant. He's still a partner, but it's clear he's being gently (and sometimes not so gently) nudged aside.

"Don't screw the pooch on this one," Scott continued, pretending not to hear Rick. "Berkowitz is one of our biggest clients."

"Screw the pooch?" I responded. "Berkowitz already screwed the pooch. I'm trying to save his ass. What idiot has the chutzpah to take a tax deduction for..."

"I know, I know," Scott said before I could finish. Everyone in the firm knew about Harvey's brazen move, which quickly became the subject of jokes that even Avery laughed at. "I realize you don't have much to work with, but watch yourself with Judge Abrams. She may not have held you in contempt today, but from here on out she'll try to keep you on a short leash, and knowing how you operate..."

"Yeah, no contempt this morning," I said, "just a friendly chat in chambers before Abrams recessed for the day."

"You told us today's session was going to be short," Avery said, "but I never expected it to be that short. If I had known you were going to be back by noon, I would have agreed to a two o'clock meeting with Martin von Beverwicjk instead of four."

The von Beverwicjk family, one of the original settlers of Troy Forge back in the eighteenth century, owned large tracts of land throughout the town, as well as numerous local businesses. Joshua von Beverwicjk, Martin's father, had been one of Rick's first clients when he opened his law practice back in the '50s. We've handled the extended family's legal affairs ever since. They were valuable, but demanding clients, hence Avery's desire to accommodate Martin's schedule.

"I love the circus," Rick said again, a bit more loudly. He had that empty look in his eyes that I had come to recognize as a sign that he was with us physically, but mentally was in a world all his own.

My partners routinely ignored Rick, but I couldn't. So I said, "You'd love this one, Rick. It's got dozens of government clowns."

"Government clowns are the best kind," Rick said. "They're always the most entertaining. Teapot Dome, Watergate, a dip in the tidal basin. Send in the clowns. All brought to you in living color. Cue the peacock." Rick was waving his arms as his voice rose, but the far-away look had been replaced by a gleam in his eye, and one corner of his mouth had turned up in a not-quite-successful attempt to smile. The old Rick was making an effort to join us once again.

Scott ignored him and continued the meeting. We spent the next half hour reviewing new cases, most of which were fairly routine and few of which would require my skills as a litigator. Then Avery launched into an overly detailed review of firm finances. As he droned on in his nasal monotone, I thought about the first, and last, argument that Aimee and I had about money.

One weekend a number of years ago, shortly after Aimee had become involved with the Art Alliance, she dragged me to a gallery in Manhattan that specialized in modern art. If you paint something that looks as real as a photograph, you're an artist in my book. But if all you do is throw paint on a canvas and call it art, you're a fraud. Aimee and I stopped in front of a very large, very colorful, and very ugly example of faux art. She asked me if I liked it, and I made the mistake of telling her the truth. I later discovered she had shelled out three thousand bucks for the damn thing, supposedly as a birthday present for me, her totally ungrateful, uninformed, no-class husband. Since then, I've let her spend whatever she wants on so-called art. It's a small price to pay to keep the peace. In court I play to win, but when it comes to dealing with Aimee, I've learned that the best way to win is to not fight the battle in the first place.

"You might want to familiarize yourself with the file before our meeting this afternoon." I snapped out of my daydream as Scott slid a file down the conference table in my direction.

I hadn't heard a word he or Avery had said so I simply picked the file up and nodded. "Will do." Scott adjourned the meeting and I headed back to my office, juggling thoughts of the Berkowitz trial with Eddie the Skunk's revelation about Aimee.

5

"Talk to Ziggy."

Back in my office I began looking through the file that had interrupted my daydream, and almost immediately realized something was drastically wrong. What should have been a relatively straightforward subdivision of a twenty-eight acre parcel into building lots had turned into a full-scale war between Martin von Beverwicjk and the Town of Troy Forge. The battle began when the town returned the original subdivision application our firm had prepared with "defective filing" written on the first page. Over the years, we've filed hundreds of subdivision applications for our clients with scores of municipalities throughout the county. Carol, Rick's secretary, probably knows more about the ins and outs of subdivisions than most attorneys. Occasionally, a planning board will ask for clarifications or additional information, but the von Beverwicjk subdivision application was the first one that had ever been returned unfiled. Although the Troy Forge planning board was kind enough to keep the filing fee, they didn't do us the courtesy of explaining why this particular application was defective.

According to the correspondence in the file, Scott and the planning board had traded a series of letters in which he attempted to find out why the original subdivision application was defective, and the town attempted to avoid providing a straight answer. Once Scott had managed to file an application that met the town's constantly shifting requirements, the next skirmish began. This one involved a series of letters from the town stating that subdivision approval, if approval was granted at all, would be contingent on our client agreeing to a number of concessions that were nothing short of bizarre. My favorite was a requirement that Martin deed the town five acres for "wetlands mitigation." Scott sent a letter politely explaining that there were no wetlands on the property. The planning board responded with a not-so-polite letter reiterating their demand on the ground that there was a small stream on an adjoining parcel that might overflow its banks, notwithstanding the fact that it had never done so at any time in the last hundred years. Moreover, the town explained, Martin owned another piece of property on the other side of town that did have wetlands, which in their collective wisdom justified their demand.

By the time I returned to the conference room at four o'clock, I was convinced our client was being singled out for special treatment, I just didn't know why. Martin von Beverwicjk was in the process of supplying the answer as I entered the room. "Bob Proctor is behind this," he was saying, referring to the mayor of Troy Forge. I had never met Mayor Proctor, but I knew all about him. Heck, everybody in the county knew about "Billboard Bob," thanks to the numerous billboards he erected, at taxpayer expense, extolling his great accomplishments. "I've been suspicious about Proctor from the moment I laid eyes on him. There's something about him that just doesn't ring true. He appeared out of nowhere, ran this aggressive campaign against Phil Johnson, who had been mayor for years, and ended up running things before anybody realized what happened."

"You knew Mayor Johnson, didn't you?" I asked Rick, as I slid into the empty chair next to his.

"Oh, yes, he and I were good friends," Rick said. "I helped him with his very first campaign for mayor. Of course that was many years ago." Rick looked out into space as if trying to conjure up a mental image of his old friend. "I don't see him around much these days."

I was trying to figure out the best way to explain that Phil Johnson had been dead for years when Rick asked Martin, "How's your father doing? I don't see him around much either. Joshua was one of my first clients when I started the firm back in the '50s. He and I used to play golf every Wednesday. But then he hurt his back."

"Dad's health has been slowly declining for several years," Martin said. "He's in hospice and we don't know how much longer he has."

"That's too bad," Rick replied. "Joshua was one of my first clients." Then the empty-eyed look returned, and the room fell silent.

"So how did Proctor end up getting elected?" Avery asked, attempting to divert attention from Rick. "I wasn't here when he first ran for mayor."

Martin was quick to answer. "He promised everything to everybody. Then he made good on those promises using the taxpayers' money. Since he's been in office, taxes have gone through the roof."

"I think we can all agree that Proctor is a shrewd politician," Scott said, "but that's beside the point. The issue is how to deal with a planning board that's giving us a hard time on what should be a routine subdivision. You have two options, Martin. The first is to give them what they want and hope they don't turn around and ask for something more."

"Not an option," the client said. "I won't lie down and play dead for that egomaniac, Proctor. Besides, what they're asking is ridiculous. If I gave them what they wanted, I'd end up losing money on the project. They have to know that."

"That brings us to your second option," Scott continued, "which is to sue the town, alleging that what it's doing constitutes a taking of your property without just compensation in violation of the Fifth Amendment."

"What are our chances if we sue?" Martin wanted to know.

"Pretty good, thanks to *Nollan*, a recent Supreme Court case that makes it more difficult for municipalities to get away with making outrageous demands like these."

"What kind of expense are we talking about?" Martin asked

Scott looked toward Avery, the firm's money man, who, in turn, looked at me and gave a subtle nod I interpreted to mean, *Go ahead and quote a fee, but leave some wiggle room.* I gave the client a number, quickly adding, "but it could be higher – potentially much higher – depending on how things play out."

The client was clearly unhappy. And when I told him how long the process was likely to take, he was even more unhappy. But he eventually said, "Do it. I'll be damned if I'll give in to Proctor's extortion."

"Talk to Ziggy," Rick said, apropos of nothing.

Everyone at the table turned to Rick, waiting for him to elaborate, but he didn't. He appeared to be staring at the painting on the wall depicting the Ford Mansion in nearby Morristown, which served as George Washington's temporary headquarters during the Revolutionary War.

We waited. Nobody spoke.

We waited some more. Martin von Beverwicjk turned around to see what Rick was staring at, then turned back with a bemused expression.

None of us had any idea what the heck Rick was talking about. Things had reached the point where it was never clear if Rick himself know what he was talking about.

Rick finally broke the silence. "We need to talk to Ziggy," he said again, this time slowly and deliberately, banging the table with his hand as he spoke.

Avery gave me a look that could only be interpreted as, *Get him out of here before the client realizes he's lost his marbles.* So I said to Rick, "Good idea. Let's go make that call and see what we can find out."

As I walked Rick back to his office, I asked, "Who's Ziggy?"

"Oh, I don't remember his name. My memory isn't what it used to be," Rick said, surprising me with a coherent sentence. "But he's worked in the Town Clerk's office for years, and Bob Proctor makes him ziggy."

"Is Ziggy his actual name or is that a nickname Proctor gave him?"

"No, no, no," Rick insisted. He was clearly trying to tell me something, but couldn't figure out how. He thought for a moment and then starting jogging in place. "Ziggy," he said. "Ziggy."

Then it dawned on me. "You mean ziggy as in scurry or run away?"

"Yes, yes, yes!" Rick said, his face lighting up with a smile.

Rick was obviously talking about Machias Phelps, a strange little man with a strange name and even stranger habits to go with it, including the peculiar habit of scurrying out of sight any time Mayor Proctor appeared. Everyone knew about Phelps' odd behavior, but nobody was ever able to figure out what caused it. The leading theory was that he had somehow displeased His Majesty, King Bob, at some point in the past, and kept out of Proctor's sight to avoid the royal wrath.

Phelps would have been the archetypal henpecked husband if he had ever married, which he hadn't. He stood about five foot nothing, weighed little more than Buddy, my cat, had big, black glasses that made his eyes look as though they were bulging out of his head, and was the only man I ever met who wore a short-sleeve white shirt and a bow tie to work every single day. Machias Phelps was an odd little guy by any measure, but he was an extremely useful odd little guy because he owed me a favor. Years ago I learned something about him that others didn't know, and to ensure others never would know, Mr. Phelps was very obliging whenever I asked for information about the goings on in town hall. So when we got back to Rick's office, I placed a call to the Town Clerk's office. Phelps answered and I identified myself.

"Hello, Mr. Reynolds," he said in response.

"No, Machias, it's me, Brendan O'Brian."

"I'm sorry, your garbage wasn't collected today, Mr. Reynolds," Phelps continued. "Please hold and I'll connect you to the Public Works Department. I'm sure they'll rectify the problem."

The next thing I knew, someone from the Public Works Department was on the line assuring me that as part of the glorious Proctor administration they were there to serve all of His Majesty's subjects. "Sorry, wrong number," I said, and hung up.

There was an outside chance Phelps had decided it no longer mattered whether or not I kept his secret, but more likely he couldn't talk because there was someone in the office with him. I waited ten minutes and tried again. This time a woman answered. I asked for Mr. Phelps, only to be told, "He just left for the day."

As we left Rick's office, I asked Carol, his secretary, to tell everyone in the conference room that we had been unable to reach Ziggy.

"Call him our town hall informant," Rick instructed. "Makes it sound like we have a spy inside the Proctor administration. Martin will love that. And we'll be able to bill for it." Rick may have been losing his marbles, but he still knew how to maximize billings.

"And tell them Rick and I are drafting the complaint against Troy Forge so we can file it first thing in the morning," I added. That elicited a snort from Carol, who knew that Linda, who runs the firm's computer, would be the one doing the work. Avery says that some day each of our secretaries will have her own computer, but I have my doubts. Having seen how Linda can use it to assemble in minutes a document that would ordinarily take hours, I'm not sure we'll ever need more than one computer operator. As it turned out, Linda was able to crank out the complaint for *Martin von Beverwicjk v. Town of Troy Forge* in less than twenty minutes using one of my old complaints as a template.

I dropped the complaint off with my secretary for her to make the requisite number of copies (a number which only the secretaries seem to know), and file it with the Superior Court in Morristown, the County Seat, on her way to the office tomorrow. Then I headed for home, still trying to decide how to deal with the warning Eddie the Skunk had delivered the previous day.

6

"I'm not happy with the way things went today."

When I got home that evening, Buddy was waiting for me in his usual spot in the middle of the front hallway. He followed me into the kitchen where Aimee was sitting at the counter reading a magazine and eating a salad. Either she didn't hear me or was deliberately ignoring me because she never looked up until I spoke.

"I didn't hear you come in last night," I said as I crossed the room heading for the bottle of Jameson's on the counter near the back of the kitchen.

Aimee looked at me, then shifted her gaze to Buddy, who had positioned himself where he could see both of us. "You and your cat were sound asleep," came the reply. "Snoring away."

I've never heard myself snore, not even once, in my 37 years. "Were you snoring?" I asked Buddy. He gave me a look that seemed to say, *That wasn't snoring, it was purring.*

I was trying to decide how to broach the subject of Eddie's revelation when Aimee announced, "I have a meeting tonight, so you'll have to handle dinner for yourself." As she carried her dishes to the sink, she added, "and your cat," nodding in Buddy's direction. Buddy looked at Aimee for a moment, then walked to where I was standing and rubbed against my leg as if to say, *You feed me every morning and every night; why should today be any different?*

I was secretly relieved when Aimee headed upstairs before I could say anything more. How do you ask your wife if she's hired someone to kill you? I knew in my heart that the idea was preposterous. Eddie the Skunk wasn't the brightest crayon in the box, and the information was third hand at best. Granted, if I ended up six feet under, Aimee would be seven digits richer thanks to an insurance policy I had purchased three years ago. But I just couldn't imagine her plotting my demise. I'm clearly worth more to her alive than dead. At least I think I am.

I filled Buddy's food dish and put fresh water in the other bowl, then made myself a tuna sandwich. I ate my sandwich and sipped my favorite Irish whiskey. Buddy ate his dinner and took a token sip of water. I often wondered if I could encourage him to drink more by adding a bit of Jameson's to his water bowl. Our makeshift meal complete, and with a replenished drink in hand and Buddy at my side, I walked to the living room and settled into my favorite chair by the fireplace. No sooner had I gotten comfortable than the phone rang. It was Harvey Berkowitz.

"I'm not happy with the way things went today," were the first words out of his mouth. Conversations with clients that begin that way usually go rapidly downhill. But Harvey settled down after I explained for the umpteenth time that Uncle Sam had a solid case, and that our best strategy was to turn the trial into a circus in an attempt to get a hung jury. My hope was that instead of re-trying the case, the government would agree to settle for a whopping fine, but no time behind bars. The strategy required me to deliberately provoke the judge into reacting in a way that would cause the jury to view her, not as a neutral arbiter of justice, but as part of a powerful government prosecuting their fellow taxpayer. It was a risky strategy, not just for Harvey, but for me as well. What I needed to do would most likely risk disciplinary proceedings at the trial's conclusion, but I'd cross that bridge when I came to it.

"But if you succeed in getting a hung jury, how can the government try me again?" Harvey wanted to know. "Isn't that what they call double jeopardy?"

"A hung jury results in a mistrial," I explained, "and the government has the right to try you again. That's been the law since the early nineteenth century, a case called *United States v. Perez*. The Supreme Court reaffirmed that a few years ago in the *Richardson* decision."

"It doesn't seem fair," Harvey complained.

"I didn't say it was fair, I said it was the law."

"Why don't you try to get the whole jury to acquit me, instead of just trying to convince a couple of jurors?" Harvey asked next. "I saw them do that on television."

"Trials on television aren't like trials in the real world," I said. "What you're referring to is called jury nullification, convincing the jury to come to a verdict that's contrary to the law or the facts."

"Yeah, jury nullification," Harvey said. "Why don't we do that?"

"Because of a case called *U.S. v. Dougherty*."

"Never heard of it," Harvey said before I had a chance to explain.

"That was the case involving the so-called D.C. Nine who trashed a Dow Chemical office to protest the war in Vietnam. The court conceded that juries have the right to acquit a defendant despite the law or the facts, but attorneys can't tell them they have that right, and courts won't issue jury instructions mentioning it."

"If you can't tell them, how are they supposed to know?" Harvey wanted to know. "That's just dumb."

"Welcome to my world."

We talked for a few more minutes about the events in court that day, with Harvey finally admitting that my abbreviated opening statement was actually pretty funny.

After ending my conversation with Harvey, I reviewed the evidence Uncle Sam had against my client. Under Rule 16 of the *Federal Rules of Criminal Procedure*, I had been able to obtain copies of documents the government would use to make its case. But unlike state court proceedings, in federal court, I wasn't entitled to the prosecution's witness list.

I didn't necessarily need to know the witnesses the government would call to prove the first two counts of the three-count indictment. I had a pretty good idea who they were by looking at the documents Lionel Newton was required to provide under Rule 16, and I could pretty much guess what they would say on the witness stand.

What I didn't know was the identity of the witness the government would need to prove the third count of the indictment. I would have already discovered his identity if the State of New Jersey had prosecuted him (and Harvey) for the incident that gave rise to Harvey's "ultimate chutzpah" tax deduction. But a person in the prosecutor's office who owed me a favor led me to believe, without actually saying so, that the state was honoring the federal government's request to delay prosecution until after Harvey's tax fraud trial. That way I wouldn't learn the identity of this crucial witness in advance. I impressed upon my contact that I'd owe him one if he happened to casually mention the name of this important witness in the course of our conversation, but he said he didn't have access to that information.

Harvey was equally unhelpful in identifying the mystery witness. He didn't know his accomplice's name, he said, because he didn't need to know it. "It's not like I wrote him a check." The physical description Harvey provided ("he was about my height") was so vague it matched ninety percent of the middle-aged men in New Jersey. "I only met the guy once," was his explanation, "and it was in the middle of the night." And Harvey had absolutely no idea where I could find his accomplice, having arranged for this person's services through the brother-in-law of a friend of a friend who lived "someplace out near Hopatcong." I hired two investigators who, after looking for two weeks, couldn't locate either the witness or the brother-in-law. In fact, they couldn't even find the street on which the friend's friend supposedly lived. I love clients who can assist in their own defense.

Although I didn't know the identity of this crucial witness, I did know two potential witnesses we probably wouldn't see in the courtroom. The first was Ray Benson, Harvey's long time accountant. Ray had initially cooperated with the IRS, turning over documents and answering questions in the hope that he could help Harvey resolve the matter by paying back taxes, penalties, and perhaps a small civil penalty. But when it became apparent that Uncle Sam intended to file criminal charges against Harvey, Ray realized he could also be indicted. At that point he stopped cooperating.

As a newbie attorney, Newton might make the mistake of calling Ray as a witness, but I assumed one of the more experienced attorneys on his team would explain that the specter of Ray pleading the Fifth to question after question could cause the jury to decide that any improprieties on Harvey's return were Ray's doing, not Harvey's. There was always the possibility that Ray could make a deal with the Feds to save his own skin, but Harvey assured me that would never happen. He and Ray were lifelong friends, college roommates, and cousins. Of course, the prospect of spending time in a federal penitentiary can be a powerful motivator to turn on old friends.

The second potential witness I was pretty certain we wouldn't see in the courtroom was Aaron Gertz, Harvey's travel agent. Like Ray Benson, Aaron was one of Harvey's college pals, someone with whom Harvey had done business for many years. Aaron told me on numerous occasions that no one from the IRS or the Justice Department had interviewed him or even contacted him. Since even a novice litigator like Newton wouldn't put a witness on the stand without first interviewing him, I assumed Gertz wouldn't be making an appearance in court, which was odd because his testimony could be extremely damaging to Harvey's case. Like Ray Benson, there was always the possibility that Gertz wasn't being truthful and would surprise us by taking the stand, but Harvey assured me that wouldn't happen.

At some point I must have fallen asleep, still stretched out in my favorite chair. The next thing I knew it was morning, and Buddy was kneading my chest with his paws and staring at me with big green eyes. I went looking for Aimee, but all I found was a note informing me she had left for an early meeting at an art gallery in Manhattan.

7

"Judge, you're detached from reality."

I nsulting a judge in open court is generally considered bad form. But it was the right way to begin the Berkowitz trial because it warmed up the jury for the circus I had planned for them. Two of the jurors were laughing outright. Two others were trying hard not to laugh, but not having much success. My breach of protocol subjected me to an evening in fashionable government accommodations, but it was an important part of my strategy to get a hung jury.

It all began when Lionel Newton attempted to introduce my client's tax return into evidence. George Boutwell, the lead IRS investigator on the case, had taken the stand and identified a document as Harvey Berkowitz's tax return for the previous year.

I immediately objected. "Your Honor, how do we know that document is Mr. Berkowitz's tax return?"

Uncle Sam's consigliore gave me an incredulous look that I interpreted to mean: *Are you out of your mind? Nobody ever objects to the introduction of routine evidence like this.* Before trial, it's customary for an attorney to give his adversary copies of the documents he intends to introduce as evidence and to ask opposing counsel to stipulate that the documents are legitimate, saving everyone time and effort in the courtroom. Unfortunately for the government, their newbie attorney had made two mistakes. The first was skipping that pre-trial ritual, apparently assuming that I wouldn't object to my client's tax return being offered as evidence. His second mistake was thinking I was interested in saving time and effort.

"Counselor, you're not seriously suggesting the government would offer a counterfeit tax return as evidence, are you?" Judge Abrams asked with a laugh.

"You're not seriously suggesting the federal government never lies, are you?" I shot back. "Have you checked the government's latest inflation statistics?" This brought a few giggles from the jury box.

"Counselor," Judge Abrams continued, using a tone of voice that was halfway between pleading and condescending, "you and I both know your client's tax return is going to be admitted into evidence eventually. There are a lot of ways Mr. Newton can do that. So be reasonable, look at the prosecution's exhibit and stipulate that it is, in fact, the defendant's tax return so we can move on."

Newton and I, having the benefit of a legal education, he at a prestigious Ivy League school and me at the same state university that Abrams had attended, knew the judge was right. But I was reasonably certain the jurors hadn't spent the previous evening curled up in bed with a copy of the *Federal Rules of Evidence*. So instead of being reasonable I said, "For starters, I object to you referring to Mr. Berkowitz as 'the defendant.' The gentleman has a name and I would ask that the court use it when referring to him."

"He *is* the defendant in this case," Judge Abrams said. Now she was getting a bit testy. A good first step. "I routinely refer to defendants in my courtroom as defendants."

"And secondly," I continued, "while that tax return may or may not be a legitimate tax return, there's no proof that it's Mr. Berkowitz's tax return. And speaking of ownership, this courtroom isn't *your* courtroom." Pointing to the jurors, I said, "It belongs to these people and their fellow taxpayers who pay your salary, the salary of Mr. Newton, and the dozen or more people who are helping you and him prosecute Mr. Berkowitz."

Judge Abrams, who by this time was visibly angry, banged her gavel so hard I thought it would break. "That's enough, counselor," she said indignantly. "I'm not prosecuting your client. I'm a federal district court judge who's taken an oath to uphold the law, and..."

"And whose salary is paid for by the taxpayers," I interrupted. "That's the problem with this whole case. We're in a *federal* court where my client is being prosecuted for not paying as much in *federal* taxes as the *federal* government wants." Criminal tax fraud cases are tried in a federal district court because it's a federal crime, but if the jury wanted to think the case could have been tried in a state court instead, I was more than happy to indulge that belief. "And what does the federal government do with the taxes it collects?" I continued. "It gives foreign aid to countries that hate us, sends politicians on fact-finding junkets that are really vacations, and pays hefty salaries and generous benefits to federal employees like you, Mr. Newton, and the dozens of investigators working behind the scenes to put Mr. Berkowitz and other innocent taxpayers in prison." I thought the reference to vacation travel on the taxpayers' dime was a particularly nice touch considering one of the charges against my client involved deductions for a business trip that was actually a family vacation.

"Counselor, you're getting perilously close to being cited for contempt," the judge warned.

Instead of pulling back at the mention of contempt, as she expected, I escalated the confrontation another notch. "You and Mr. Newton and all the people prosecuting him are on the federal payroll and have a vested interest in prying more money out of Mr. Berkowitz and his fellow taxpayers." I looked straight at the jury when I delivered that line to convey the message that they were taxpayers first and jurors second.

The judge was getting angrier with each passing second. "One more word and I'm going to hold you in contempt."

"You're going to hold me in contempt for pointing out the obvious? You're going to throw me in jail so you and Lionel Newton the fifth, and the small army of taxpayer-financed attack dogs working with him can prosecute my client without me being here to defend him?"

"That's enough!" Judge Abrams yelled.

It was time to bring the confrontation to its inevitable conclusion. "If you think you can collect a salary from the same federal government that's trying to put Mr. Berkowitz in jail for not offering up another pound of flesh, and remain objective, you're..." I paused as if trying to come up with the right word, although I knew exactly what I was going to say. "Judge, you're detached from reality."

That comment elicited an audible gasp from the heavyset blond woman in the front row of the jury box. I wasn't surprised. During jury selection I learned that she was a public school teacher who, like the judge and Newton, depended on taxpayer dollars for her livelihood. On the other hand, the black electrician and the white plumber sitting next to each other in the back row were nodding and smiling at my antics. And Lionel Newton, originally looking very satisfied that I was digging a hole for myself, was now dumbfounded, apparently unwilling to believe that he had just heard a member of the bar deliberately insult a federal judge.

Judge Abrams set a new speed record for holding an attorney in contempt of court. "Reality" was barely out of my mouth before she instructed two rather large deputy marshals to "get him out of my court room."

"Let's see if a night behind bars and a five hundred dollar fine teaches you some respect," she said, pointing a finger at me.

"Five hundred dollars?" I said with mock incredulity. "The government wants even more money? You didn't get enough from Mr. Berkowitz and his fellow taxpayers?"

"Now I know you've lost your mind," Harvey Berkowitz whispered as the two marshals frog marched me past him on my way to spend a night in luxurious government accommodations.

8

"Thank your benefactor."

My luxurious government accommodations turned out to be a six-by-eight-foot holding cell with concrete block walls on three sides and metal bars on the fourth. There were ten of these cells in the basement level of the courthouse, five on each side of a corridor accessed through a thick glass door. A federal marshal was stationed at a desk outside the corridor to monitor the holding cells and the elevator that was used to shuttle prisoners to and from the courtrooms on the floors above.

"Can I make a phone call?" I asked as the two deputy marshals ushered me into one of the cells farthest from the glass entry door.

"If you were under arrest, we'd let you call your lawyer," came the answer. "But you're not technically under arrest. And besides, you *are* a lawyer." Neither one smiled, but it was clear that they both found my predicament hilarious. I was somewhat less amused.

"Hey, there's no television in this room," I shouted at the marshals as they walked away. "And no coffee maker. I'm certain I reserved a room with a coffee maker." If they were impressed by my attempt at humor, they didn't show it.

I circled the room, much as Buddy does before lying down, then stretched out on the not-at-all-comfortable bed along the back wall of my cell. I assumed Harvey Berkowitz was already on the phone to Avery Glickman, his primary contact at the firm. It was just a matter of time before Scott sent someone from the firm to pay my fine, at which point Judge Abrams would hopefully decide to let me out. I don't mind spending a few hours behind bars if it helps me win a case, but that doesn't mean I want to spend more time than necessary caged like a zoo animal.

I took stock of how my strategy was working out. I knew my antics would play well with some jurors, but alienate others. The key was getting at least one holdout on the jury, one person who was strong enough to withstand the inevitable pressure from other jurors to fall in line and return a guilty verdict warranted by the facts. I needed someone who would see Harvey as the ordinary taxpayer's David standing up to a government Goliath. I've never used jury consultants who claim to be able to predict how potential jurors will act. In my opinion, they're a waste of the client's money. I'd prefer to trust my gut. It's been my experience that when I go with my instincts, I'm right more often than I'm wrong. My gut was telling me that the public school teacher in the front row would probably vote to convict Harvey, and the plumber and the electrician in the back row were my best bet for getting a hung jury. The retired accountant, who knew firsthand how complicated and contradictory the Tax Code is, might also swing over to our side now that he no longer had to worry about earning a livelihood filling out indecipherable tax forms. The rest of the jurors were a toss-up at the moment.

"Yo!" The shout snapped me out of my thoughts. I looked up to see a much older version of the deputy marshals who had unceremoniously escorted me from the courtroom earlier that day. He was about my height, but paunchy, with white hair, a ruddy complexion, and saggy jowls. He had the look of a man who was counting down the days to retirement. "Lunch," he said, holding up a white paper bag and a can of Coke.

"Thanks."

"Don't thank me. Thank your benefactor," he said, motioning over his shoulder to the glass door at the end of the hallway. I jumped to my feet and got to the front of the holding cell in time to see a bald man with a goatee disappear into the elevator.

"Who's he?" I asked the deputy.

"How should I know?" he answered. "I assume he works for you. Why else would he be bringing you lunch."

Since our firm didn't employ a tall bald man with a goatee, I was about to decline the proffered meal. But just then my stomach rumbled and I gave in to temptation. "Good point," I said to the deputy, taking the meal that he slipped between the bars of my cell. Mr. Goatee was probably just a deliveryman from the local eatery that Harvey or someone from the office had contacted.

After devouring my lunch I hunkered down on my not-at-all-comfortable bed and waited for someone from the office to show up and get me out of my cage. I used the time to analyze the warning Eddie the Skunk had delivered two days earlier. I was pretty certain that whatever Eddie's original associate had overheard had become so distorted by the time it reached Eddie that the best thing to do would be to ignore it. Eddie was probably just trying to repay the favor he thought he owed me, or perhaps he thought delivering this warning meant I owed him a favor. I spent another hour trying to decide who owed whom, and then gave up. What I did decide was that I had spent enough time in a holding cell, so I called for the guard. The same deputy who had brought me lunch got up from his desk outside the glass door and slowly walked back to my holding cell.

"I'm an attorney," I said.

"I know. Heard all about your courtroom exploits."

"Any chance you could let me make a phone call? I need to call my office."

"Against the rules," he said as he reached for the ring of keys on his belt. "But I suppose I can bend the rules for someone who has the balls to call Abrams deranged." That wasn't exactly what I had called the judge, but if that's what the custodian of the keys wanted to believe, so be it. As long as it got me my phone call.

The deputy unlocked the door and I followed him to the desk in the elevator lobby.

"You can use that," he said, pointing to the phone on the desk. He settled into his chair, picked up the paperback he'd been reading, and made a concerted effort to pretend to ignore me as I dialed the phone.

When Elaine, our receptionist, answered, I had her connect me with my secretary.

"I wondered when I'd hear from you," were the first words out of Carolyn's mouth. I started to explain my predicament, but she cut me off. "I know; we all know. Harvey Berkowitz called Avery a few hours ago. Scott sent a messenger to Newark with a check."

"Great," I said, assuming Abrams would order my release as soon as she got her pound of flesh. "The accommodations here are first rate, but I'd rather sleep in my own bed tonight."

"Not going to happen," Carolyn said. "Scott asked, begged, pleaded, threatened, cajoled, and demanded, without success. The judge won't budge. Make yourself comfortable; you're spending the night."

Before I could respond to the bad news, my jailer tapped me on the arm and pointed to the clock-like mechanism over the elevator that was counting down to the "B" at the left side of the semi-circle, signaling that we were about to have company. "You need to be back in the holding cell before that elevator gets here," he said, "or my ass is grass."

I told Carolyn to arrange a meeting with Machias Phelps for Saturday before heading back to my luxurious accommodations *sans* coffee maker. "Thanks," I said to the deputy as I slipped through the glass door.

"You owe me one," came the reply.

9

"Oh, you did something wrong, all right."

The next morning my zookeepers let me out in time to go home, shower, and put on clean clothes before court began. Instead, I headed for a diner six blocks away and had a hearty breakfast, arriving in court fashionably late in a rumpled suit and bathed in the trendy new cologne, *Eau de Jail*. Lionel Newton was dressed in his expensive, gray three-piece suit, providing the jury with a striking contrast. Exactly what I wanted.

Judge Abrams took one look at me and shook her head. She declined to comment on my appearance, so I did it for her. "I apologize profusely to the court for my appearance," I said with mock sincerity. "Even when I don't spend the night in a government gulag I can't match the sartorial splendor of a taxpayer-paid government attorney like my esteemed colleague, Lionel Newton the seventh."

"What's needed, counselor," Judge Abrams shot back, "is an apology for yesterday's behavior."

"No apology necessary, Your Honor," I replied with a smile. "I realize you were just doing your job."

That crack should have gotten me another contempt citation, or a rebuke at the very least. But Abrams, who was on to my strategy and had come up with one of her own to deal with it, didn't take the bait. Instead, she said to Lionel Newton, "Call your first witness."

George Boutwell, the IRS investigator Newton had called as a witness yesterday, took the stand and promptly identified the document handed to him as Harvey Berkowitz's tax return. This time I didn't object, at least not directly.

"I would renew my objection from yesterday," I said, standing to face Judge Abrams, "except for the fact that protecting my client's interests would probably land me in jail again."

"Overruled," was the judge's curt response. "Continue, Mr. Newton."

One of Newton's assistants – I counted six of them that morning – rolled a large bulletin board into position where everyone in the courtroom could see it. Oversized copies of the relevant pages from Harvey's tax return were in the center, his questionable deductions highlighted in yellow. Surrounding the pages from Harvey's tax return were three folders, numbered one through three, each filled with the exhibits the government would use to prove that particular count of the indictment, and connected to the relevant portion of the tax return with colored-coded lines. It was a very artistic presentation, worthy of praise. So I did just that.

"I commend my adversary on his artistic skills," I said, rising to my feet. "I'm sure many man hours and tax dollars went into creating this work of art." That brought snickers from some of the jurors.

"Sit down, Mr. O'Brian," Judge Abrams said. Apparently she didn't appreciate fine art the way I did. Perhaps she should have spent some time with Aimee.

Newton began by having George Boutwell testify about his training and experience with the IRS. Next, Boutwell provided the jury with a summary of the questionable deductions my client had taken, starting with those referred to in the first count of the indictment and concluding with the ultimate chutzpah deduction in the third count. Newton was obviously saving that one for a big finish, concluding his case with something he was hoping the jury would consider so outrageous they'd demand that Harvey be drawn and quartered right there in the middle of the courtroom.

Harvey and I watched the jurors' reactions as Boutwell outlined the government's case. When he finished explaining the first count of the indictment, Harvey scribbled, "What do you think?" on a legal pad and slid it over to me. I wrote, "10% chance of acquittal," giving him some hope, but not wanting to raise his expectations. After Boutwell finished his overview of the second count, Harvey repeated the process, and this time I wrote, "20% chance of acquittal." When Boutwell finished explaining the third count, I scribbled "ultimate wild card" and slide the pad over to Harvey.

Having provided the jury with an overview of the government's case, Boutwell got into the specifics of the first count of the indictment, which charged Harvey with filing a fraudulent tax return by deducting the cost of repairs to one of his rental properties. He had claimed a total of two hundred and seventy-eight thousand dollars for plumbing, carpentry, and all the other costs you would ordinarily expect to incur for extensive repairs to a building. The problem was that although Harvey really had spent the money, those expenses were for an addition to his already oversized home, not repairs to a rental property. As such, they were personal, non-deducible expenses, but that hadn't stopped Harvey from deducting them anyway.

Boutwell had a veritable mountain of incriminating evidence, some obtained from Harvey and his accountant before our firm became involved, and some the handiwork of IRS Special Agents. There were statements for building materials supposedly delivered to the rental property, and photos showing trucks unloading those same materials at Harvey's residence. There were bills from carpenters detailing projects done at the rental property, and photos showing the work had actually been done at Harvey's home. As the morning wore on and the stack of incriminating documents grew higher, my discomfort grew. It was partly the result of seeing the evidence against my client piling up, but it was something else as well.

Finally, unable to take it any longer, I rose unsteadily to my feet. "Your Honor, I hate to derail Lionel's train of thought," I began, generating snickers from a few jurors who appreciated both toy trains and word play, "but I wonder if we might recess. I'm afraid the food at the luxurious government lodgings where I spent the night isn't agreeing with me, and I would hate to have to return it here in your nice clean courtroom."

To my surprise, Judge Abrams said, "You are looking a little green around the gills, Mr. O'Brian. We'll recess for the weekend and continue on Monday morning."

As I was leaving the courtroom I spotted a man sitting in the back row of the public gallery who looked vaguely familiar. Then I realized he was the person who had brought lunch to my holding cell the previous day. Apparently he wasn't a delivery-man after all. "Thanks for lunch," I said when I got to where he was seated, hoping his response would tell me who he was. But he didn't say anything. Instead, he nodded in acknowledgement, got up and made a beeline for the elevator. I considered going after him, but decided against it. Better to let him think I knew who he was than to reveal I was clueless. Besides, barfing on his shoes seemed a bit undignified.

After a quick stop at the restroom, which wasn't nice and clean like the judge's courtroom, and was even less so by the time I left, I made my way out of the building and down the street to the lot where I had parked my car. I bundled myself into my Mustang and pulled into traffic, keeping a close watch on the cars around me. In my experience, urban areas have more than their fair share of overly aggressive drivers. I spotted one almost immediately, a dark blue or black sedan six or seven cars behind me that kept changing lanes.

For the next fifteen minutes I snaked my way through city streets, eventually arriving at the ramp onto Interstate 280, which would take me westward to my office in Troy Forge or my home in Mountain Springs, my ultimate destination being determined by how I felt when I got off the interstate. The dark sedan followed me onto I-280, but stayed behind me. I didn't think anything of it at the time since 280 was the logical route for anyone heading west out of Newark.

As I drove, I tried to figure out who the bald man with a goatee was. One possibility was an IRS agent keeping tabs on me. If Harvey had been a mobster or a drug kingpin, then perhaps that was possible. But the Berkowitz case, although potentially life changing for my client, wasn't important enough to the government to justify the expense of assigning someone to tail me. And if Mr. Goatee were with the IRS, why would he buy me lunch? Just then my guts rumbled and cramped, and I conjured up a mental image of Lionel Newton laughing his ass off after one of his flunkies had delivered a tainted lunch to my holding cell. Then I remembered how quickly the judge had agreed to adjourn for the day. Could she be in on it as well? *Calm down*, I told myself. *You're imagining things. Attorneys from the Department of Justice and federal court judges don't go around poisoning people.*

That's when I remembered the warning Eddie the Snake had delivered, and another possibility came to mind that was more horrifying. I was troubled by Eddie's warning, but still thought of it as third- or fourth-hand information that had been misunderstood or misinterpreted. Things between Aimee and me had been strained for some time, but I couldn't imagine her hiring someone to kill me. It's a big jump from marital discord to murder. Eddie was an idiot, a well-meaning idiot, but still an idiot. On the other hand, a seven-figure insurance payout can cause people to do a lot of things you might not expect.

I got off the interstate at the exit for Troy Forge and turned left onto Route 46, where I was greeted by the image of Bob Proctor smiling down at me from a billboard next to one of the town's many strip malls. Billboard Bob was giving me the thumbs up and making sure I knew that *Troy Forge is a great place to live.* Because of traffic, I was forced to drive well under the speed limit, so I ignored the Troy Forge police car that pulled in behind me shortly after I passed another of the Lord Mayor's billboards, this one making sure everyone knew that *Troy Forge is a great place for business.*

Unfortunately, although I had ignored the cop, he didn't ignore me. His flashing lights and a short whoop of his siren made it clear he wanted me to pull over, which I did. I ran through a mental checklist as I waited for the cop to get out of his cruiser. Driving under the speed limit for a change, check. Not changing lanes, check. Not tailgating another vehicle, check. I was running out of possibilities when a very large flashlight began tapping on my window. I rolled the window down.

"I thought that was your Mustang," a familiar voice said. The cop holding the flashlight bent down, and I found myself face to face with Sean McDermott, one of my buddies from high school. Sean, who had been captain of the school's football team, was drooled over by the school's bad girls. The only girls who showed any interest in me, the captain of the debating team, were considerably less – how shall I put this? – open-minded than the ones drawn to Sean. I couldn't wait to get out of high school. He hated the thought of leaving.

"Always happy to see you, Sean," I said, "but why did you stop me? I wasn't doing anything wrong."

"Oh, you did something wrong, all right," Sean said. "You got yourself on Mayor Proctor's enemies list with that lawsuit you filed"

"I consider that a high honor," I replied. "Only the best people in town make it onto Bob's shit list."

Sean laughed. "Yeah, that's probably true, but Mayor Proctor has a lot of power and he's not afraid to use it."

"What, exactly, does that mean?"

"It means you need to watch your back." Sean and Eddie the Skunk now had something in common. They were both concerned about my welfare, although I had my doubts that either Aimee or Mayor Proctor really intended to do me bodily harm. Aimee might take me to the cleaners in divorce proceedings, but Proctor was all bark and no bite. Or so I thought until Sean said, "Proctor uses the police department as his own personal palace guard. Don't be surprised if you get stopped for speeding, even though you weren't speeding. And if you fight it, it'll be your word against the cop's. We both know how that will go. And if you stop for a beer someplace in town, there'll be a cop with a Breathalyzer waiting for you when you come out. You get the picture?"

"You really think guys in your department would do that?" I asked.

"Some of them. It's tough to get ahead in the department when you ignore orders that come down from the top."

"But why is Proctor so bent out of shape? I realize our client's property is the last big open space in that part of town, and

I hate to see it developed as much as the next guy, but it's just a matter of time. Proctor has to know that."

Sean laughed. "His Highness doesn't give a crap about open space. Word is he has other plans for that property."

"What kind of other plans?"

"That I don't know. It's not like I'm one of Proctor's trusted lieutenants. All I know is what I hear. Supposedly he has someone lined up to develop the property, and that someone isn't your client."

"But why go after me?" I asked. "I don't own the property. How can making my life difficult help Proctor?"

"I'm guessing he thinks that if he makes your life miserable, you'll drop von Beverwicjk as a client."

"Not going to happen," I said. "You should know me better than that."

"What I know doesn't matter," Sean replied. "The only thing that counts is what Proctor thinks. In his world, you're either with him or against him. And if you're against him, you're an enemy who has to be crushed. You might not ditch von Beverwicjk as a client, but what about all the other people he needs for that project? A surveyor shows up to survey the property, and Proctor's guys hassle him. An engineering company shows up to do soil logs, and they get the same treatment. After awhile, nobody wants to do business with your client." Sean arched an eyebrow as if to say, *I'm not making this stuff up.*

"Thanks for the heads up," I said as Sean straightened his six-foot frame and looked around. I didn't think anything of it at the time, but I later realized he was scanning the area to make sure we weren't being watched. That should have been the first clue that Proctor was more dangerous than I realized, something I eventually learned the hard way.

"No problem," Sean said. "I don't like Proctor any more than you do." Half the town thought Bob Proctor walked on water, and the other half thought he was as crooked as they come. Sean had always been tight lipped when it came to local politics, but it was pretty clear what he thought about our illustrious mayor. "And by the way, you didn't hear any of this from me."

Sean headed back to his patrol car, but not before adding, "You owe me one."

10

"I'm tired of sharing a bed with your cat."

As I turned off Route 46 onto the main boulevard leading into Mountain Springs a dark sedan that had been sitting in a side street pulled in behind me. It looked like the one I had first noticed back in Newark. Or was I just being paranoid? After all, the world is filled with dark sedans. But as I made the left turn onto my dead end street, the vehicle continued straight and I caught a glimpse of the driver in my mirror. It was Mr. Goatee.

I pulled into my driveway and immediately slammed on the brakes when I spotted a white pickup truck parked near the enclosed back porch by the kitchen. A man dressed in a blue coat was standing behind the vehicle, his back toward me, removing something from the bed of the pickup. All kinds of crazy thoughts went through my head. Was he taking out a gun to fulfill the terms of Aimee's purported contract? Was he someone sent by Bob Proctor, or perhaps an accomplice of Mr. Goatee? But when he turned around with an armful of firewood, I realized the mystery man was only Jorge, our gardener in the summer and firewood purveyor in the winter. Jorge gave a perfunctory nod to acknowledge my presence before continuing to the back porch to stack the logs.

Jorge knows that if I had my way, he'd never set foot on our property again. I don't like the way our yard looks when he's finished with it. And I sure as hell don't like the way he looks at my wife. The two of them belong to a mutual admiration society, although I suspect for Jorge it's more adoration than simple admiration. He never misses an opportunity to stop working and chat with Aimee when he thinks I'm not looking. During the spring and summer, lilacs appear on our back porch. I view them as inappropriate love offerings, but Aimee says they're just byproducts of Jorge's pruning work. More likely pining than pruning, in my opinion. I've never caught the two of them doing anything truly inappropriate, but I'm always uneasy when Jorge is alone with Aimee.

Right after starting to work for us, Jorge convinced Aimee that every woodlands creature carries rabies, and to protect her it was necessary for him to poison every last squirrel, skunk, and groundhog on the property with something that made the animals go crazy with thirst. Aside from the fact that there's never been a known case of a squirrel carrying the rabies virus, I was opposed to Jorge's extermination campaign just on general principle. I initially looked the other way to keep the peace, but when I caught Jorge attempting to poison the neighbor's dog, I finally put my foot down. Granted, the mutt was digging up our flowerbeds, but still...

That was the first time Aimee and I had words about Jorge's tenure at Casa O'Brian, but it wasn't the last. After the poisoning stopped, the lawnmower rodeo began. I came home early one day to find Jorge hooting and hollering and having a grand old time chasing squirrels while driving the lawnmower at full tilt. Even worse, Aimee was standing on the front porch laughing at his antics and cheering him on. Jorge and I had words while Aimee watched silently. She didn't take Jorge's side, but neither did she back me up. And she refused to go along with giving Jorge his walking papers because, according to her, I was "overreacting." I was also "overreacting" when I wanted to fire Jorge for throwing rocks at Lucky, the neighbor's cat

I'm never happy to see Jorge, but on this particular occasion I reasoned it was better to have a hunter of four legged creatures on the premises than one who had been hired to hunt me.

I parked in the circle in front of the house so the Great Humanitarian could back out of the driveway when he finished stacking firewood. I went inside, expecting to find Buddy waiting for me in his usual spot by the front door, but he wasn't there. The house was silent except for Simon and Garfunkel's rendition of *The Dangling Conversation* coming from the radio in the kitchen. I started in that direction, hoping (but not expecting) to find my bride whipping up a delicious meal, when I heard a sound from the second floor and headed for the stairs instead. As I reached the landing, Aimee came out of our bedroom with an armful of clothing.

"I'm sleeping in the unused room from now on," she said. "I'm tired of your snoring. And I'm tired of sharing a bed with your cat."

Aimee referred to the room next to her office as "unused" instead of calling it a guestroom or a spare bedroom. In her mind, the room should have been used for the child we could have adopted after we learned we were unable to have children of our own. Aimee's insistence on calling the room "unused" was her way of letting me know I would never be forgiven for refusing to go the adoption route.

Buddy had been sitting under the table on the landing, keeping a watchful eye on everything. As Aimee was announcing the new sleeping arrangements, he crawled out, deliberately brushed against her leg, and dashed into our bed-room. He hesitated a second and then jumped to the middle of the bed, hunkered down with his paws straight out in front of him like a miniature Sphinx, and looked straight at Aimee as if to say, *I win.*

Aimee looked from me to the cat, then without a word crossed the hallway, entered the so-called unused room and closed the door behind her. I thought about following her and hashing things out, but decided the timing was wrong. A discus-sion at this point would quickly escalate into an argument, one that I would most likely lose. So instead, I went into what had been our bedroom, but was apparently now my bedroom, and stretched out on the bed. Buddy curled up beside me and rested his chin on my shoulder, something he hadn't done since he was a kitten. He was staring right at me, and I'm sure it was just my overactive imagination fueled by fatigue, but I thought I saw sadness in his eyes. When I started to scratch behind his ears, something he likes even more than eating, he began to purr. I once read that cats purr to calm themselves. It must work on humans too because the next thing I knew it was morning, the sun streaming through the window and Buddy curled up in his usual spot at the foot of the bed.

The sound of a car door caused me to jump out of bed and run to the window in time to see Aimee's red Miata speeding down the driveway. When I went downstairs for breakfast, I found a note from Aimee informing me that she was spending the weekend with one of her friends in New York.

11

"If they see us, we'll both be in danger."

Buddy and I spent most of Saturday doing chores and watching television, with me doing the chores and Buddy doing the watching. By late afternoon when I set off for my meeting with Machias Phelps, my contact in the Town Clerk's office, the temperature had dropped to just above freezing and wind-whipped snow flurries filled the iron gray sky. I had asked Carolyn, my secretary, to have Phelps meet me at the von Beverwicjk property at the center of the escalating war between our client and the current rulers of Troy Forge. I wanted to see the property for myself, and to find out if Phelps knew why the town was giving us such a hard time about subdividing it.

I spotted my town hall informant, as Rick had dubbed him, the moment I turned off Beverwicjk Road, named for one of our client's ancestors. Phelps was peddling a bicycle that was much too small for his boney, spindly legs, causing him to weave from side to side as he slowly made his way along Fairgrounds Circle, so named because it traces the perimeter of the property where the county fair was held each August back in the 1950s.

Phelps peddled to the back of the property, as far from Beverwicjk Road as he could get, then stopped and got off the bicycle, losing his balance and almost falling head first in the process. I pulled alongside him and rolled down the window of the Mustang. "Good afternoon, Machias."

"You have to get out of here. We're being watched."

As I got out of the car, I looked around but didn't see anyone. "Machias, there's nobody here."

"They're here somewhere," he said, frantically looking in every direction. "They're always nearby."

"Who is always nearby?" I wanted to know.

"Proctor's people," came the answer. "They follow me everywhere I go. I should never have agreed to meet you."

I tried to reassure him. "There's nobody here but you and me, and no place for anyone to hide."

"They're here somewhere," came his anxious response. "We might not see them, but they're here. They're always nearby, watching and listening."

I knew Machias Phelps was an odd little man, but I had never considered him paranoid. The information he had provided in the past had always been reliable, but now I was beginning to wonder if I could trust anything he said. He began walking in a small circle, each hand under the opposite armpit as though he were trying to hug himself. "We shouldn't meet in person," he insisted. "We should talk on the phone instead. But not office phones, pay phones. They can't listen in on pay phones." I noticed that his breathing was ragged and irregular, perhaps from the exertion of riding a bicycle that was much too small for him or perhaps out of fear. Either way, I was afraid he was going to hyperventilate, so I tried to calm him down. But the more I tried, the more agitated he became.

In desperation, I finally grabbed his shoulders to stop his circular pacing and said, "Okay, just answer a couple questions and you can go." That seemed to calm him a bit, and he shook his head in agreement. "Why is the planning board giving us such a hard time on our subdivision proposal for this property?" I asked, releasing my grip on his shoulders and pointing to the large open tract behind him.

"It's not the planning board, it's Mayor Proctor. He has other plans for this property," Phelps said, confirming what Sean McDermott had told me.

"What other plans?" I wanted to know.

"That I don't know. All I know is Proctor has been meeting with someone who wants the property, and he's afraid the deal won't go through if your client gets subdivision approval."

"So he's issued marching orders to the planning board to drag their feet?"

"Exactly."

"Who's the buyer, one of Proctor's political cronies?"

"I don't know that, either," my paranoid informant said. "But he's had a bunch of meetings about the property with some religious guy with a beard." At the mention of a beard, I thought of Mr. Goatee. Somehow he didn't strike me as particularly religious, but who knows?

"What kind of deal is Proctor's crony looking for?" I assumed it wouldn't be the sort Martin von Beverwicjk would consider, but who knows? A quick sale for a decent price would avoid litigation expenses and could generate a nice commission for the firm.

Phelps looked at me as though I was crazy to have even asked the question. "Bob Proctor only makes deals that benefit Bob Proctor. You should know that."

As we spoke, Phelps had calmed down, or so I thought. But it proved to be the proverbial calm before the storm. Without warning, he became frantic. "I have to go," he said. "I have to go. If they see us, we'll both be in danger." He pulled away from me and scurried to his undersized bicycle.

"Machias, calm down."

"No, you don't understand. I have to go." He jumped on the bicycle and began to peddle furiously, looking like a modern day Ichabod Crane, his bony knees sticking out on either side of him, as he retraced his route back to Beverwicjk Road. I watched him for a few moments then got back in my Mustang and continued to drive in the opposite direction on the perimeter road.

Phelps and I both came out to Beverwicjk Road at the same time, he at the northern end of the fairgrounds property and me at its southern end. Hunched over to fight the wind, Phelps turned left and headed back toward the highway. I didn't really think we were being watched, but he obviously did, so I decided to go in the opposite direction. As I passed Yukon Lane, the side street on my left, a police car pulled in behind me. Mindful of Sean McDermott's warning, I checked my speedometer to make sure I was safely under the speed limit. The police car followed me down the hill, over the bridge, and then up the next hill by the nursing home. He continued on Beverwicjk Road, and I turned right toward a part of town I hadn't been to in years, the reputed location of the eighteenth century forge that gave the community its name. When I was a kid growing up in Troy Forge, this area was filled with farms and forests. Now the open space is almost completely gone.

If you look at Troy Forge on a map, you'll see that five major highways cut through it. Back in the 1960s, shortly after Rick started the firm, this road network, coupled with lower taxes and relatively cheap land, was a powerful lure for corporations headquartered in Manhattan, twenty-five miles to the east. The farms and forests disappeared, replaced by corporate headquarters, warehouses, and industrial parks. Housing developments sprang up for the influx of executives, and apartment buildings for those on lower rungs of the corporate ladder. The population exploded and the farming community I remembered from my youth completed its transformation into suburbia.

I was driving aimlessly through this commercial wasteland with no real destination in mind, just killing time to avoid going home to an empty house, when I realized I had no idea where I was. The landmarks I remembered from my childhood had long since disappeared. I continued driving and eventually came to an intersection that I recognized. If I turned right, I could head home to Mountain Springs. A left turn would eventually put me on Interstate 287 heading south. It would soon be dusk and I was low on gas, so the logical thing to do was hang a right and go home. I turned left instead.

It was a decision I was soon to regret.

12

"You don't want Eddie pissed at you."

I got off the interstate at one of the exits for Morristown, the small city (or large town, depending on your point of view) that serves as our County Seat. I've been here countless times over the years, first as one of the throngs of children who came to see Santa Claus on the town green that stands in the center of the commercial district. In recent years, after trading my belief in Santa for an equally valid belief in justice, I've confined my visits to the courthouse and the surrounding buildings that house a variety of state agencies.

I drove aimlessly for the better part of an hour, punching the buttons on the Mustang's radio in search of something worth listening to. I stopped when I came to a station playing an instrumental version of "Boogie Woogie Bugle Boy Of Company B." It was from before my time, but better than most of the stuff that passes for music these days. As the last light of day drained from a steel gray sky, I found myself in an unfamiliar part of town. Here the commercial buildings had long ago been boarded up and their residential counterparts hadn't seen a paintbrush in years. The Prosperity Fairy had clearly passed over this kingdom of despair.

Suddenly my car jerked to the right and I had to fight to retain control. I pulled over, got out, and walked around my hobbled steed. Even in the fading light it was easy to see the gaping hole in my right front tire. I opened the trunk and was about to retrieve the spare tire when two men sauntered around the corner. The first was a large black man who looked like he should have been playing in the NBA. He must have been close to seven feet tall, with wide shoulders and huge hands. He had long hair like a hippie from the '70s and a scar running down one cheek. His companion was a short, slightly built guy with a mustache and a gold earring in one ear.

"I'm Joe," the smaller of the two said. "And my buddy is Barry. We're here to help you." Apparently I had wandered into a section of town populated by good Samaritans instead of muggers. I had visions of Barry lifting the car with one hand while Joe changed the tire.

My relief was short lived, however, when Barry explained how he planned to help me. "I'll hold your wallet for you, while you change the tire."

They say humor can defuse a tense situation so I countered with some of my own. "Gee, thanks, that's awfully kind of you. You're right that it's tough to change a tire when you're weighed down with a heavy wallet in your pocket. Unfortunately, I just paid this month's alimony so my wallet is pretty light right now."

Either Barry's sense of humor wasn't as well developed as I had hoped or he had never paid alimony because, without a word, he grabbed me around the throat with one massive hand and lifted me off the ground. Joe, who had been standing back several yards, watching the cross street while Barry and I did our comedy routine, moved closer and scrutinized my face, now clearly illuminated by a street light, thanks to Barry's levitation.

"Put him down," Joe instructed Barry as he came up beside his partner. I knew that was a euphemism for euthanizing pets, but I didn't realize it applied to people as well. Joe's choice of words made me think of Buddy. Once this monster choked the life out of me, who would take care of Buddy? Certainly not Aimee. She'd probably put him down the minute she got news of my death. Maybe even bury him with me like the pharaohs in ancient Egypt. It's amazing the crazy stuff that goes through your mind when you think you're about to die. It's probably a defense mechanism to distract you from contemplating what's about to happen.

"I said put him down." This time there was a real urgency in Joe's voice. I closed my eyes and waited, expecting Barry's grip to tighten. But instead, I felt my feet touch the ground as the hand around my throat disappeared.

"Sorry, buddy," Joe said to me. "We didn't recognize you at first." From the expression on Barry's face it was clear he still didn't, so Joe explained it for him. "This here's Eddie's lawyer. You mess him up and Eddie will be royally pissed. And you don't want Eddie pissed at you. Trust me on that." The only Eddie I had as a client was Eddie the Skunk. I knew he was a bad apple with an incredible number of equally rotten associates, but until now I had no idea how much weight he carried with northern New Jersey's less-than-solid citizens. I couldn't decide whether to thank him when this was all over or steer clear of him.

I had been so focused on my two assailants I didn't realize we weren't alone. Now that my feet were back on terra firma, however, I saw the tall, bald man who had been watching from down the block. As he got into a dark blue sedan, I recognized him as Mr. Goatee.

"You know that guy?" I asked, pointing down the street.

By that time Mr. Goatee was already in his car, prompting Joe to ask, "What guy?"

Was Mr. Goatee there to supervise my two assailants, or was he about to come to my rescue? Or was he there to fulfill Aimee's purported contract, and been thwarted by the appearance of Joe and Barry? Not knowing was really starting to get to me. But at least I was going home in one piece.

13

"In the real world you get two meals a day, that's it."

After Barry changed my flat tire, I drove home to Mountain Springs, fed Buddy, fell into bed exhausted and had the most bizarre dream of my life.

I dreamed I was an ancient Egyptian pharaoh. Wearing a kilt-like garment belted at the waist, with a lion's tail hanging from the belt, I was seated on a raised throne in a columned hallway filled with my adoring, loyal subjects. Aimee, seated on a throne to my right, was my queen. Buddy was on my left, sprawled out on a purple pillow rimmed with pearls. One of Lionel Newton's assistants was peeling grapes and dropping them into Buddy's waiting mouth. "Don't get used to that," I told the royal feline. "In the real world you get two meals a day, that's it."

Scanning the crowd that lined both sides of the hallway, I saw familiar faces. Scott was there, wearing a cowboy hat, as were several of my clients. Avery was there as well, dressed in a kilt like mine, but with a purse instead of a lion's tail hanging from the belt. Jorge, our gardener, was on the left side of the hallway, hacking away at a lilac bush with an electric hedge trimmer. It wasn't plugged in, of course, since there was no electricity in ancient Egypt. But because this was a dream, it worked anyway, the power cord trailing along the stone floor as Jorge worked. Machias Phelps poked his head from behind the lilac bush, only to scurry away when he realized I had seen him.

Directly across the columned hallway, Bob Proctor was sitting on an elevated chair that looked suspiciously like a miniature version of my throne. Half a dozen men in Troy Forge police uniforms were bowing before him. I made a mental note to pass a decree making it a crime to bow before anyone but me.

Looking down the length of the hallway to the rust orange desert beyond, I saw an immense pyramid with a giant eye carved into its side. A crumbling Statue of Liberty stood to the left of the pyramid with a giant "for sale" sign plastered across the front. A second sign, reading 'Caution: slaves at work' stood at Lady Liberty's feet, along with a pile or rocks. To the right of the pyramid was a Ford Mustang chained to an Old West hitching post. In the distance I saw Martin von Beverwicjk and a survey crew dividing up the desert into building lots.

"Great Pharaoh," Queen Aimee said, interrupting my review of my kingdom, "to celebrate your birthday I have arranged for the royal artisans to paint your portrait." She clapped her hands and several servants stepped forward, bowed before me, and scurried to the far wall where a linen sheet was hanging. My faithful queen clapped her hands again, and the servants pulled the sheet down, revealing brightly colored paint splattered on the wall.

"When will they start this portrait?" I asked my adoring queen.

"Start?" came the startled reply. "They have finished, and it is the finest portrait in the kingdom."

I got up from my throne and walked toward the wall, hoping a closer view would allow me to see the fine portrait that Aimee apparently saw. My queen joined me, and together we stared at the wall for several minutes while the assembled multitude waited in silence for a cue to what sort of reaction was expected of them. Finally, Aimee spoke. "The royal artisans have portrayed you arrayed in battle gear, riding to victory on your chariot," she said. "There you are," she continued, pointing to a purple blob in the middle of the masterpiece she had commissioned, "swinging your sword above your head, preparing to slay your enemies." She pointed to another section. "And there are three soldiers following behind you. And over there," she continued, pointing to a patch of red that looked as though one of the royal artisans had raided the royal wine cellar before starting work, "is the Nile flowing with the blood of your enemies."

I decided to play along. "What's that yellow blob over in the corner?"

Queen Aimee looked hurt. Or perhaps she was shocked that I was unable to recognize something that was so obvious, at least to her. "That is the royal cat asleep on our bed. He is napping while you are fighting."

"Oh," was all I could think to say as I stood there gazing at my queen's wonderful birthday present, trying to decide whether to thank her or order the execution of the royal artisans who had crafted this mess. Apparently satisfied that I was satisfied, Aimee turned to face the crowd and began to clap. They followed her lead, and the ceremonial hallway erupted in thunderous applause. When it died down, Aimee and I returned to our thrones.

As soon as I sat down, the royal cat stopped his grape gobbling, jumped onto my lap, made an airplane-circling-to-land maneuver, put his front paws on my royal chest, and began to lick my royal face.

I awoke in my king-sized (but non-royal) bed in Mountain Springs, New Jersey to find Buddy perched on my chest, and my cheek covered in cat slobber. Satisfied that he had done his alarm cat duty, he jumped off the bed and silently padded his way to the bedroom door. He paused long enough to give me his *are you going to get up or what?* look before running downstairs to his food dish on the back porch by the kitchen.

I got up and followed him, but instead of going downstairs, I headed for the so-called unused room, which was now apparently Aimee's bedroom. Halfway down the hallway I remembered that Queen Aimee was spending the weekend in the necropolis of New York, so I turned and joined Buddy downstairs for breakfast.

14

"Ever write a cookbook?"

Buddy and I spent Sunday watching old movies on television. Aimee is partial to all things modern, so old black and white movies have little appeal for her. Buddy, on the other hand, seems to enjoy them immensely. Perhaps it's because cats don't see colors the same way humans do. Or perhaps it's because he has better taste than Aimee.

Monday morning found me back in federal court, which looked much the same as it had when I left on Friday, except there were more spectators in the public gallery, including two who I guessed were reporters. Telling a federal district court judge that she's detached from reality is apparently considered a newsworthy event.

When I arrived, the giant bulletin board displaying pages from Harvey's tax return was positioned in the center of the courtroom, and Lionel Newton and his government entourage were huddled near the prosecution's counsel table. When he saw me, good old Lionel said, "Glad to see you're looking better. The shade of green you were wearing on Friday didn't do a thing for you."

"My mistake," I replied. "Got my dates mixed up and thought Friday was St. Patrick's Day." Lionel just shrugged, but one of his minions actually smiled at my wisecrack. I settled into my chair and exchanged a few words with Harvey Berkowitz. Outwardly he seemed calm and composed, but the stress of a federal trial and everything leading up to it had to be taking its toll. I did my best to assure him things were going as planned, and reiterated my previous instructions not to react to anything I did in court.

Judge Abrams entered the courtroom a few minutes later and the circus began anew. Newton called his first witness, George Boutwell, the IRS Investigator who had spent Friday morning identifying the exhibits the government intended to use to make its case. Boutwell continued the process, with Newton piling each document on top of the previous one to produce a stack the very size of which was designed to convince the jury that the government had such an overwhelming amount of incriminating evidence against my client that they should quickly return a guilty verdict and get a head start on the Thanksgiving holiday.

When Boutwell identified prosecution exhibit 244, Harvey leaned toward me and whispered, "I never filed that."

"I know," I whispered in response, "but Newton apparently doesn't. That's our ace in the hole."

Mid-morning, having completed his mountain-building exercise, Newton shifted gears and had Boutwell outline the procedures the government had used to collect all this evidence.

Then it was my turn to cross-examine the witness. "Mr. Boutwell, you said that you've been an IRS Special Agent for twelve years, correct?"

"Correct," came his one word answer. Boutwell had testified numerous times during his career and knew to give the shortest answer possible, something attorneys preach to their clients, but which clients routinely ignore.

"During that time did you ever participate in a so-called B-O-P or Business Opportunity Project?"

Boutwell hesitated and looked over to Lionel Newton, who was conferring with one of the members of his team.

"I would ask the court to instruct the witness to answer my question," I said to Judge Abrams.

Before she could respond, Newton stood up and objected. "That question is totally irrelevant. This case doesn't involve a Business Opportunity Project."

"How do we know that," I asked. "The witness hasn't even had a chance to explain what a Business Opportunity Project is." I knew what a B-O-P was and that the IRS hadn't used one with Harvey, but I was pretty sure the jury didn't know what the term meant, and I was hoping Judge Abrams didn't know either.

The judge hesitated. If my hunch was right, and she didn't understand what a B-O-P was, she could call for a sidebar conference and ask Newton. But I had Abrams pegged as the kind of person who was loathe to admit she didn't know something. My hunch was confirmed a moment later when she said, "The witness may answer," quickly adding as she looked right at me, "but it better be relevant to this case."

Realizing he had no choice but to answer my question, Boutwell said, "A Business Opportunity Project is when an IRS Special Agent poses as a prospective purchaser of a business."

"Why would you do that?"

"Because the businesses we approach are usually cash businesses, and the information we gather allows us to construct cases against taxpayers who aren't reporting all their income."

"But when you target a taxpayer for one of these operations you don't have any proof he's not reporting all his income, do you?"

"We may not have proof, but we have our suspicions."

Before he could explain why Uncle Sam would have suspicions, I asked, "Isn't it true that in addition to posing as prospective business buyers, IRS agents routinely pretend to be brokers, clergymen, lawyers, pretty much everything under the sun to entrap innocent taxpayers?"

Newton was on his feet objecting just as Boutwell said, "We don't entrap innocent taxpayers, counselor."

"Oh, you just entrap the guilty ones?" I responded sarcastically. "In that case, it's perfectly alright. A great use of the taxpayers' money."

"That's enough, counselor," the judge said. "None of this is relevant. I'm ordering it stricken from the record." Turning to the jury, she instructed, "The jury will disregard everything you've heard thus far during Mr. O'Brian's cross-examination. It's not relevant to this case and you may not consider it in reaching a verdict." The public school teacher in the front row was nodding assent, but the electrician and the plumber in the back row showed no reaction at all. I know from experience that once a jury has heard something, they're not going to disregard it just because a judge declares it stricken from the record.

Instead of moving on, I decided to see how far I could push this. "It's not irrelevant, Your Honor. It shows the ridiculous lengths the government will go to persecute innocent people like Mr. Berkowitz. It's an indication of bad faith, a colossal waste of the taxpayers' money, and the jury has a right to know about it."

Before Judge Abrams could respond, a highly indignant Saint Boutwell defended the honor of his beloved organization. "The IRS doesn't persecute taxpayers, counselor, we serve the taxpayers."

"Ever write a cookbook?" I shot back, eliciting chuckles from those who caught my reference to an old *Twilight Zone* episode. Boutwell apparently hadn't because he looked at me as though I had lost my mind.

Judge Abrams leaned forward and said, "Mr. O'Brian, you're trying my patience. None of this is relevant to the case. If you want to ask questions that are relevant, you may continue with your cross-examination. Otherwise, you're done and the witness may step down."

Boutwell took that as his cue to leave the witness stand. As he got to his feet, I said "Hold on, I'm not finished with you yet." He sat back down.

To Judge Abrams I said, "I assume my client's tax return is relevant to the case, so is it okay if I ask Secret Agent Boutwell about that?" Abrams was clearly irked by my use of "secret" instead of "special," but she just waved her hand to indicate that I should proceed.

Before continuing with my questions, Harvey and I set up two easels that were deliberately smaller and far less impressive than the huge bulletin board Team Newton had been using. With our two scrawny easels positioned so Boutwell and the jury could see them, I turned to the witness and asked, "You've shown the jury a few selected pages from Mr. Berkowitz's tax return, but his complete return is well over a hundred pages, isn't it?"

"I couldn't say; I haven't counted the pages," Boutwell responded. I picked up a copy of Harvey's return, which was almost half an inch thick and fanned it like an oversized deck of cards so the jury could see how big it was.

"Let's look at some of the pages you conveniently forgot to show the jury," I said, putting a blow-up of the second page of Harvey's return on one of the easels. I had circled in red the amount of tax Harvey had paid. It was a five-digit sum, more than what many people earn all year. I asked Boutwell to read the amount shown, and he did.

"Mr. Berkowitz paid a lot of taxes, didn't he?" I asked.

"Mr. Berkowitz had a pretty hefty income," Boutwell responded.

"Is that why he was audited and then charged with a crime?" I asked. "Because he's a successful businessman who provided jobs for a lot of people, and made a lot of money in the process?"

Before Boutwell could respond or Newton could object, I said, "Let's look at some of the ways Mr. Berkowitz made money and provided jobs in his community."

On one easel I put a large blow-up of the tax form Harvey had filed for his car wash half a mile from my office in Troy Forge. On the other easel I put a photograph of the car wash. "Did you and another agent visit the car wash at some point before Mr. Berkowitz was indicted?" I asked Boutwell.

"Yes," came his one word answer.

"And isn't it true that during that visit you interfered with my client's business by questioning employees who were trying to service customers?"

"I may have talked to employees, but my actions certainly didn't interfere," Boutwell responded.

I replaced the original page from Harvey's tax return with a second one he had filed for the dry cleaning establishment he operated in Morristown. I put a photo of the store on the second easel and asked Boutwell, "Did you visit this business in the course of your investigation?"

"Yes" came the one word answer.

"And did you subsequently arrive unannounced at the office of Mr. Berkowitz's accountant to grill him about this business?"

"We spoke to him," Boutwell said. "We didn't grill him."

I put another ten tax forms and related photos up for the jury to see. I realized there was some risk to this approach. Jurors could begin to think of Harvey as some fat cat Wall Street type who deserved to rot in jail. So I made it a point to ask Boutwell two questions about each of the businesses he and his colleague visited. The first was, "Did you see Mr. Berkowitz when you visited this business?" I knew from what Harvey had told me that Boutwell would say he had, if he answered honestly, which he did. I wanted the jury to see Harvey as a hard working small businessman who was successful not because he traded pork belly futures, but because he put in long hours at his neighborhood businesses. My second question was, "How many employees did you see at that business?" Boutwell's answer varied depending on the business, but in each case his response signaled to the jury that Harvey was providing employment for people in the community, jobs that could possibly disappear if Harvey spent time behind bars.

Boutwell's testimony also served to demonstrate the techniques he and his IRS colleagues used to collect information about taxpayers. The highlight came when I asked him about an incident involving a delivery van operated by one of Harvey's companies.

"Did you, during the course of your investigation, have occasion to speak to the driver of a van operated by one of my client's businesses?"

"I believe so," Boutwell responded.

"And did that conversation take place on the side of the road?" I asked. "State highway ten, to be precise."

"Correct."

"Did you enlist the cooperation of a local police officer to bring about that conversation?"

"Yes."

"At your request, did the police officer turn on his flashing lights and siren to signal the driver of the vehicle to pull over?"

"Yes, I seem to recall that's what happened," Boutwell said.

I established that Boutwell and another IRS agent were in a car behind the police cruiser before asking, "Was the driver of the van speeding at the time he was pulled over?"

"He didn't appear to be."

"Was he weaving in and out of traffic?"

"I don't believe so."

"Was he tailgating another vehicle?"

"I don't think so," Boutwell said.

"Was he committing any driving violations at all?"

"None that I'm aware of."

"Was he wanted by law enforcement for any reason?"

"None that I know if."

"Was he under investigation by the IRS?"

"I don't believe so."

"So would it be accurate to say that you and another agent of the federal government used a local police officer to force an innocent person to pull his vehicle off the road because you wanted to interrogate him about his employer?"

"All we wanted to do was ask him a few questions."

"In the middle of the workday while he was trying to earn a living," I pointed out. "And standing on the side of a highway while traffic whizzed by at sixty miles an hour."

Jurors' reactions to Boutwell's testimony ranged from disbelief to outrage. Hopefully, they were thinking, *If the government can use tactics like this against an innocent van driver, it could use them against me.*

I abruptly changed topics, an old trial lawyer's tactic to keep witnesses off balance. "You previously testified that the government indicts approximately three thousand taxpayers for criminal tax fraud each year, correct?"

"Sounds about right."

"How many of those three thousand cases involve a member of Congress?" I asked, hoping at least one of the jurors was aware that a congressman from a nearby state was under investigation for cheating on his taxes.

Newton objected to the question on the grounds that it was irrelevant, and Judge Abrams upheld his objection.

"How many cabinet officers have been indicted for criminal tax fraud?" I asked next, thinking of a certain politician who had "forgotten" to declare some of his income.

Newton again objected and the judge again upheld his objection.

"How many senators?" I wanted to know.

Newton objected for a third time and Abrams once again sustained his objection. At that point I turned to the judge and said, "I realize a federal judge and a federal prosecutor think they have a duty to protect other federal employees from scrutiny, but this is getting ridiculous."

Abrams was so shocked that at first she couldn't do anything but stare at me incredulously. But then, in a very measured tone of voice that was barely above a whisper, she said, "I've had it with your shenanigans. We'll take a one hour recess for lunch, and when we come back, I'll deal with you."

Judge Abrams was clearly not a happy camper. But then again, I don't think Shelly Abrams has ever been happy. Or a camper.

15

"I've had it with your courtroom antics."

When we recessed for lunch, Harvey and I headed for the diner where I had eaten breakfast after my night in luxurious government accommodations. After we had walked in the cold for several minutes, Harvey suggested that the digestive distress I experienced on Friday was more likely caused by my choice of an eating establishment than a prosecutorial poisoning plot. Since the wind was picking up and the temperature was dropping, I conceded that he was probably right, and we retraced our steps to the courthouse. Stale sandwiches from the lunch counter in the ground floor lobby would have to suffice.

As we were eating what passed for lunch, I realized that I couldn't remember the last time I had shared a meal with another human being. When Aimee and I were first married, we ate dinner together almost every night. I had just started at the firm, and although I did some litigation, most of my time was spent in the office helping Rick prepare for appearances before planning boards and zoning boards. I was almost always home by six o'clock. But after winning my first "unwinnable" case, the firm got an influx of litigation and I found myself spending more and more time in court, making it difficult to tell Aimee when I'd be home for dinner. I suspect Aimee's involvement with the Art Alliance was a form of retaliation, her way of letting me know she wasn't about to sit around waiting for me to come home. These days we almost never eat dinner together. Come to think of it, we almost never do anything together.

I was finishing off my tuna on rye when a familiar face emerged from the elevator, weaved through the midday crowd in the lobby and disappeared out the courthouse doors. It was Mr. Goatee. I considered following him outside, but decided that was a bad idea. Even if I managed to catch up with him, what would I do then? Harvey must have sensed my unease because he asked, "Something wrong?"

I considered telling him about my stalker, if in fact that's what Mr. Goatee was, but decided Harvey had enough on his plate at the moment. With the possibility of a prison sentence in his future, he didn't need to think his attorney, the only person standing between him and a guest pass to Club Fed, was too distracted to give his case the attention it deserved. So I answered his question with a lie. "No, just thinking what I can do to shake things up this afternoon."

I checked my watch and saw that it was almost time to head back upstairs to resume the judicial circus. "I'll meet you in the courtroom," I said to Harvey. "I have to call the office to check in."

He pulled what looked like a skinny brick out of his monogrammed briefcase. "Here, use this."

"What's that thing?"

"A portable phone," he said, raising the antenna and pushing some buttons before handing the object to me. "Just talk like you would with a regular phone."

I put the phone to my ear, and a second later I heard the voice of Elaine, our receptionist. I had her connect me to Carolyn, my secretary, and we had a short conversation that concluded with her telling me to hold on for Scott, who had left instructions that he had to speak to me when I called in. "It's important," she said.

She put me on hold, and moments later Scott came on the line. "We have a situation here," he said.

"What kind of situation?"

"Two Troy Forge police cruisers were camped out in our parking lot, pulling over everyone who left the office and ticketing them for pretty much every traffic violation you can think of."

I was about to tell him about the conversation I had with Scott McDermott, but decided that was something best discussed in person. I assumed portable phones used some sort of radio signal, meaning they weren't necessarily private.

"So what did you do?" I asked. "Are they still there?"

Harvey was eyeing me nervously, presumably because he thought whatever problem we were discussing involved him. I shook my head and waved my hand to signal that we weren't talking about his case.

"I called Jeff LaSalle," Scott said, referring to the local attorney who serves as the town's municipal court judge. Since municipal court is where traffic offenses are heard, he was the one who would ultimately have to deal with the result of the police department's ticket writing spree. "He called the police chief and a couple minutes later the cruisers disappeared, but not before ticketing another three clients, one of whom was Martin von Beverwicjk, who's mad as hell."

I checked my watch and realized I had to hurry or run the risk of incurring more of Judge Abrams' wrath. "Gotta run," I told Scott. "We're due back in court. We'll talk about this later." I handed the phone to Harvey who did something that I assumed was the portable phone equivalent of hanging up.

"Pretty nifty gadget," I said as Harvey put the brick-with-antenna back in its genuine simulated-leather carrying case. "What's a gizmo like that cost?"

"About a thousand bucks," came the answer.

"A thousand bucks? You've got to be kidding. I can use a pay phone for a decade for less than that."

"Perhaps," Harvey said, "but you can't put a pay phone in your briefcase. Someday everyone will have one of these, and the pay phone will go the way of the horse and buggy."

I snorted. "Yeah, right. That'll happen the year they make me Pope."

Harvey just smiled. "Wait and see. The times they are a changing."

As I threw the sandwich wrapper in a nearby trashcan, I had a thought. "What do you do if you don't have a briefcase, put the phone in your pocket?" A line from an old W.C. Fields movie popped into my head. "Is that a portable phone in your pocket or are you just glad to see me?'"

"You have a weird sense of humor," Harvey said, turning on his heel and heading for the elevators that would take us to the courtroom upstairs.

I started to follow him, but almost immediately bumped into a man dressed in gray slacks, a turtleneck, and a tweed sports jacket with elbow patches. He was younger and taller than me, with a physique I'd never have even if I spent every waking minute in the gym. His choice of clothing made him look like a university professor, but I guessed he was more likely a plain-clothes cop or a private investigator. He looked ordinary enough to blend into a crowd, but clearly more than capable of holding his own in a fight.

"Sorry," I said.

"No, my fault," he replied. "You okay?"

I assured him I was fine and continued on my way. It wasn't until I was riding in the elevator that it dawned on me that our collision might not have been accidental. Good grief, I thought, a pickpocket has just used the classic bump and grab in a federal courthouse in full view of who-knows-how-many private security guards and federal marshals. I reached into my jacket pocket and was relieved to discover my wallet was still there.

My relief was short lived, however. As I stepped off the elevator, one of the deputy marshals who had escorted me to the holding cell on Friday informed me that Judge Abrams wanted to see me in her chambers. "Now," he added at the end of the message to ensure I knew the judge was expecting me to hop in my time machine and show up ten minutes before I got her summons. I left Harvey in the hallway and wound my way back to the judge's chambers. Her secretary looked up when I entered the outer office, and without saying a word, jerked her thumb toward the closed door behind her. The judge's secretary apparently didn't like me any more than Abrams did.

I knocked to announce my arrival and, without waiting for a response, entered the inner sanctum of Judge Shelly Abrams, federal district court judge, protector of courtroom decorum and all that is right and holy. Lionel Newton was already there, seated in one of two chairs facing the judge's desk, his face festooned with a very satisfied Cheshire cat smile. The judge pointed to the empty chair, apparently assuming that without her direction I would have sat on Lionel's lap. A millisecond after my rear end made contact with the chair, Judge Abrams launched into her tirade.

"I've about had it with your courtroom antics, Mr. O'Brian," was the opening salvo in what was to become a completely one-sided war of words. "I know what you're trying to do, and let me make it clear that you will not succeed in turning my courtroom into a three-ring circus."

"That was not my intent, Judge." I briefly considered adding, "One ring will do quite nicely," but decided that probably wasn't a good idea.

She picked up a document from a stack of papers, slammed it down in the middle of the desk, and pushed it in my direction. The words *Guidelines for Litigation Conduct* were clearly visible at the top of the first page. "This copy is for you," the judge said. "I strongly suggest you read it thoroughly and take it to heart." She was holding what I assumed was another copy of the same document. "Turn to page five," she instructed. I did so and found a series of numbered paragraphs under the heading: *Lawyers' Duties to the Court.*

"Item number one," the judge began, reading from the document she was holding. "Lawyers appearing before a federal court will speak and write civilly and respectfully in all communications with the court." She stopped reading and looked right at me. "Do you seriously think calling me detached from reality in open court is respectful?" I tried to think of a way to answer her question in the affirmative without actually using the word "yes," but before I could formulate a response, she supplied one for me. "No, it is not respectful. Not even close."

"Item number two," she continued, once again reading from the document. "Lawyers will not engage in any conduct that brings disorder or disruption to the courtroom." Looking up at me, she asked, "Do you think your antics disrupt my courtroom?" Once again, she answered her own question. "Yes, they most certainly do."

For the next forty-five minutes Judge Abrams went paragraph by paragraph through the various duties an attorney owes to the majesty of the court, and how I had failed miserably in all of them, thereby besmirching the honor of our sacred, ancient, and honorable profession. While she was excoriating me, I flipped to the first page of the document and confirmed my suspicion that the guidelines had been written by a federal court judge. Throughout Abrams' tirade, Lionel Newton sat quietly, the smug smile never leaving his face.

Judge Abrams concluded by asking me, "Do you understand, Mr. O'Brian?"

"Absolutely," I replied.

The typical attorney is more careful after a tongue lashing from a federal court judge who, with one phone call to the Office of Attorney Ethics, has the power to create a disciplinary debacle. Fortunately for my clients, I'm not the typical attorney, as I demonstrated minutes later.

16

"Government always wants more."

Shortly after our conference in chambers concluded, Harvey's trial resumed with Judge Abrams instructing Newton, "Call your next witness."

"Prosecution calls Joseph J. Lewis," Newton responded. But before the witness could get out of his seat, I was on my feet.

"Judge," I began, "before the government continues to persecute Mr. Berkowitz, I think the jury has a right to know why this afternoon's session was delayed."

"Sit down, Mr. O'Brian," came the judge's response. I could tell by her clenched jaw that she hadn't cooled off from her tirade in chambers.

I didn't sit down. Instead, I said, "You delayed proceedings so you and Mr. Newton could harangue me in your chambers. And the jury has a right to know what took place."

"For starters, Mr. O'Brian, nobody was harangued. And secondly, as you well know, the jury does not have a right to know what takes place in chambers." That statement was factually correct, but it made the jurors think the judge was trying to hide something from them, which is exactly what I wanted.

Before she had a chance to explain why jurors aren't privy to discussions in the judge's chambers, I said, "A delay like the one we had is prejudicial to my client. It creates a false impression in the minds of the jurors."

"It does no such thing," the judge replied in a tone of voice that made it clear she was getting even more annoyed, assuming that was possible.

"Give me one minute, just sixty seconds, to address this issue and I promise I won't say a single word until it's time for me to cross examine Mr. Lewis." Ordinarily, it would be dangerous to make that kind of promise, but I had a pretty good idea what Lewis would say and didn't think it would be necessary for me to make an objection. And if it was necessary, I could always break my promise. Besides, I didn't really expect Abrams to grant my request, which was admittedly ridiculous. I just wanted the jurors, who didn't understand the finer points of courtroom procedures, to think Abrams was being unfair by turning down my request for a mere sixty seconds to satisfy their curiosity about what had happened in their absence.

It may have been the prospect of me sitting quietly like a good little defense attorney with hands folded and mouth shut, or perhaps its was the realization that muzzling me would play into my hand, but whatever the reason, Abrams said, "You've got one minute, no longer. And you say anything that's inappropriate and I'll hold you in contempt."

"Nothing inappropriate," I said, keenly aware that she and I were undoubtedly operating with different definitions of inappropriate. "During our conversation in your chambers, you quoted from this," I continued, holding up the document she had given me, *Guidelines for Litigation Conduct*, which states on page two that lawyers have a duty to, and I quote, zealously advance the legitimate interests of our clients."

Judge Abrams didn't stop me, so I turned to look directly at the jury and continued. "In this case, to zealously advance the interests of my client, as required by the litigation guidelines,

I have to make sure you understand that the deck is stacked against Mr. Berkowitz from the outset. He has only me to protect him from a government with virtually unlimited resources. Mr. Newton has two attorneys to assist him, along with a forensic accountant, two clerks, a veritable army of Special Agents, secret agents, and investigators from both the IRS and the Department of Justice, and who knows how many other people working behind the scenes." As I said this, I pointed to the table where Team Newton was arrayed.

"Mr. O'Brian," Judge Abrams said in exasperation, "your client can employ experts to help in his defense if he so chooses. You know that."

"He has a right to employ experts," I agreed, "but he doesn't have the virtually unlimited budget that the federal government has. And what's particularly unfair is the fact that Mr. Newton's prosecutorial army is being paid for by Mr. Berkowitz and his fellow taxpayers." As I said "fellow taxpayers" I pointed to the jury to make sure they knew their tax dollars were helping to foot the bill for Newton's army. "It's like forcing a man to supply the rope that's used to hang him."

With that I sat down. Abrams stared at me, deciding the best way to deal with my inappropriate little speech. She must have concluded that no response was the best response because she turned to Newton and said, "Call your next witness."

Joseph Lewis took the stand and testified that he was an air conditioning contractor who had done work for Harvey Berkowitz many times over the years. Newton showed him one of the documents that George Boutwell had identified that morning. Under questioning by Newton, Lewis testified that, yes, the document was a contract for his company to install an air conditioning system, that, yes, he had delivered and installed the air conditioning system specified, and yes, he had been paid the contract amount.

Newton walked to the bulletin board displaying pages from Harvey's tax return and pointed to an oversized copy of a Schedule E used to report profits and losses from rental real estate. "The address on the work order matches the address of one of the defendant's rental properties, doesn't it?"

"Yes," came Lewis' answer.

The string of "yes" answers ended when Newton asked, "But you didn't install the air conditioning system at that property, did you?

Lewis, an older gentleman with a receding hairline and a nervous habit of rubbing his hands together, didn't answer the question. Instead, looking down at his shoes as though embarrassed to make eye contact with Harvey, he said, barely above a whisper, "Mr. Berkowitz is a good man. I've worked on his properties for many years. Never had a problem. He always paid me on time, never tried to renegotiate once we agreed on a price."

"The witness will answer the question," Judge Abrams directed.

Lewis sat silently for several seconds, then shook his head and said, "No, that's not where I installed it."

"Where did you install the system?" Newton wanted to know.

"At Mr. Berkowitz's home in Upper Montclair."

Upper Montclair is just north of Montclair, yet despite their proximity and similar names, the two towns could have been on separate planets. Homes in Montclair come in three varieties: reasonably nice, not bad, and who-in-his-right-mind-would-live-there. Homes in Upper Montclair also come in three varieties: extremely nice, over-the-top nice, and is-that-a-house-or-a-hotel? nice. Harvey's place was hotel-sized even before Joseph Lewis and his brethren constructed an addition. It was definitely not the sort of abode that would make the jurors feel that Harvey was one of them. So when it came time for me to cross-examine Mr. Lewis, I started by asking him if he knew how much my client paid in property taxes each year. Before he could answer or Newton could object to my completely irrelevant question, I supplied a number that was probably more than what many of the jurors earned in a year. "And Mr. Berkowitz is on trial because the government wants more money. Government always wants more," I concluded.

Judge Abrams was banging her gavel even before Lionel Newton got to his feet. "The jury will disregard Mr. O'Brian's cross-examination," she instructed. "The amount of property tax paid by the defendant is irrelevant. This case is about whether or not the defendant filed a false federal income tax return, not about the amount of property tax he paid." Then, to me she said, "The purpose of cross-examination is to ask questions of the witness, not to make a speech. If you have more questions, ask them. Otherwise, you're finished."

"Just doing my duty to zealously advance my client's interests," I responded. "Local government, federal government, it's all government. Local taxes, federal taxes, it's still taxes."

"Sit down, Mr. O'Brian," Judge Abrams instructed in a tone of voice that made it clear that I was one word away from another night in luxurious government accommodations.

I sat down, and Lionel Newton spent the rest of the day putting on a parade of witnesses, all of whom provided testimony that was a carbon copy of that offered by Joseph Lewis. The jury heard from an electrician, a general contractor, a plumber, a drywall installer, and the owner of an insulation company. Each admitted billing Harvey for repairs to a rental property identified in his tax return, but performing the work on the megasized addition to his home in Upper Montclair. All seemed profoundly uncomfortable, the drywall installer in particular, who perspired so profusely it looked as though he had just come out of a steam room. The body language of the electrician and plumber in the back row of the jury box told me they were as uncomfortable as the witnesses. I wondered how many times they had helped an important customer play fast and loose with the tax laws by supplying less-than-accurate paperwork.

When it came time for me to cross examine each witness, I stood, faced the jury box and said, "Out of respect for the jury's time, no questions." Each time I did that, Judge Abrams looked pleased that I wasn't using the opportunity for more courtroom antics. Newton had a look of smug satisfaction, happy in the belief that the testimony he elicited from the witnesses was so damaging to Harvey that there was nothing I could do to lessen its impact. He was about to learn otherwise.

I changed tactics after William Orton, the owner of Orton Insulation, testified. I started by asking, "Were you recently audited by the IRS?"

"Yes," he answered.

"Had you ever been audited before?"

"No, never," he said with a certain amount of pride. "I've been filing a tax return for decades and never had any problems with the IRS."

"And during the course of that first-time audit were you asked to testify against Mr. Berkowitz?"

"Yes," he answered, more hesitantly this time.

"And did the IRS tell you that testifying against Mr. Berkowitz would affect the outcome of your audit?"

Orton looked toward Newton and his small army of government assistants. I was almost positive he had made a deal to testify against Harvey in exchange for a favorable conclusion of his audit, and he was now wondering if answering my question would allow Uncle Sam's revenuers to renege on that arrangement. I turned to Judge Abrams and said, "Would the court please instruct the prosecution to assure the witness that providing truthful answers under oath won't invalidate the deal he was pressured into making with the IRS?"

Newton shot to his feet. "Mr. Orton was not pressured into making a deal or doing anything else for that matter."

"Does the government deny making a deal with Mr. Orton?" I asked.

Before Newton could answer, Abrams said, "The witness will answer the question."

I turned back toward William Orton and nodded for him to continue. "I was told that if I testified against Mr. Berkowitz, the IRS would close their audit and accept my return as filed."

"And what was it about your tax return that they were questioning?" I asked.

"They said I didn't report all of my income." Before I could ask my next question, an indignant Mr. Orton added, "But that's not true. I reported every penny I made, just as I have every year."

"You weren't selling your business, were you?"

"No," he responded, apparently confused by my question.

"Then I guess they weren't using their notorious B-O-P operations to entrap you," I said, taking the opportunity to remind the jury of the tactic George Boutwell had testified about that morning.

Newton naturally objected, and Abrams upheld his objection, but it was too late. I had made my point.

"Did they tell you what would happen if you refused to testify against Mr. Berkowitz?" I asked William Orton.

"They said my audit would continue," came his answer. "And they made it clear that it was just a matter of time before they found something wrong with my tax return."

"So you were blackmailed into becoming a stool pigeon for the government," I said. Then, turning to face the jury, I added.

"And all the other contractors who testified here today were also blackmailed."

Abrams banged her gavel so hard it broke, and a piece of it went flying across the courtroom. "You apparently didn't learn your lesson on Friday," she said to me. "Let's see if another five hundred dollars will teach you not to pull a stunt like that in my courtroom."

I had instructed Harvey, as I do with all my clients, to never react to anything that happens in the courtroom. But I was pleased when he disregarded my instructions by standing, pulling a checkbook out of his pocket, and asking Judge Abrams, "Should I make it payable to IRS or to you?"

The judge was caught by surprise. In the few seconds it took for her to process Harvey's question, he whispered to me, "I guess we're both out of our mind."

17

"This doesn't change anything."

Judge Abrams dismissed the jury for the day and then spent the next half hour reading the riot act to both Harvey and me before a public gallery that had grown larger as the day progressed. Word of my antics had apparently spread throughout the courthouse. Judging by the number of three-piece suits, I estimated the majority of spectators were attorneys who, having concluded their business in the courthouse, decided to experience vicariously what they would never do in a courtroom. I also suspect that Abrams decided to deliver her tongue lashing in the courtroom, instead of in her chambers, to ensure her message was delivered to any other attorney who might attempt to emulate my tactics.

Abrams made it abundantly clear that if she had to endure "any more nonsense" from either of us, she'd hold us in contempt, and the five hundred dollar fine would grow to a sum large enough to convince us that she meant business. She concluded by asking, "Mr. Berkowitz, do I make myself clear?"

"Yes, Your Honor," Harvey answered.

"And Mr. O'Brian," she said, directing her attention to me. "Do you realize how close you are to being brought up on disciplinary charges?"

Since the jury was out of the room, there was no point in continuing the confrontation, so I decided my best move was to let her think I was conceding defeat. "If I went overboard in my zeal to protect my client's interests, I apologize to the court," I said.

That seemed to placate her, and she recessed proceedings for the day. As Harvey and I were leaving the courtroom I saw the gentleman who had bumped into me in the lobby at lunchtime. Mr. Tweed Sports Jacket was sitting in the back of the courtroom, in the seat that Mr. Goatee had occupied on Friday.

"We seem to keep bumping into each other," I said, stopping at the last row of seats. I decided to do a little fishing. "You an attorney?" I asked. His only response was to lean back in his seat, drape his arm over the back of the seat next to him and look at me. "An Investigator?" He didn't answer. "Bondsman?" No response to that either, except for a slight smile. "An IRS agent, perhaps?"

He laughed when I mentioned the IRS. "Not even close. Name's Reynaldo. I work for someone who from time to time has his own problems with the IRS. If he ever needs an attorney, I'll recommend you," he said, as he got up and headed for the elevators, having tactfully evaded answering my question. As he was walking away, he looked over his shoulder and added, "assuming you haven't been disbarred by then."

Rather than join the crowd waiting for an elevator, Harvey and I ducked into a nearby conference room. "That was a nice touch with the checkbook," I said as I closed the door.

"Least I could do," he replied. "Felt bad for you since you're already out five hundred bucks."

"No, actually you're already out five hundred bucks. I have to pay the fines, but they're showing up on your bill. Part of your litigation expenses." He didn't say anything, just arched an eyebrow in response. "Don't complain. You're getting a break. Your litigation expenses are a fraction of what they'd ordinarily be for a trial like this. Hell, your expert witness fee is just a few thousand dollars," I reminded him.

"That's something I've been meaning to talk to you about," Harvey said. "Are you sure we don't need more than one expert witness?"

"One expert is all you need," I assured him, "if it's the right expert. And, trust me, C.M. Clay is the right expert. By the time he's finished the jury will want to lynch Newton and give you a medal. If you think I can put on a show, wait till you see Professor Clay in action. He makes me look like an amateur."

"Speaking of witnesses," Harvey continued, "if you knew all those contractors who testified against me made deals with the IRS, why didn't you object to them testifying?"

"Knowing and suspecting are two different things. Besides, the fact that they made deals with the government doesn't necessarily prevent them from testifying," I said. "Having the jury think the IRS had to coerce people to testify against you helps our case. And Newton may have run afoul of the *Giglio* case by failing to tell us about the deals beforehand. That gives us a potential bargaining chip when it comes time to discuss a deal.

As I was trying to come up with a way to explain the prosecution's duty to reveal potentially exculpatory evidence, Harvey asked, "You really think you'll be able to negotiate a deal that keeps me out of jail?"

"That's the game plan," I said.

Harvey visibly relaxed when he heard that, and we chatted for another ten minutes about sports, the weather, the lousy parking situation in Newark, anything but his trial. When we emerged from the conference room, the lemming-like rush to the elevators had ended. We caught the next car to the ground floor, made our way through a nearly empty lobby and emerged into a drizzle that was turning to sleet as the temperature dropped. Traffic was light, the city's office workers having already gotten out of town before the sun disappeared. The sidewalks were also deserted, the plunging thermometer acting as an additional deterrent to anyone who would brave an after-dark walk in Newark.

Harvey turned left toward the lot where he had parked his car. I turned right and began the trek to a more distant lot. The parking lot next to the courthouse that I usually use when I come to Newark was closed, having been flooded by a ruptured water pipe and then turned into a veritable skating rink by the falling temperature. The parking garage across the street, where I would have liked to park, still hadn't opened even though construction had been completed three months ago. According to the story I heard, the city building department had a beef with the state's compliance officer, who, in turn, was fighting a turf war with someone at the federal level. The end result was a perfectly good parking garage constructed at taxpayer expense that the taxpayers couldn't use because of government infighting.

I had walked about halfway down the block when I heard footsteps behind me. They were speeding up. Whoever was following me wasn't running, but was walking faster in an apparent effort to catch up with me. Not a good sign in a place like Newark, particularly after dark. I stopped and turned around, expecting to be confronted by an urban thug, but came face to face with a judicial varmint instead. It was Judge Abrams.

"Counselor," she said.

"Your Honor," I replied.

She fell into step beside me without an additional word being spoken by either of us until we came to a narrow alleyway. I turned into the alley and the judge stopped, apparently deciding whether to follow me and have company or stay on the reasonably well-lighted sidewalk and continue her trek through the urban jungle alone.

"Shortcut to the parking lot," I said, pointing toward the alleyway. She joined me after a moment's hesitation. An attorney isn't supposed to converse with a judge outside the courtroom in the middle of a trial unless opposing counsel is present, but Lionel Newton was nowhere to be seen, and five words don't constitute a conversation in my book.

We were about fifty feet into the alley when a dark shape next to a dumpster emerged from the shadows and took on human form. The teenager who materialized before us was decked out in the latest urban thugware – black stocking cap, black sweatshirt, black jeans and black boots – fashionably accessorized with a six-inch knife, which he cheerfully displayed in his right hand. We stopped and I instinctively raised my briefcase in front of me like a shield.

"Wallets," the kid said, as he swaggered toward us, casually tossing the knife from hand to hand. The oversized predator's smile never changed as he calmly surveyed his prey.

Acting purely on instinct, I grabbed the judge's elbow and pulled her with me as I backed away, never taking my eyes off our assailant, who continued to approach, certain that he had the upper hand. We hadn't taken more than a few steps when I heard a metallic click behind me at the same moment that our would-be mugger's predatory smile vanished. Glancing over my shoulder, I saw Reynaldo in the traditional shooter's stance, legs planted shoulder width apart, his right hand holding a pistol and his left under the right wrist to steady his aim.

"Bad idea," Reynaldo said, aiming his pistol at the knife-wielding teenager. The kid took one look at the gun and the man holding it, and realized his odds of winning an altercation were less than zero. Without a word, he slowly placed the knife on the ground, raised his hands, palms outward, in a sign of submission, and backed slowly down the alley. After taking several tentative steps, he turned and ran into the darkness.

"Thanks," I said to Reynaldo as he returned the pistol to a shoulder holster that I was pretty certain wasn't there when I had seen him earlier in the courthouse.

"Just doing my civic duty," came the reply. "You probably want to stay on the sidewalk," he added.

We followed his suggestion, and for the next couple blocks he followed us, apparently to ensure against a return visit by our urban fashion maven.

When I was sure Reynaldo was out of hearing range, I asked the judge, "You know him?"

"I was about to ask you the same question."

I told her about our meeting in the lobby, and later seeing him in the back of the courtroom. "I'm guessing he's law enforcement of some type, otherwise he wouldn't be permitted to have a gun in the courthouse."

The judge's response surprised me. "Even if he were law enforcement, he wouldn't have a gun in my courtroom without my knowledge."

We continued to the parking lot without further incident or conversation. At some point during our trek, Reynaldo vanished in the night as silently as he had appeared.

I walked the judge to her car. She got in, started the ignition, and lowered the window. "This doesn't change anything, Mr. O'Brian. I'm still not going to let you turn my courtroom into a circus." She paused and I waited for what would come next. But she just closed the window and drove away.

18

"Blind men don't drive."

Tuesday morning I set out for the office instead of Newark, having received a phone call the previous evening from Judge Abrams' clerk informing me the judge had recessed the Berkowitz trial for the day. The clerk didn't provide an explanation, and I didn't ask, assuming, incorrectly as it turned out, that the judge was so traumatized by her attempted mugging she was taking the day off to recover. The spring-like weather we had enjoyed the previous week was now a distant memory, replaced by gray skies, a chill wind and intermittent snow flurries.

I took my usual route: a short drive along my quiet side street onto the tree-lined boulevard that serves as Mountain Springs' main thoroughfare to the highway, and then east on Route 46 into Troy Forge. As I crossed the town line, an oversized image of Billboard Bob greeted me with a reminder that *Troy Forge is a safe community*. A moment later a Troy Forge police cruiser appeared behind me and I discovered just how safe the town had become under Bob Proctor's rule.

Mindful of Sean's warning, I immediately checked my speedometer and saw that I was driving just under the posted speed limit. I was in the right hand lane, dutifully observing all traffic laws, and under normal circumstances wouldn't have any reason to be concerned that a police car just happened to be occupying the stretch of highway behind me. But recent events convinced me my circumstances were somewhat less than normal. Since the start of the Berkowitz trial I had been shadowed first by Mr. Goatee, then the mysterious, though seemingly benign, Reynaldo. I had been the target of two attempted muggings, one in Morristown and one in Newark. And now I had the local constabulary waging a campaign of intimidation. Perhaps the police car behind me was just a coincidence, but I was too cynical to think so.

What happened next proved my cynicism was justified.

The police cruiser accelerated, shot by me, and pulled back into my lane so close to my Mustang's front bumper that I had to tap the brakes to avoid hitting it. I was so focused on the kamikaze cop that I didn't see the second police car until it appeared just a few inches from my rear bumper. Maybe Proctor's principality is a safe community because everyone has a protective police escort.

I drove sandwiched between the two police cruisers for about half a mile, trying to determine the best way to deal with the situation. The car in front of me had slowed down, apparently daring me to pass him. I considered doing just that, but decided that if I did, he would pull me over for speeding. But then I realized that perhaps the cops were setting me up for a violation of the statute that prohibits driving too slowly. Most people don't know that law exists because it's rarely enforced, probably because motorists are more likely to drive too fast than too slow, but it's the law nonetheless.

To pass or not to pass, that was the question. The decision was made for me a few moments later when a third cruiser pulled alongside me in the left lane. I was now surrounded on three sides by Bob Proctor's private palace guard, and had no choice but to remain where I was. The driver of the car ahead of me started playing the brake light game. He'd tap the brakes for no apparent reason, making me do likewise, increasing the chances of being rear-ended by the car behind me.

Although my focus was fixed on the brakes lights ahead of me, I kept tabs on the car to my left, afraid that he might up the ante in our little game by "accidentally" drifting into my lane. Out of the corner of my eye I saw the passenger's window in that cruiser slide open. The uniformed cop in the passenger's seat was wearing sunglasses, not because he needed them on this gray November morning, but probably because he thought they made him look more intimidating. He was right. When he realized I saw him, the bastard smiled. A big toothy grin that let me know he and his buddies were having great fun at my expense.

As we came down the hill by the industrial park, clustered together in our tight little formation, I looked for a place where I could pull off the highway. The strip mall up ahead was a possibility, but I decided against it. I'd have to hit the brakes to make a quick right turn into the parking lot, practically assuring the car behind me would become intimately acquainted with my Mustang's rear bumper.

It was at this point that I wished I had an expensive portable phone like the one Harvey Berkowitz carried. But then I realized it wouldn't do me any good. Who could I call? The nearest state police barracks was a good forty minutes away, and even if they already had a car in this area, it would be my word against half a dozen local cops. Not likely the state trooper would be taking my side on that one. I could dial 911 and hope the local cops who showed up weren't part of Proctor's private army, assuming the 911 dispatcher even believed me. Or maybe she would believe me and send more of Proctor's people. Until I had a better idea of which cops worked for Bob Proctor and which ones worked for the people of Troy Forge, Sean McDermott was the only one in the department I could really trust. And I couldn't very well call 911 and ask for him by name.

At some point very soon I would have to get in the left lane to make the turn for our office, but the police car to my left was blocking me. I put on my left turn signal. The cop in the passenger seat said something to the driver, and both of them laughed. Then he removed his sunglasses, looked right at me, smiled a big toothy smile, and slowly moved his head from side to side. They had no intention of allowing me to make a left turn.

Fortunately, while the cop was auditioning for a toothpaste commercial, the traffic light at Baldwin Road turned red, forcing our automotive entourage to slow. I took advantage of the opportunity to make a sharp right into the parking lot of a fast food joint, realizing too late that I was entering an exit. I half expected the police car behind me to follow me into the parking lot and issue a summons, but he and the other two cars continued on their way when the light turned green. I sat in the parking lot for a few minutes to compose myself before completing my drive to the office without further incident.

When I got there, I went straight to Scott's office. He and Avery were discussing the tax implications of a particularly nasty divorce case Scott was handling. "Sorry to interrupt," I said, "but something's come up you guys should know about."

I must have looked rattled because Scott didn't hesitate for a second. Pointing to the sofa against the far wall, he said, "Grab a seat." Then he picked up the intercom and told his secretary to see if she could find Rick.

Although I should have waited for Rick to get there, the adrenalin was still flowing, so I told Scott and Avery about my run-in with the Troy Forge cops, making a mental note to tell Rick the story later.

"I'll call Jeff LaSalle," Scott said, referring to the local attorney who serves as the part-time judge for the municipal court in Troy Forge. Our firm has had numerous dealings with Jeff over the years, both in his capacity as a judge and as an attorney, and had come to regard him as someone who was scrupulously honest and fair-minded. But I had my doubts that there was much he could do.

"I'm not sure Jeff will be able to help us with this," I said. "He can dismiss cases that end up in his court, but he can't stop the cops from harassing us or our clients. Proctor's goons know that, which is why they didn't bother writing me a ticket on some bogus charge. I think their game plan is to intimidate, not drag us into court. They want to keep this little war on their turf, not ours." I told them about my conversation with Sean McDermott, concluding with the prediction, "This is just the opening salvo in Proctor's war against Martin von Beverwicjk and everyone helping him on that subdivision project. I have a feeling things are going to escalate."

No sooner had I made that prediction than Rick walked into the office clutching a copy of the local newspaper that confirmed my status as a soothsayer. He was obviously upset, but clear-eyed. The Rick of old was with us, at least for the moment. "Machias Phelps is dead," he said, tapping the newspaper. "Proctor's people killed him."

Avery, who was closest to Rick, walked toward him, hand outstretched, and Rick gave him the newspaper.

"He was an odd little man," Rick said.

"You don't know the half of it," I muttered.

Either Rick hadn't heard my comment or chose to ignore it. "But odd or not, he didn't deserve to die like this."

"Hold on," Avery said, scanning the newspaper article. "This says Phelps died in an auto accident. He drove a town-owned car into a tree."

"Nonsense," Rick shot back. "Blind men don't drive. Phelps never had a driver's license, never tried to get one, and never would have gotten one if he had tried. He was legally blind. Rode a bicycle everywhere. There's no way he died in a car accident. He was murdered, and Proctor's people made it look like an auto accident."

I knew Phelps wore glasses that made his eyes appear to bulge out of his head, but I didn't realize he was legally blind, just unfashionable.

Avery wasn't convinced. "Even if that's true, it doesn't mean Proctor had anything to do with this."

"How did he end up behind the wheel of a car owned by the Town of Troy Forge?" Rick wanted to know.

"There are any number of possibilities," Avery replied.

Before he could regale us with a list of those possibilities, I jumped into the conversation. "I think Rick might be right. I met with Phelps on Saturday and he was convinced that Proctor's people were following him everywhere he went. In fact, he told me that he and I were both in danger if Proctor found out about our meeting." I gave them details about my meeting with Phelps, concluding with, "And my run-in with the local cops this morning convinces me Proctor has more in store for us."

My prognostication, unfortunately, turned out to be correct.

19

"In how many of those photos is she naked?"

Wednesday morning I made the trek to Newark to continue the Berkowitz trial. Word of my antics had apparently been circulating because almost every seat in the public gallery was filled by the time I arrived. Judging by the number of suits I saw, it was likely that my fellow members of the bar accounted for the majority of spectators. But I also saw the same two people I had pegged as reporters on Monday. I made a mental note to confirm my hunch at the noontime recess. A little publicity might be just what I needed to turn my courtroom circus into something Barnum and Bailey would envy.

Proceedings began when Judge Abrams instructed Lionel Newton to call his next witness, who turned out to be an IRS agent named Edward Rollins. Agent Rollins was tall and thin, with slicked-back hair and a pointed nose. He licked his lips constantly, and his eyes never stopped moving, making him look like a predator scoping out his next meal. I first encountered him during a pre-trial motion and immediately nicknamed him "Mr. Shifty." If Hollywood needed someone to play a sadistic IRS employee who loved his job way too much, Mr. Shifty is the guy central casting would send.

Mr. Shifty was the agent in charge of collecting evidence to prove the second count of the indictment, which charged Harvey with fraudulently claiming deductions for a business trip that was actually a two-week family vacation in Hawaii. For the next ninety minutes, he treated the jury to an exclusive showing of *The Berkowitz Family Vacation*. Jurors saw photos of Harvey and his family getting into a taxi at the airport in Honolulu, entering a posh hotel, on a boat, at the beach, at the hotel pool, and a number of other venues that certainly didn't look like they had anything to do with business. There had to have been more than a hundred and fifty photos. I don't know the exact number because I stopped counting at fifty-four. In addition to the photos, Rollins had a stack of paperwork, much of which Harvey and his accountant had handed over during an audit in a futile attempt to convince the IRS that Harvey's expenditures were legitimate tax deductions.

Throughout Mr. Shifty's presentation, I sat quietly at the counsel table, slumped down in my chair, my body language signaling to the jury, *This isn't important, so feel free to just ignore it.* There were several times when I could have objected, but I didn't. Instead I let Mr. Shifty drone on, putting the jury to sleep with his endless presentation of photos and paperwork.

Like many of the jurors, I fell into that nether world that lies between waking and sleep. My eyes were wide open, but unfocused, as my mind wandered uncontrolled into the back alleys of my subconscious. I couldn't visit ancient Egypt as I had in my dream Saturday night, but I conjured up an image of me walking through the empty rooms of my home in Mountain Springs. Aimee was nowhere to be seen, but Buddy was at my side as I strolled from one room to the next to the sound of Simon and Garfunkel singing *The Sounds of Silence*. For reasons I can't explain, my dreams – and even my daydreams – all come with a soundtrack.

In my daydream the furniture was gone, but the walls were covered with abstract paintings, all of which were crooked. Aimee, the art expert, can tell you what an abstract painting is supposed to represent, but she can't tell that it's hung crooked. As I wandered through the daydream version of my house, I stopped at each painting and straightened it. I was in the process of leveling a particularly ugly work of faux art when I heard a noise in the kitchen and went to investigate. I found Rick pouring himself a Jameson's, which was odd since Rick's been a teetotaler ever since he got stopped by the local constabulary at one of their sobriety checkpoints. But I guess Rick assumed daydream cops wouldn't stop him without probable cause.

With glass in hand, Rick joined Buddy and me as we went out through the kitchen door onto the enclosed porch, and then out the back door to what should have been the driveway leading to our detached garage. But instead of finding ourselves outdoors, we were back in the living room. And all the paintings had been rearranged. The large orange and black one that I thought was a witch on a broomstick, but which Aimee assured me was an abstract representation of sunrise, was over the fireplace instead of on the opposite wall. Its former home was now occupied by Aimee's latest find, entitled *Blowing in the Wind,* which, in an effort to charm her into bed, I had readily agreed was a clever abstract representation of Peter, Paul and Mary. Unfortunately, I was supposed to have seen a wheat field, not three folk singers.

I snapped out of my near-dream when I heard Newton say, "Your witness."

I began my cross examination of Edward Rollins, aka Mr. Shifty, with a series of innocuous questions.

"Did you take all these photos?"

"Most of them," Agent Rollins replied.

"The ones in Hawaii?"

"Yes."

"Do you have any photos of just Mr. Berkowitz by himself?"

"Yes."

"Do you have any photos of Mrs. Berkowitz alone?"

"Yes." Like Agent Boutwell, Rollins was trained to give the shortest possible answer.

"How about my client's son? Any photos of just him?"

"Yes, I believe so."

"And my client's sixteen year old daughter, Leah? Any photos of just her?"

There was a momentary hesitation before Mr. Shifty answered that question. "Yes, I believe we have photos of just the daughter."

My next question was guaranteed to snap the jury out of the late morning siesta that Mr. Shifty's direct testimony had induced. "In how many of those photos is she naked?"

Before Lionel Newton could jump to his feet and shout "objection," Mr. Shifty's eyes stopped moving and locked on mine. And in that brief instant, I saw a mix of shame and fear in his eyes.

"In my chambers," Judge Abrams demanded. "Now."

Lionel Newton and I made our way to the judge's inner sanctum and took our seats, he at the right hand of the Almighty Abrams and me at her left. A nanosecond after my rear end made contact with the chair, Abrams unleashed her fury.

"Mr. O'Brian, you know you need a good faith basis for making a claim like that, and you damn well better have one."

"I do," I lied.

"And what is it?" the judge wanted to know.

Since I didn't have one, I said, "I can't reveal that information, judge. It's protected by attorney-client privilege."

"Nonsense," Abrams said. "Let's hear it. Now."

"Judge, revealing that information would seriously undermine my trial strategy and prejudice my client's rights."

Judge Abrams wasn't buying it. "I've had enough of your nonsense. You're either going to give me your good faith basis for asking that question or I'm going to hold you in contempt. And for good measure, I'm going to call the Office of Attorney Ethics." She put one hand on her telephone, apparently to let me know she was serious about making the phone call that would most certainly lead to disciplinary action.

At this point I had no choice but to stand my ground and brazen it out. So I said, "Yes, you could do that, or you could simply direct Mr. Newton to let you examine all the photos he has of my client's sixteen year old daughter so you can see for yourself that the photos I'm referring to actually exist." I thought my suggestion was a logical way to proceed, which is why I assumed the judge wouldn't accept it. Which would be fine since I didn't really believe Mr. Shifty had taken photos of Leah naked. I was stalling for time, trying to come up with a plausible explanation that would satisfy the judge.

Unfortunately, the one time I wanted Abrams to ignore my suggestion, she followed it. "Okay," she said. "I'll give you a bit more rope and see if you hang yourself." Then to Newton she said, "Have someone bring me all the photos of the defendant's daughter that were taken in Hawaii."

"Judge," Newton said, "under Rule 16, Mr. O'Brian only has a right to see documents we intend to use at trial. Even if the photos he's referring to existed, we wouldn't use them as evidence. O'Brian is fishing."

"I suspect you're right, at least about the fishing part" the judge said. "And if I go through those photos and don't find the ones Mr. O'Brian is talking about, they'll be hell to pay. But Mr. O'Brian won't be looking at the photos, I will. So Rule 16 doesn't come into play."

Newton wasn't happy with the judge's decision, but he stepped into the outer office and relayed Abram's instructions to one of his assistants. A few minutes later, a different member of Team Newton appeared with a file box. Abrams pointed to her desk and Newton's assistant set the box down and left the office, closing the door behind him. The file box was filled with folders containing hundreds of photographs. Abrams scanned the labels on the file folders. "These are organized by location rather than by who's shown in the photos, so this may take some time," she said.

Judge Abrams began looking through the photos. Five minutes passed. Then ten. Then fifteen. Then twenty. With each passing minute my chances of facing disciplinary action increased. With each passing minute Newton looked more satisfied. But my apprehension and his satisfaction abruptly ended when Judge Abrams muttered, "Oh, my God."

The judge removed the top photo from the stack she was holding and placed it face down on her desk. Looking at the next photo in the stack, she repeated, "Oh, my God" again, only a bit more slowly. This was followed by an "Oh ... my ... God" as she looked at the third photo in the stack. Another minute passed as Abrams leafed through the remainder of the photographs in that group. She then spread five photos face up on her desk so Newton and I could see them. All had been taken through a window, presumably with a telephoto lens. The first showed Leah getting out of the shower, stark naked, and reaching for a towel. The remaining four were obviously shot in quick succession, with the last showing Leah partially covered by the towel.

The judge looked at me with an expression I interpreted to mean, *How the heck did you find out about these?*

"I want those entered into evidence," I said calmly, not letting on that I was just as surprised as she was.

"Absolutely not," Lionel Newton said.

That was the wrong thing to say, because it prompted a now less-than-happy Judge Abrams to tell him, "I decide what's entered into evidence in my court, not you."

Newton wasn't about to be deterred. "Judge, these photos have nothing to do with the case. They're highly prejudicial and completely irrelevant. It's highly likely that Agent Rollins took these particular photos by mistake."

"Mistake, my ass," I said.

"For once, counselor," Judge Abrams said to me, "you and I agree on something. I think it's highly unlikely Agent Rollins took all five of these by mistake. The first one maybe, but not the others. Nevertheless, Mr. Newton has a point. And perhaps more importantly, I don't think your client or his daughter would like these photos shown in open court."

She was right about that, but I wasn't about to give in. "Those photos demonstrate bad faith on the part of the government," I said. "They show how far the government will go to prosecute my client."

"I'll allow you to question Agent Rollins about how he came to take these photos," Judge Abrams said, "but the jury isn't going to see them."

That was fine with me. Talking about the photos without actually showing them would allow the jurors to use their imagination and, hopefully, conjure up something even more prurient and tawdry. Of course, I'd help them do just that.

Judge Abrams looked at her watch. "I had planned to discuss this with the two of you when we recessed for lunch," she began, "but since we're already here and looking at photos, we might as well look at one more." She removed a photo from a drawer, placed it on her desk facing Newton and me, and then pushed it forward so we could both see it. The photo showed the fuzzy image of a man who looked a lot like Reynaldo. "This is an image pulled from one of the ground floor surveillance cameras," she said.

She turned to me and asked, "Would you agree with me that this is Reynaldo?"

"Looks like him," I said.

"Who's Reynaldo?" Newton wanted to know.

Judge Abrams recounted the story of our attempted mugging two nights earlier and how Reynaldo appeared out of nowhere to save us from the urban fashion maven. When she finished, she pushed the photo directly toward Newton and asked, "Do you know this man?"

Newton picked up the photo and studied it more closely before answering. "No, I don't recognize him."

"You sure?" Abrams wanted to know.

"The photo's kind of blurry, so I can't be a hundred percent sure, but, no, I don't recognize him."

"He doesn't work for DOJ?"

"Not that I know of," Newton replied.

"And he doesn't work for IRS?"

Again Newton answered, "Not that I know of."

"Well, find out," the judge told him. "This man apparently had a weapon in my courtroom and I'm supposed to know everyone who has a weapon in my courtroom. I don't know who this man is, and I want to know."

"I'll look into it," Newton said. His tone of voice made it clear that he was as much in the dark as Abrams and I were.

"I spent most of yesterday on the phone with people I know in Washington," Abrams said, continuing to direct her remarks to Newton. "If I find out this man is connected with the prosecution and you haven't told me about him, I won't be happy."

I had thought the judge was taking the day off to recover from our attempted mugging, but apparently I was wrong. She had spent the day working the phones, but came up empty-handed. I guess federal judges don't carry as much weight with Uncle Sam as I thought.

"Judge," Newton protested, "even if he was with my team, how could he get through security with a gun?"

"I don't know," Abrams said, "and that's what bothers me."

20

"I haven't invented it yet."

When I emerged from Judge Abrams' chambers, I found Harvey waiting for me in the hallway outside the courtroom.

"What the hell was that all about?" he wanted to know.

I took his elbow and steered him toward a nearby conference room, closed the door behind us, and proceeded to fill him in on what had transpired in the judge's chambers. He was understandably upset. "It's one thing for the IRS to come after me, but why my family?" he wanted to know. "My daughter isn't on trial."

"Neither is your delivery driver or your accountant or any of your employees," I said, "but that didn't stop the IRS from grilling them. These guys can basically do any damn thing they want. But for what it's worth, I don't think they meant to photograph Leah. Remember, you had adjoining hotel rooms. I think Rollins was snapping away at all the windows and Leah just happened to be there." That explanation may not have been entirely convincing, but hopefully it was enough to put Harvey's mind at ease, at least for the moment.

"Can we make a deal and end this trial?" he asked.

"No, I don't think so. Not at this point, and certainly not on terms you'd be happy with. I know these photos are upsetting, but things are going better than we could have hoped. Hang in there."

I continued my pep talk for a few minutes more, and Harvey began to feel a bit better. We went downstairs for another gourmet meal from the lunch counter, and then came back upstairs to continue our battle with the government.

When we got off the elevator, a very attractive redhead with a short hairdo was waiting for us. I recognized her as one of the people I had seen at the back of the courtroom that morning. When she saw us, she walked over, stuck out her hand and said, "Stacey McCain," adding "Star Ledger," apparently meaning she worked for the newspaper bearing that name.

"Sorry," I said, "I don't have a copy of the *Ledger* to give you." To my surprise, she laughed. It's nice to know someone other than me finds me funny.

"Can you tell me what happened in the judge's chambers?" she asked.

"No, I can't talk about that," I said. "What happens in chambers stays in chambers. But if you want to know, stick around for the afternoon session. I think you'll find it highly entertaining." Then I had a thought. "And if you meet me after we recess for the day, I'll give you some inside information nobody else knows." That sent Ms. McCain scampering back to the courtroom, her cute little head filled with visions of the news scoop that would soon be hers.

"What information are you going to give her?" Harvey asked.

"Damned if I know," I replied. "I haven't invented it yet."

We returned to the courtroom, took our seats and waited for Judge Abrams to take the bench. When she arrived, she immediately turned to the jury box and said, "Before Mr. O'Brian continues with his cross-examination of Agent Rollins, I want to explain to the jury what took place in my chambers. I examined the photographs that Agent Rollins took in Hawaii and found five of the defendant's daughter. These show her unclothed, and appear to have been taken without the young lady's knowledge. These photos will not be entered into evidence, as they have no probative value. In other words, they have no bearing on whether or not the defendant is guilty of the crime for which he is on trial, and I am directing you to give them no weight in reaching your verdict. I have, however, ruled that Mr. O'Brian may question Agent Rollins regarding how these photographs were taken." Abrams then nodded for me to proceed.

For the next half hour I asked Rollins, aka Mr. Shifty, every question I could get away with about the circumstances surrounding those photos. Newton objected constantly, and it may have been my imagination, but I thought the judge overruled almost as many of his objections as she sustained. I took that as a sign that he had joined me in the doghouse, at least for the time being.

I managed to get Mr. Shifty to admit that he and another agent had deliberately rented a hotel room that gave them a direct view into the rooms Harvey had rented for his family. He also admitted that he knew who was staying in what room, and that Leah was not under investigation. That, of course, made it difficult to explain why he was photographing her room in the first place. None of this testimony really had anything to do with tax fraud, but it made Rollins look like a voyeur and a pervert, and hopefully made the jury more sympathetic toward Harvey.

The testimony most embarrassing to Rollins came when I asked him about the camera he used to take the photos. He testified that it was a single lens reflex camera with a manual film advance. That meant he had to crank the lever on the top of the camera to advance the film to take the next shot. "So, to get the five photos of my client's teenaged daughter in the nude, you couldn't just press the shutter once, you had to press the shutter and crank the film advance five times, correct?"

"That's correct," Rollins replied.

By the time I finished that line of questioning, the jurors didn't seem at all happy with Mr. Shifty, not even the public school teacher in the front row, who I considered the most sympathetic to the government's case.

I followed up my questions about the photos by asking Mr. Shifty about money, or more specifically, the taxpayers' money.

"Is your office in Hawaii?" I asked for openers.

"No." The one word answer again.

"Where is it?" I wanted to know.

"Here in Newark."

"So the IRS flew an employee from New Jersey all the way to Hawaii?"

"Correct."

"The IRS has agents all over the country," I said, adding, "kind of like the Gestapo in Nazi Germany or the KGB in the Soviet Union."

Newton naturally objected, and Abrams naturally sustained his objection. I was waiting for her to rebuke me for my comment, but instead she simply said, "Move on, counselor."

"Why didn't the IRS send agents from an office in Hawaii or California?" I asked Rollins. "That would have been a lot easier than having you fly there from New Jersey, and it would have saved the taxpayers a lot of money."

"Because I had been working the case and was familiar with the file," Mr. Shifty responded.

"And that brings up an interesting question," I said, glancing at the jury to signal they were about to hear something important. "When did you buy the plane tickets and make the hotel reservations for your little junket to Hawaii?"

I caught Rollins off guard with that question. Unlike his other answers, this one took a moment for him to formulate. "I can't answer that question," he said, "our travel department makes those arrangements."

"Fair enough," I replied. "Here's a question you can answer. How long before the date of that trip did you know you were going to Hawaii?"

Mr. Shifty's eyes stopped scouting the room and locked on mine. This time I'm quite certain I saw anger in his eyes. "Approximately two months."

"So this wasn't a last minute response to Mr. Berkowitz's plans."

Rollins said nothing since my question was actually a statement.

"That means," I continued, "the IRS knew about the trip in advance."

Again, no response.

I looked over to the jury box and saw several furrowed brows, which I interpreted to mean they were wondering how the IRS could have known about the trip. So I asked Rollins the obvious question. "How did the IRS know?"

Mr. Shifty looked toward Lionel Newton for instructions, or perhaps trying to signal that this would be a good time to object to my question.

"Would the court please instruct the witness to answer my question," I said to Judge Abrams.

Newton was halfway out of his chair when Abrams said, "The witness will answer the question."

"How did the IRS know of the trip in advance?" I pressed Rollins.

"Answering that question would reveal operational details that I'm not at liberty to disclose," he responded.

The judge wasn't at all happy with that answer. She looked directly at Rollins, and I'm sure was about to tell him to answer my question when I put my hand up and said," That's okay, Your Honor, I won't press the issue." Abrams game me a look that said, *What the hell are you up to now?* But she didn't say anything to Rollins. "Agent Rollins doesn't have to answer," I said. "I know the IRS has secrets it doesn't want to reveal to the public."

I started back to my seat, but after taking a few steps, turned to face the jury and added, "just like the Gestapo and the KGB."

21

"To the IRS, Harvey Berkowitz is a disease."

Instead of chastising me for comparing the IRS to the Gestapo and the KGB, Judge Abrams recessed court for the day. Was she going easy on me because she was still ticked off at Newton for the nude photos of Leah? That was too much to hope for. More likely, she decided the jury had heard enough for one day. Or maybe she had heard enough. Judges have told me that I tire them out. I can't imagine why.

As I was packing up my briefcase, Harvey asked, "So how exactly did the IRS know about my trip to Hawaii?"

"Mysterious are the ways of the IRS," I replied.

That answer apparently wasn't satisfactory. "No, seriously, how could they have known? I made all the arrangements through Aaron Gertz. And we know he didn't tell the IRS because they never contacted him."

"That's what Aaron says," I replied. "You better hope he's being straight with us because if he shows up to testify, we've got a problem. A big problem."

"Don't worry," Harvey said. "Aaron and I are old friends. If he says he never discussed the Hawaii trip with the IRS, then he never discussed it with them."

Stacey McCain was waiting for me as we left the courtroom. When I saw her, I told Harvey to head home and I'd see him in the morning. He started to say something, but stopped when he saw the *Star Ledger* reporter. "Hope you've invented something good," he whispered, before joining the crowd shuffling toward the elevators.

Ms. McCain and I went into a nearby conference room. It was a different one than the one Harvey and I had used two days earlier, but it looked exactly the same. The same conference table and chairs, designed for durability rather than comfort. The same ugly carpet. The same institutional paint job. The same portrait of President Reagan on the wall. I often wondered how much money Uncle Sam could save by hanging a portrait of George Washington in public buildings instead of changing to the current Oval Office occupant every time we elected a new president.

Stacey and I took seats across from each other, and I began by asking, "Ever been to the circus?"

"Absolutely," she replied, "I've recently been enjoying the performance at the Barnum, Bailey, and O'Brian circus."

"Then you've seen one of the things every circus needs: clowns."

"Lots of clowns," she agreed, without elaborating on whom she considered a courtroom clown, which is probably just as well.

"But the clowns are just the warm-up." I continued. "The main attraction is always the lion tamer. Here's a guy who goes into a cage with a bunch of wild animals that could rip him to shreds, and all he has to protect himself is a whip and a chair. People come to a circus to see the lion tamer for the same reason they slow down to gawk at a traffic accident. Everyone's waiting to see if the lion tamer will end up as dinner for one of the animals."

"And he never does," Stacey said.

"Exactly. And that's because when he's training the lions, the first thing he does is make sure they know he's the boss."

"Sounds plausible," Stacey said, "not that I'm an expert on lion taming. But what does that have to do with this case?"

"It's the reason the government charged Harvey Berkowitz with criminal tax fraud, instead of handling this as a civil matter," I said. "There are only a few thousand criminal tax fraud cases brought each year, but there are tens of thousands of civil actions."

"What's the difference?" Stacey asked.

"With civil tax fraud, you pay a penalty if you lose. But if you lose a criminal case, you end up in prison." I should have stuck a "probably" in there since losing a criminal tax fraud case won't necessarily land you behind bars. And had I wanted to be really accurate, I could have explained that the minimum-security facilities where tax cheats end up are a bit more pleasant than the prisons where murders and rapists go. But I didn't want to burden Stacey with too many details, particularly ones that didn't fit my narrative.

I paused while Stacey wrote something in her notebook. When she looked up, I continued. "Criminal tax cases cost the government money, sometimes a lot of money. In this case, for example, the government paid agents to follow my client all the way to Hawaii. Even if the government wins – and I'm not saying they will – the money they collect won't begin to pay what it cost to prosecute this as a criminal case." That wasn't necessarily true, but it fit in nicely with the story I wanted to convey.

"So why did they charge him with criminal tax fraud?" Stacey asked.

"Because Harvey Berkowitz is a dangerous lion and the government, the lion tamer, has to make sure he and other taxpayers who think like him know that Uncle Sam's the boss."

"So they want to make an example out of him," Stacey said.

"Exactly."

"So what's the big inside information you were going to give me?" she asked. I got the distinct impression Stacey thought I was wasting her time.

"From the moment I got involved in this case, I wondered why the government was bringing a criminal case instead of treating this as just a plain vanilla, civil fraud case. The defendants in criminal tax cases are almost always famous people - entertainers, politicians, mafia dons, big-time drug dealers. The government wants defendants who are in the spotlight. That maximizes publicity and let's them send a warning to millions of taxpayers by winning a single case."

"So what's your point?" Stacey asked.

"The point is that Harvey Berkowitz isn't famous. Not even close. He's a small businessman who runs a handful of mundane local businesses in suburban New Jersey. Not the kind of person the IRS goes after with a criminal prosecution. That's what makes this case stick out like a sore thumb."

I picked up the photos of Harvey's businesses that I had used in the courtroom earlier. "A car wash," I said, laying the first photo on the conference table. "A furniture store," I said, laying the second photo down in front of Stacey. I repeated the process with all of Harvey's businesses until the table was covered with photographs. Then I asked, "What's the common denominator in all these photos?"

She studied the photos for a minute or so and then looked up at me. "I'm not sure what I'm supposed to see. Like you said, they're pictures of businesses."

I picked up the photo of the car wash and pointed to the trailer-mounted sign sitting in the parking lot. Then I picked up the photo of the dry cleaners and pointed to a similar sign in the front window. There were two signs in the furniture store photo, one on the front of building and another on a delivery truck by the loading dock on the side.

Stacey went through the photos and found the same sign in all of them. "You're telling me that because of that sign, the IRS decided to make this a criminal case?"

"That's the only reason I can come up with." I knew it was a lie, of course. After Harvey's "ultimate chutzpah" deduction caught their attention, the IRS undoubtedly went back though his previous returns, realized he had engaged in some extremely creative accounting for years, and decided enough was enough.

The IRS version of events was more accurate, but mine was better fodder for a newspaper article. So I pushed my version.

"To the IRS, Harvey Berkowitz is a disease, an extremely contagious disease. And they're determined to eradicate the disease before it can spread. He could infect hundreds of people, who in turn could infect thousands more. Next thing you know, Uncle Sam has to contend with a full-blown epidemic. The IRS wants to put Harvey behind bars today so they won't have to deal with hundreds of thousands of taxpayers like him in the future." I realized I had morphed Harvey from a lion to a contagious disease, mixing my metaphors, or perhaps mangling my metaphors. My high school English teacher would be so proud.

Stacey studied her notes for a moment and then looked up. "What's the name of your client's organization?"

"There is no organization," I said. "That's the point. With a formal organization, the government would know who to keep tabs on. The organization's leaders would end up being audited every year, as well as the organization itself and the people who contribute to it. There are a million things the government could do to harass an actual organization. But if there is no formal organization, just a bunch of individual citizens who believe in the same thing, it makes it much more difficult for the government to crack down on them. To Uncle Sam, a lone wolf with an idea that inspires others is more dangerous than an organization." I had gone from lion tamer to disease to lone wolf in the course of fifteen minutes. My high school English teacher would definitely be pleased with my verbal virtuosity.

Unfortunately, Ms. McCain was a different story. I could tell from her body language she wasn't buying what I was trying to sell her. She confirmed that by saying, "Nothing personal, but I find all this a bit hard to believe. I'm not sure there's much of a story here. This just seems like a routine tax case."

I was ready with a response. "I thought so too at first, but then crazy stuff started to happen."

"What kind of crazy stuff?"

I told her about Mr. Goatee and Reynaldo, crafting the story to make it sound as mysterious as possible and leaving her with the impression Uncle Sam had me under round the clock surveillance. I told her about being poisoned while in federal custody, carefully omitting any mention of the local diner where I had breakfast.

"You're not seriously suggesting the federal government hired someone to poison you or mug you, are you?" Stacey asked.

"No," I answered, "but what are the chances of being mugged twice in one week? And both times having some mysterious individual appear out of nowhere?"

"Pretty slim," she admitted, adding, "note to self: stay away from this guy, he's a magnet for muggers." She smiled when she said it, an impish smile that, combined with her short red hair, big green eyes, and freckled face, made her look like a very feminine leprechaun - with an empty ring finger. I made my own mental note. It was X-rated.

"So, you're saying this Reynaldo and the bald guy work for the government, and they're following you?" Stacey asked.

"I have no idea who they work for," I said, perhaps the first completely truthful thing I had told her. "All I know is that they keep showing up. And remember on Monday when Special Agent Boutwell testified about using a local cop to stop the driver of Harvey's delivery van?"

"Yeah, that seemed pretty extreme," Stacey said.

"Well, local cops have been tailing me. And on Monday, while Boutwell was testifying, the cops ticketed every car leaving my firm's parking lot." I was pretty certain my hometown constabulary was following orders from Bob Proctor rather than the IRS, but I didn't mention that to Stacey. Why ruin a good story?

"I don't know," she said skeptically, "all this seems pretty far fetched. Next thing you know you'll be claiming the government taps our phones and reads our mail."

I pulled back, afraid that I might have gone too far. "No, I'm not suggesting that at all. This is the USA, not the USSR. The government needs a warrant to tap someone's phone, and the mail is sacrosanct."

For the next ten minutes I embellished the story as much as I could without making it sound too outlandish, adding as many details as I thought would help my case. Stacey scribbled away in her notebook, but then abruptly stopped, looked at her watch, gathered up the photos from the conference table and said, "Gotta go. I have a story to write." I had no idea whether or not she believed me, or if the story she planned to write would be about the Berkowitz case or something else.

I followed her out of the conference room, intending to ride down to the ground floor with her, but she darted across the lobby and hopped on an elevator just before the door started to close. I hurried after her, thinking she would hold the elevator for me.

She didn't.

"By the way, do you like modern art?" I yelled just before the door slid shut.

"Hate it," she said.

And then she was gone.

22

"That BOLO was bogus."

My drive home from Newark was uneventful until I got off Interstate 280 in Troy Forge and turned onto Route 46, heading west to Mountain Springs. I hadn't driven more than a few hundred yards when a police car pulled in behind me. Flashing lights and a siren informed me that I was once again being invited to interact with Bob Proctor's palace guard.

I pulled off the road next to yet another of Billboard Bob's public proclamations. In the time it took me to learn that *Troy Forge parks are the best in the county,* the cop got out of his patrol car and made his way to the side of my Mustang. He was young, in his mid-twenties, tall, and slender. He had the confident gait and neutral, no-nonsense facial expression that every cop in the country must learn on his first day of police training. "Good evening, sir," he said when I rolled down my window. The word "sir" can be either a sign of respect or contempt, depending on how it's said. The cop was using it as a sign of respect. So far, so good. "May I see your license, registration, and insurance information, please?" It was a request rather than a demand, another good sign. I retrieved the documents from the glove compartment, and as I handed them to the cop, I realized he was resting his right hand on his holster. It may have been an instinctive reflex or perhaps standard procedure, in case I pulled a weapon out of the glove compartment, but given all that had happened recently, having his hand hovering above a presumably loaded gun made me more than a little nervous. "Thank you," he said. "Please stay in your car; I'll be back shortly."

The cop returned to his police cruiser where I assume he checked my paperwork. He came back a couple minutes later, handed my documents back to me and then, to my surprise, said, "Sorry for the inconvenience, Mr. O'Brian. The reason I stopped you is because your car matches the description of a stolen vehicle."

"Having checked my registration, I assume you know the car is mine," I said.

"Yes, sir. No problem. I didn't recognize you at first, but when I ran your registration I realized who you were." I didn't know what to make of that comment until he added, "You represented my sister last year on that drug charge in Dover. The drugs weren't hers; they belonged to that creep she was living with at the time."

"Oh yeah, I remember that case." I didn't really, but I wasn't about to tell him that. "How's your sister doing?"

"That trial was a wakeup call. She dumped her boyfriend and went back to school."

"Glad everything worked out." That was true, even if I didn't remember the case or the sister.

"By the way," he said, pointing to the documents he had handed back to me, "that's last year's insurance card." Before I could say anything, he continued, "But I owe you one for taking care of my sister, so I'll assume this year's card is either in your glove compartment or your wallet. You're free to go."

"Thanks, officer," I said. I was so relieved that our little encounter had ended, and even more relieved to discover that not all the cops in Troy Forge were part of Mayor Proctor's private army, that I added, "Give my regards to your sister."

My relief lasted only a few minutes. As I passed another one of Billboard Bob's public proclamations, a different police cruiser appeared behind me with lights flashing and siren wailing. This was getting ridiculous, but what could I do? I pulled to the side of the road and waited. This time two cops got out of the police car and approached, one on each side of my Mustang. I rolled down the window and waited. "Good evening, officer," I said to the one on my side of the car. "This is not the Mustang you're looking for."

Either the cop had never seen *Star Wars* or my Obi-Wan Kenobi impression wasn't up to par because he never cracked a smile. "License, registration, and proof of insurance," was all he said. This time it was a command, not a polite request. I complied, noting that I now had two cops resting their right hand on a loaded gun when I reached into the glove compartment. Perhaps I should leave my documents out in plain view before I drive through Troy Forge in the future.

The cop on my side of the car grabbed the papers out of my hand and started back to his cruiser, but not before ordering me to keep both of my hands on the steering wheel. His partner remained by the passenger side door, presumably to ensure I was a good little driver and did as I was told.

Five minutes passed. The cop standing sentry duty on the passenger's side folded his arms. I wanted to do the same, but decided to keep my hands on the wheel, not knowing what would happen if I moved. Probably nothing, but at this point, who knew?

Another five minutes passed. My arms started to ache, and I tried to stretch them by pushing against the steering wheel. The slight movement caught the cop's attention and he rested his hand on his holster. It was the sort of subtle move that was designed to intimidate but allow him to truthfully say he never drew his weapon if we ended up in court. I had had enough.

I was tired and hungry, and my arms were getting numb, so I looked right at the cop and began a staring contest to see who would blink first.

The contest was interrupted a moment later when the first cop re-appeared by my window and said, "We seem to have a problem here." I was about to explain that I really did have insurance, but had simply forgotten to put the latest insurance card in the glove compartment when he added, "We stopped you because you have a broken tail light."

"That's news to me," I said. "Last time I checked, both tail lights were working fine."

"You calling me a liar?" the cop asked.

"No, I'm telling you I was unaware my tail light wasn't working."

"Well maybe we should double check." He nodded to his partner, who disappeared from my view. I couldn't see where he went, but the sound of shattering plastic told me the first cop was correct: I now had a broken tail light.

The second cop reappeared next to his partner. "Yup, your tail light is definitely not working," he said, slapping his night-stick into the palm of his hand.

Suddenly the first cop was all smiles. "But hey, it's not that big a deal, so we won't write you up. Just make sure you get that fixed." There was no mention of my expired insurance card. The whole point of the stop was obviously lawyer harassment, not law enforcement.

As Proctor's bullies in blue walked back to their car, I hit the accelerator, anxious to get out of Troy Forge as quickly as I could.

I almost made it ... but not quite.

I had gotten to within sight of the town line when a third police cruiser pulled in behind me. Almost immediately his lights went on and a whoop of his siren made it clear that he wanted me to join him on the side of the road for another session of Mustang bashing. Instead of pulling over, I stepped on the accelerator, and my pony car took off like the thoroughbred it is. The cop was driving a late model Police Interceptor, a version of the Crown Victoria that Ford manufactures for police departments. I wasn't sure what kind of engine he had in that car, but whatever it was, it was no match for my Mustang. The cop made a valiant effort to catch me, but I made it to the Mountain Springs town line.

As soon as I crossed that invisible, but legally significant boundary I slowed down to just above the speed limit and checked my rear view mirror, expecting to see the Troy Forge police car make a U-turn at the median opening just inside the town limits. The cop turned off his lights and siren as he entered Mountain Springs, but instead of turning around, he stayed right behind me for the rest of my journey on Route 46.

When I turned onto the town's main boulevard, he followed me. When I turned left onto my quiet side street, he followed me. I pulled into my driveway and the cop followed me. At this point it was obvious I was in real danger. I had no way of knowing what Proctor's henchman would do when he caught up with me, but I was reasonably certain whatever was about to happen wouldn't be by the book.

I parked the Mustang in the circular driveway in front of the house, jumped out and sprinted to the front door before Proctor's bully with a badge had even gotten out of his police cruiser. My hands were shaking, partly from the cold but mostly from the apprehension of what the huge shape getting out of the police car in my driveway had in store for me. I fumbled with my keys and almost dropped them. The simple task of unlocking the door, which would ordinarily take a few seconds, seemed to take an eternity. At one point in the process, the cop yelled something, but I was so intent on getting inside that I didn't hear what he was saying. I finally got the door open, slipped inside, immediately re-locked it, and threw the seldom used deadbolt for good measure. I leaned up against the door, catching my breath and listening to my pounding heart. Despite the cold, sweat was trickling down my back.

Buddy was waiting for me in his usual spot in the middle of the foyer. He looked up at me with his big green eyes and started to purr. "What are you purring for?" I asked. "I thought cats were supposed to be able to sense danger. There's a guy outside with a gun." Buddy gave the feline equivalent of a shoulder shrug and headed for his food dish on the back porch. I headed for the phone on the hallway table. The Mountain Springs police would probably side with their Troy Forge counterpart, but maybe not. At least I'd have a witness to whatever was about to happen. I had just dialed the "9" in "911" when the doorbell rang and a familiar voice on the other side of the door said, "Brendan, open up. It's me, Sean."

I put the phone down, walked to the sidelight next to the door, parted the curtain and saw Sean McDermott standing on the porch. "I'm alone," he said when he saw me peering through the glass. "Open up, it's cold out here."

The first words out of his mouth when he got inside were, "You do realize you're supposed to pull over when a police car signals you to stop, don't you?"

"I did stop," I said, as we went into the living room and sat down. "Twice. The first time because a guy from your department thought I was driving a stolen car. The second time I stopped so two guys from your department could smash my tail light."

"That BOLO was bogus," Sean said. "When I saw that we were supposed to be on the lookout for a red Mustang, the kind of car you just happen to drive, I got suspicious and checked with other departments in the area. They didn't know what I was talking about. A real BOLO goes out to all the departments in the area, but ours was the only one looking for a red Mustang."

"Proctor's doing?" I asked.

"I can't prove it, but most likely."

I described the two cops who had stopped me for the second time that evening. "Sounds like Clark and Pagano," Sean said. "Those two are bad news. They're not only happy to do whatever Bob Proctor wants, no matter how shady, but seem to get off on it."

"Sean, what's going on? Ever since we filed that lawsuit, all hell has broken loose."

"I don't know," he said. "But you're right, you guys have stirred up a hornets' nest."

"You've heard about Machias Phelps, haven't you?" I asked.

"Yeah, in fact, that's why I'm here." He handed me a large manila envelope.

23

"No Guinness record for you."

Thursday morning I once again journeyed to beautiful downtown Newark to continue as ringmaster of the Berkowitz and O'Brian circus. The day's performance began when I continued my cross-examination of Edward Rollins, aka Mr. Shifty, by asking him if he was alone when he took the photos the jury had been shown the day before.

"No," came the one word answer.

"Who was with you?" I asked.

"Agent Delano."

"Did you and Agent Delano ever operate separately? For example, did you follow Mr. Berkowitz while he followed another family member?"

Mr. Shifty must have thought I was setting a trap because he answered, "Absolutely not. IRS procedures require us to work in pairs so we have verification of everything we observe."

I was setting him up, but not in the way he thought. "So, that means while you were photographing Mrs. Berkowitz poolside, for example, nobody was watching where Mr. Berkowitz or other family members went?"

Rollins hesitated, not quite sure where I was going with my questioning. "That's correct," he finally said.

"And while the two of you were photographing Mr. Berkowitz at the hotel spa, nobody was following his wife to see where she went?"

"Also correct," Rollins said.

I shifted topics to keep him guessing. "You previously testified that you're familiar with the various businesses that my client operates, correct?"

"Yes, that's correct."

"So you're aware that he operates a car wash?"

"Yes."

"A dry cleaning franchise?"

"Yes."

"A copy center?"

"Yes."

"A florist?"

"Yes, I believe so."

"An apartment building?"

"Yes."

"An auto salvage yard?"

"You mean a junkyard? Yes, I know he operates a junkyard," Rollins answered in a way that was clearly designed to denigrate Harvey. Little did he realize that Harvey's "junk yard" was a veritable cash cow that made more money than several of the other businesses combined. Of course, how could anyone at the IRS be expected to know that since most of the cash never showed up on Harvey's tax return?

Mr. Shifty had become a real yes man, albeit not willingly, and he certainly didn't seem happy about it. In fact, he looked so unhappy that I decided to cheer him up by ensuring him an entry in the *Guinness Book of World Records* for the most consecutive, one-word, negative answers by a shifty-eyed government employee.

"Were you aware that on the day you were photographing Mrs. Berkowitz at the hotel swimming pool, and weren't following Mr. Berkowitz, that there was a trade show for the car wash industry in another hotel a few miles away?"

Lionel Newton shot to his feet. "Objection, Your Honor. There's no proof that such a trade show was held, much less that the defendant attended it."

"Here's the program for that trade show," I said, holding up a brochure so the jury could see it. "And I don't recall asking the witness if Mr. Berkowitz attended it. I simply asked him if he knew about it." Of course, Harvey not only hadn't attended that trade show, neither he nor I even knew about it until I came across an article in a Honolulu newspaper while preparing for trial. I fully expected Judge Abrams to sustain Newton's objection, but that was fine. The jury had already heard the question and could use their collective imagination to conjure up an answer.

But to my surprise, Abrams said, "I'll allow it. The witness will answer the question."

Newton was about to respond to the judge's ruling, but she shot him a look that I interpreted to mean, *If he knew about the nude photos of his client's daughter, he probably knows more than you think.* Newton got the message and sat back down.

I looked at Rollins and our eyes locked. "No," he said, unknowingly starting his quest for a *Guinness* world record.

"Were you aware that during the time my client was in Honolulu there was a meeting of dry cleaning franchisees?" I asked.

"No."

"A trade show for owners of copy centers?"

"No."

Newton stood to make another objection, but Abrams waved him back down.

"A meeting of the American Florists Society?"

"No."

"Were you aware that on the day you took nude photos of my client's sixteen year old daughter without her knowledge or consent, the National Multi-Family Property Owners Association was holding its annual meeting two miles away?"

Newton started to get up again, and again Abrams waved him back down.

"No," Rollins answered, making admirable progress on his quest for a *Guinness* record.

"And were you aware that one of the largest Japanese manufacturers of equipment used in auto salvage yards has its U.S. headquarters within walking distance of where Mr. Berkowitz and his family were staying?"

"No, I was not," Mr. Shifty said, breaking his string of one-word answers.

"No *Guinness* record for you," I said at the same moment Lionel Newton got to his feet yet again. This time he managed to have his say without the judge waving him down.

"None of this is relevant," he said. "It has no probative value, even if it's true, and the prosecution is not conceding that it is. Even if these events took place, there's no proof that the defendant attended them."

"How would you know whether or not he attended these functions?" I shot back. "Your government voyeurs were so busy photographing my client's naked teenaged daughter they had no way of knowing where he was most of the time."

Newton continued to protest, and before Abrams could rule, I threw up my hands in my best imitation of sincere disgust and said, "Right, it's just a coincidence that there were trade shows, meetings, and conventions for the various businesses my client owns, all held while he just happened to be there, and all a stone's throw from the hotel where he just happened to be staying."

I headed back to the counsel table and pulled out the chair to sit down. But before I did, I added, "And it's just a coincidence that my client's family members are officers in the corporations that operate these businesses, and would therefore have a bona fide reason to be there."

Newton made a good argument, so Judge Abrams sustained his objection and then told the jury to disregard my cross examination of Mr. Shifty.

Somehow I didn't think they'd do that.

Abrams checked her watch and said, "I think we'll recess for lunch at this point, but before we do, I want to inform the jurors and counsel that I have to hear motions in connection with another case tomorrow morning. So when we finish this afternoon's session, we'll be in recess until Monday."

A three-day weekend! And it's not even a federal holiday.

24

"Things are more complicated than you realize."

During the noon recess, I bought a tuna sandwich from the lunch counter and headed for the bank of pay phones with a pocketful of change. Harvey had offered me the use of his fancy portable phone before leaving for a more upscale dining venue, but the thought of discussing firm business over what to my mind was nothing but a glorified (and expensive) CB radio struck me as a bad idea. I ate my sandwich and waited until a middle-aged man in a three-piece suit finished his conversation and left the end phone booth, the one I prefer because it means having only one potential eavesdropper sitting next to me instead of two. I slid in, closed the door, took a seat, and dialed the office.

When I got my secretary on the line, the first words out of her mouth were, "I'm glad you called. Scott needs to talk to you. He says it's urgent."

After running through a list of things I needed her to do in connection with other cases I was handling, I had her connect me with Scott. "How's the trial going?" he asked when he came on the line.

A request for a routine trial update clearly didn't qualify as urgent, but I answered his question. "Better than I have any right to expect. The prosecution has the law and the facts on their side, but I don't think they've got the jury in their corner. Fortunately for us, pretty much everyone hates the IRS. It's all theater, and the government has a rank amateur as its leading man."

Scott laughed. "Having seen you in action, I'm pretty sure you're managing to upstage him. And when your old law school professor takes the stand, things should really get interesting."

"Yes, indeed," I said. "Yes, indeed."

Scott then got to the real reason he needed to speak to me. "Someone broke into my garage last night and slashed all the tires on both of our cars. Like most people, we don't lock the door from the garage into the house, so whoever was in the garage could have walked right in while we were all asleep."

"Most likely Proctor's people," I said.

"Most likely, although there's no way to prove that. It really spooked my wife. She's got a guy at the house right now installing new locks, a deadbolt, and an alarm system."

"Did they do anything else?" I asked. "Did they take anything?"

"No, all they did was slash the tires."

"Anything like this happen to Avery or Rick?"

"No," Scott said, "but like you, they don't live in Troy Forge. It's unlikely Proctor would send his guys where they might be caught in the act by another police department."

I was about to tell him about Sean's foray into Mountain Springs the previous evening, but decided it made more sense to start at the beginning and lay things out chronologically.

"Things are more complicated than you realize. Let me tell you about a few crazy things that have happened to me, and see if you can figure out how they're connected, if in fact they are." I started by telling him about my visit from Eddie the Skunk.

"Could someone have put Rizzo up to that to mess with you?" Scott asked.

"Interesting theory. I hadn't thought of that."

"Possible?" Scott asked.

"Possible, but Eddie the Skunk isn't the kind of guy to play errand boy for somebody. It's more likely that he misinterpreted whatever it was he heard. Besides, he told me about this before we filed suit against the town, so if he was doing this for someone, it wouldn't be Proctor."

"IRS?" Scott asked.

"Not likely. Eddie would want to stay as far away from the IRS as possible."

"Maybe he had no choice. Maybe he had a tax problem you didn't know about and this was a way to make it go away. Remember, the feds used a tax evasion case to take down Al Capone."

That angle hadn't occurred to me, but it should have. Maybe all this was messing with my head and causing me to lose focus.

"You said crazy things, plural," Scott said, "so I'm guessing there's more."

I told him about Mr. Goatee bringing me lunch and about the aborted mugging in Morristown, about bumping into Reynaldo in the courthouse lobby on Monday and how he saved Judge Abrams and me from a mugging on our way to the parking lot that evening.

"What are the chances of being mugged twice in the space of a week, and walking away unscathed each time?" Scott asked.

"I told you crazy stuff was happening."

"Anything else?"

"I told you about my encounter with the Troy Forge cops on Tuesday, the day we read about Machias Phelps being killed."

"Right."

"Well, yesterday I had three more encounters with the cops." I told him about the bogus BOLO for a red Mustang and my run-in with the two cops who smashed my tail light. "And then last night, my friend who's a member of the department shows up at my home and hands me an envelope he found when he and three other cops went through Phelps' apartment."

"What were they doing in Phelps' apartment?" Scott asked. "And what was in the envelope?"

I was about to tell him when someone rapped on the door of the phone booth. I looked up to see Harvey Berkowitz standing there, pointing to his wristwatch.

"I have to get back to court," I told Scott, "but the judge is hearing motions tomorrow morning so I'll be in the office. Let's have a meeting and I'll fill everyone in."

As we rode the elevator upstairs to the courtroom, Harvey said, "I just spoke to Aaron Gertz. He's in his office, which means he's not here, which means he won't be testifying."

"At least not today," I replied.

"Not today, not ever. I take care of my friends, and they take care of me."

As it turned out, Harvey was right. Aaron Gertz never testified, which was extremely odd. It wasn't until the trial was almost over that I learned why the government had failed to call a witness who could have severely damaged our case.

25

"No, the taxpayers are footing the bill."

After the lunch recess, Lionel Newton called John Douglas as his next witness. Douglas, the manager of the Honolulu hotel where Harvey and his family had stayed, spent the next forty minutes explaining how the Berkowitz family had availed themselves of all the wonderful amenities his hotel had to offer, from poolside happy hours and luaus to massages and sightseeing trips. Rollins had already testified to all the essential elements of Harvey's alleged crime, making the hotel manager's testimony completely unnecessary. There were only two reasons for Newton to have put John Douglas on the stand. The first was that Newton wanted an "ordinary Joe" to counterbalance the serious, unsmiling shifty-eyed IRS agent who had testified that morning. That would be consistent with how he had gone about proving the first count of the indictment involving the addition to Harvey's house in Upper Montclair. Have the IRS agents lay out the elements of the crime and present the documents needed to prove the government's case, and then follow with the contractors, with whom the jurors were more likely to identify. It was a version of the old "put a human face on the crime" tactic.

The second possibility was the one that worried me. It was conceivable Newton had called Douglas as a witness so he could conclude his testimony with some bombshell that would seal Harvey's fate. As the minutes dragged on and Douglas piled one tedious detail on top of another, it seemed more and more likely that this was the real reason. Just as the jury was about to tune out the hotel manager's day-by-day accounting of Harvey's activities, Newton would spring the surprise.

But when John Douglas concluded his testimony with no surprise ending, I realized there was a third possibility: the government's newbie attorney was an idiot.

"Welcome to lovely downtown Newark," I said as I approached the lectern to begin my cross-examination. "Our beaches aren't as nice as the ones you have in Hawaii, but at least our weather is better."

Douglas laughed, as did some of the jurors and many of the spectators in the public gallery.

"Had a chance to do any sightseeing yet?" I inquired.

"A little," Douglas said.

"What's the most interesting thing you've seen so far?" I asked, keeping the seemingly casual conversation going.

"The Museum of Natural History," Douglas said.

"Hey, wait just a minute," I said in mock indignation. "That's in Manhattan. We want you to spend your tourist dollars here in Newark."

That elicited more laughter, as well as an objection from Lionel Newton that my questions weren't relevant.

"Just trying to make the witness comfortable," I explained.

Abrams said, "Move on, counselor."

So I did. "Let's talk about those tourist dollars for a minute. Did you fly here from Hawaii?"

"Yes."

"When?"

The hotel manager didn't have an immediate answer. Apparently he had to do a mental calculation. He finally said, "I flew in five days ago."

"Did you pay for the plane fare yourself?"

"No," Douglas said.

"How about your hotel, are you paying for that?"

Newton objected to my question as being irrelevant. "This line of questioning is highly relevant," I said to Judge Abrams. "It goes to the witness' credibility."

Abrams overruled Newton's objection and instructed Douglas to answer my question.

"No, I'm not paying for the hotel," he said.

"Are you paying for your meals?"

Douglas hesitated, seemingly unsure how to answer my question. He finally said, "I have a per diem allowance for meals."

"Do you have a rental car while you're here?" I asked next.

"Yes," came his answer.

"And are you paying for that yourself?"

"No."

"Well, if you're not paying for the airfare, the hotel, the meals, and the rental car, who's paying for all that?"

"The IRS is footing the bill," Douglas said.

"No, the taxpayers are footing the bill," I corrected him. Out of the corner of my eye I saw two jurors shaking their heads. "So you've been here for five days, spent a few hours in court, and the rest of the time you've gone sightseeing on the taxpayers' dime." Then, looking directly at the jury, I added, "But when Harvey Berkowitz spends his own money to go to Hawaii, the government prosecutes him because he didn't spend every waking minute in business meetings."

That got Newton out of his seat with an objection. He and I then had an unpleasant exchange of words that escalated into a shouting match that morphed into all out verbal warfare that only ended when Judge Abrams banged her gavel repeatedly and yelled, "Enough." We waited as she massaged her temples with both hands. "You two are giving me a headache," she finally said.

Lionel Newton started to speak, but Abrams held up her hand to silence him. "Mr. O'Brian," she said, looking directly at me, "the purpose of cross-examination is to ask questions, not to make a speech. Save your remarks for your closing argument. If you have more questions for Mr. Douglas, you may continue. Otherwise, sit down." Little did any of us know at the time that there would be no closing argument.

"I have a few more questions," I said, "but out of respect for the jurors' time, I'll be brief."

"Then get on with it," the judge instructed.

"Mr. Douglas, do you keep tabs on the comings and goings of all the hotel's guests as you did with Mr. Berkowitz?" I asked.

"We respect our guests' privacy," he answered indignantly.

"And yet you're able to give a day-by-day, hour-by-hour account of what Mr. Berkowitz and his family did while they were staying at your hotel," I persisted. "Why is that?"

"Well, Agent Rollins asked me to let him know what I saw."

"Did Agent Rollins make any promises or threats in connection with that request?"

Douglas hesitated, so I added, "For example, did he threaten you with a tax audit if you didn't cooperate?"

"No."

"Then why did you agree to violate the privacy of a hotel guest?"

Douglas began to fidget; he was clearly uncomfortable. If it hadn't already occurred to him that his violation of hotel policy could cause problems with his employer, it did now. He finally said, "What choice did I have? This is the IRS we're talking about."

"What choice, indeed," I said as I returned to my seat.

Lionel Newton was about to call his next witness when Judge Abrams stopped him. "In view of the hour, I think we'll recess until Monday. Enjoy your three-day weekend."

If only I had known what the weekend had in store for me.

26

"You love that cat more than you love me."

By the time I got home to Mountain Springs it was almost dark. Jorge's white pickup truck was parked by the back porch on the section of driveway leading to the garage at the rear of the property, so I parked in the circle in front of the house, behind Aimee's red Miata. The temperature had dropped and snow flurries were falling as I walked back to see what Jorge was doing. I had almost reached his truck when he emerged from behind the house carrying what looked like a pillow-case, but which I realized was a burlap bag when I got closer. Whatever was inside the bag clearly didn't want to be there. It was putting up a tremendous fight, making the bag appear to have a life of its own, and almost causing Jorge to lose his grip. When Jorge got to the pickup, he swung the bag underhand like an accomplished softball pitcher, arcing it into the truck bed where it landed with a thud. The creature inside continued to thrash around, trying desperately to free itself.

"Raccoon?" I asked.

The animal inside the bag answered my question before Jorge could by letting out a plaintive meow. I walked over to the truck and was reaching for the bag when Jorge said, "I wouldn't do that. It's wild." Remembering Jorge's treatment of Lucky, the neighbor's cat, I assumed that Lucky had once again gotten unlucky at the hands of my soon-to-be former gardener. I carefully untied the bag, keeping it at arms length just in case Jorge had rounded up a stray instead of the neighbor's pet, but instead of Lucky or a stray, Buddy emerged from the bag.

His ears were flattened against his head, his fur was standing on end and his tail was puffed up in fear. I picked him up and he snuggled against my shoulder, shaking visibly. I tried to comfort him by scratching him behind the ears. "Relax, you're safe now," I said.

Then I turned to Jorge. "What the hell were you doing with my cat?" I asked through clenched teeth.

"I didn't know it was your cat," he said, shrugging his shoulders as he started to get back in his truck. "Cats all look the same to me. I found this one outside and thought it was a stray."

"Bullshit. You've seen Buddy countless times in the three years you've worked here. You know what he looks like, and you also know he never leaves the porch."

By this point Jorge had gotten into his truck and started the engine. I was flabbergasted, thinking that he was about to just drive away without even bothering to respond to what I had said. But after lighting a cigarette, he rolled down the window, looked me in the eye and said, "Lighten up, man. It's only a cat."

"That's it," I said. "You're fired. Get the hell out of here and don't come back."

Jorge laughed. "You can fire me, but Mrs. O will hire me back."

"No she won't. I pay the bills around here, and you'll never get another dime. And if you set foot on my property again, I'll call the police."

He gave me the finger, backed out of the driveway, and disappeared.

With Buddy in my arms, I walked up the porch steps, passed the logs that Jorge had apparently just stacked there, and entered the kitchen. I called for Aimee, but got no response, so I headed for her office upstairs next to the "unused" room that was now very much in use as her bedroom. She must have heard me coming, or perhaps she had been watching from her office window, because when I got to the second floor landing, I found her standing there with arms crossed.

I put Buddy down and he darted under the hallway table, his favorite second floor hiding spot. I recounted the incident with Jorge. To my surprise, she said, "You must be mistaken. Jorge wouldn't do that."

"Aimee," I said, "you know Buddy never leaves the back porch. He sits by his food dish and watches Jorge stack wood, but he never goes outside, even though the door is wide open."

"There's always a first time," Aimee said.

"But even if that were true, why would Jorge put Buddy in a sack and throw the sack into his truck? Why wouldn't he just pick Buddy up and put him back on the porch?"

"You just don't like Jorge," Aimee said.

"This has nothing to do with whether or not I like Jorge. It's about what he did to Buddy."

"You never liked Jorge," she insisted.

"Okay, I never liked Jorge," I agreed. "But that doesn't give him the right to mistreat my cat. Or the neighbor's cat. Or any cat, for that matter."

"I still can't believe he'd do that," Aimee said.

"Well, believe it, because he did. And then he has the gall to justify what he did by telling me Buddy is just a cat." I glanced over to Buddy, who was taking all this in from his hiding place under the table. I don't think he understood what we were saying, but I'm pretty sure he knew we were talking about him.

"He *is* just a cat," Aimee said, still defending Jorge.

"No, he's not just a cat, he's *my* cat, a member of my household, and I expect the hired help to treat members of my household with respect."

Aimee started to laugh. "You should hear yourself," she said. "Members of your household? You sound like some feudal lord from the Dark Ages." *No, actually, more like Great Pharaoh.*

"I let Jorge go," I said.

"You let him go?"

"I let him go," I repeated. "As in fired. Dismissed. Terminated."

"No," Aimee said. "You can't do that. Hire him back."

"Absolutely not. My decision is final."

"Your decision?" Aimee said. "This should be our decision, not your decision. Since when do you get to make these decisions by yourself?"

"Since I'm the one paying the bills around here, I get to say who gets paid," I said. "And Jorge doesn't get paid another dime."

"You're just mad because Jorge brings me lilacs."

"This has nothing to do with lilacs, and you know it."

"No," Aimee said, "it's about your damn cat. It's always about your damn cat. You love that cat more than you love me."

I was tempted to say, *that's because Buddy wouldn't dream of hiring someone to kill me,* but I still wasn't sure I should take Eddie's warning seriously. So instead, I said, "And Buddy loves me more than you do."

That was apparently the wrong thing to say. Aimee just stood there for another moment, then without a word, walked back to her office and slammed the door.

Buddy crawled out from his hiding spot under the table, a bit more slowly than usual, I thought. He rubbed against my leg, and made the sound he uses to announce, *I'm here; give me some attention.* I picked him up and carried him downstairs to the kitchen where he and I had dinner: a tuna sandwich for me, and a can of salmon flavored cat food for him. A few minutes later I heard the front door slam shut, and got to the porch in time to see Aimee drive away in her Miata.

I spent the remainder of the evening staring at the flames in the fireplace, drinking Jameson's, and listening to music from the sixties and seventies. Buddy kept me company, curled up on my lap. Aimee didn't come home, and she didn't call. I couldn't call her because I didn't know where she went. And even if I could reach her, I wasn't sure what I'd say. The hours went by and the fire in the fireplace eventually burned out.

Still no Aimee.

Just before midnight, the phone rang. It was my mother-in-law, who informed me in an icy tone that Aimee was with them at their home outside Philadelphia. She ended the short, one-sided conversation with, "You can join us for Thanksgiving if you want." And then she hung up.

I put the phone down and just stood there for a moment, replaying the argument with Aimee in my mind, trying to make sense of everything that had happened. Clearly I had some decisions to make, but after doing battle in federal court as well as on the home front, I was too tired to decide anything at the moment. So I trudged up to my bedroom with Buddy at my side and, fully clothed, flopped down in the center of the king-sized bed. Buddy curled up next to me and put his chin on my shoulder. I wasn't sure whether he was seeking comfort after his ordeal with Jorge or if he was trying to comfort me.

27

"You have to paint this one."

Rick was in the waiting room when I arrived at the office the next morning, his usual coffee mug in hand. He was talking to Elaine, our receptionist, but he broke off the conversation when he saw me. Elaine started out as Rick's secretary when he opened the office thirty years ago, but when her arthritis got so bad she had trouble using a typewriter, he made her the firm's receptionist.

"You look like hell," he said, eyeing me up and down. He was his old self, at least for the moment. "Out carousing till the wee hours, were you?" he added playfully, knowing full well I'm usually sound asleep right after the eleven o'clock news, and sometimes even before that.

I told him about the previous evening, starting with Jorge and Buddy and concluding with the midnight phone call from my mother-in-law. I thought about telling him about Eddie the Skunk's warning, but decided the idea was so crazy it would make me sound like I had lost touch with reality. But I did finally tell him, "There's no us anymore. There's her and there's me, but there's no us."

As my story unfolded, Rick changed from playful rogue to the concerned, avuncular mentor I regarded as my one true friend. "We have a partners meeting in half an hour," he said when I finished. "But under the circumstances, I'm sure Scott and Avery wouldn't mind if you skipped it. I'll join you in your office after the meeting and we'll talk."

"Looking forward to the talk," I said, "but I'll be at the meeting."

"Ever the trooper," Rick replied before heading back to his conversation with Elaine.

Half an hour later, I entered the conference room to find Rick seated at the large rectangular table instead of in what had become his usual wing chair in the corner.

"I see you made the newspaper," he said, as I took the seat across from him. He slid a copy of the *Ledger* toward me, folded back to expose a story with the headline: Uncle Sam Targets Tax Protestor.

Stacey McCain had come through big time for Harvey. She portrayed him as a patriotic American fed up with politicians' misuse of our tax dollars. According to her article, he was now being persecuted for his "courageous stand against government waste and corruption." The article couldn't have been better if I had written it myself, which in some respects I had by supplying Stacey with the subtle blend of fact and fiction that served as raw material for her story. There were half a dozen bulleted paragraphs listing some of the more egregious examples of the government's financial follies, including the $880,000 Uncle Sam spent to study snail sex and the $386,000 study of rabbit massage. Her article even included five of the photos I had given her, each one prominently displaying a version of Harvey's *Tax Politicians, Not Patriots* sign. She described me as a champion of the underdog, fighting to keep a man of principle out of prison, who was now being shadowed by Troy Forge cops and by unknown people who I suspected of working for the IRS or some other government agency.

"Lionel Newton will have a fit when he sees this," I said.

"Judge Abrams will be equally happy," Rick said. He had that mischievous look I had come to know so well over the years, and I hoped the Rick of old would stay with us today, at least long enough for us to have our conversation after the meeting. "And Bob Proctor will be overjoyed that Troy Forge got a mention."

"We all know how much Proctor loves publicity," Scott added, causing everyone to laugh. If we had known then how far Proctor was willing to go in his private war with our client, we wouldn't have laughed.

"Just don't get yourself thrown in a holding cell for contempt," Avery said.

"Abrams never issued a gag order," I said. "And I'm not the author of this masterpiece. In fact, I had nothing to do with it. I'm completely innocent."

"You don't think the judge will ask how the reporter got those photos?" Avery wanted to know.

Pointing to one of the photos that prominently displayed Harvey's sign, Rick said, "Catchy slogan Harvey came up with. I'm not sure what he meant by it, but it's catchy."

"Actually, his daughter, Leah, is the one who came up with that," I explained. "And the irony is that it has nothing to do with income taxes. Harvey put up those signs because of a dispute he had with a local politician who wanted to impose a new countywide business tax. But if people want to think the signs refer to income taxes, that's their prerogative."

Rick laughed, Avery shook his head, and Scott said, "Let's get down to business. Avery has a new billing system he wants to explain, but before we get to that, Brendan, tell us about that envelope you mentioned during our phone call yesterday."

I told them about my latest run-in with Bob Proctor's private army Wednesday afternoon on my way back from Newark, concluding with my conversation with my friend Sean. "He gave me this," I said, holding up the oversized manila envelope with my name and the firm's name written across the front. I removed the document that was inside it, and then turned the envelope over, allowing a key to fall on the conference table. I unfolded the document and held it up. "This is Machias Phelps' Last Will and Testament."

"How did your friend end up with that?" Scott asked.

"After Phelps died, Proctor sent four cops to Phelps' apartment to gather up any documents they found and bring them back to town hall. Sean was one of the four cops."

"Why would they do that?" Avery wanted to know.

"Proctor told them that Phelps had taken sensitive town documents without authorization, leading them to believe they were recovering stolen property."

Scott and Avery both looked skeptical, but before either could say anything, I explained, "These marching orders came directly from Proctor, and apparently nobody who works for the town, and wants to continue working for the town, questions a direct order from His Majesty. But because this envelope had my name on it, Sean gave it to me instead of delivering it to Proctor."

"Gutsy move," Rick said. "I assume your name's on the envelope because Phelps appointed you Executor of his estate."

"No, actually, he appointed you as his Executor."

That caught Rick by surprise. "Me? I hardly knew the man. Only met him a few times over the years. He was your contact in town hall. I would have thought he'd have made you Executor."

"He probably thought that would look like a conflict of interest," I said.

"Why would that be a conflict of interest?" Scott asked.

"Because he named me as his sole beneficiary."

That revelation brought the conversation to a halt. Scott tipped his chair back and looked at the ceiling. "Now isn't that interesting."

Avery pointed to the Will and held out his hand. "May I?"

I handed him the document and he quickly scanned the two pages. Then he began to read part of it aloud. "I give, devise, and bequeath my entire estate, wherever it may be situate, to Brendan O'Brian of the law firm Santorini, Woodson, Glickman & O'Brian of Troy Forge, New Jersey. He was the closest thing I had to a friend, having kept my confidence for many years." Avery stopped reading and asked, "What does 'kept my confidence' mean?"

"When I was hiking around the reservoir one Saturday several years ago, I caught Phelps *in flagrante delicto*," I said. "If what I saw had become public knowledge, Phelps could have lost his job at the very least."

"That's it?" Scott asked. "Sounds like public lewdness at worst, and arguably it's not even that, depending on the specifics."

"It's not so much what he did," I said, "but with whom he did it. The person he was with looked pretty young."

"You're suggesting he was having sex with an underage girl?" Avery asked.

"Well, you're half right."

"Half right? How could I be half right? You just said..."

"You're half right," I repeated.

Rick jumped into the conversation, surprising everyone. "For heaven's sake, Avery, the underage girl wasn't a girl."

"Oh," was all Avery could say.

"Is that right?" Scott asked.

"That's pretty much it."

"And you never reported it?"

"Why should I? The kid seemed to be enjoying himself as much as Phelps, and I had no definitive proof of his age."

"Even so," Avery began, "you should have..."

"I should have done exactly what I did, which is mind my own business," I said, before he could finish.

"And Phelps became your inside contact in town hall because he was afraid if he didn't, you'd reveal what you'd seen," Scott said.

Rick shook his head. "No, based on what Phelps wrote in his Will, it sounds more like gratitude than fear." I didn't know if Rick actually believed that or he was just saying it to make me feel better.

"What about the key?" Scott asked. "What's that for?"

"I have no idea," I said. "This whole thing is a complete surprise. When I finish with the Berkowitz trial I'll look into it. In the meantime, I'm going to put the Will and the key in the firm safe, and add this to my list of recent bizarre happenings."

After our discussion about Machias Phelps, we turned to more mundane matters: a new billing system that, if I understood Avery correctly, would allow us to charge clients for eighty minutes of work every hour. Assuming the new system was based on warping the fabric of space-time, and having little or no interest in quantum physics (or even understanding what that was), I promptly tuned out Avery's presentation.

Although I was looking in Avery's direction as he spoke, I was focusing on the painting of the Ford Mansion behind him. Avery's new billing system was apparently so powerful that just talking about it warped space-time, transforming the Ford Mansion into my home in Mountain Springs, and transporting me to the middle of the living room. Rick was there with me, standing on my right, and Buddy was on my left. Every wall in the room was covered with artwork, not the terrible faux art paintings that Aimee likes, but pictures that looked real, almost like photographs. Slowly turning clockwise, I scanned them and realized they were pictures of Aimee and me. The first picture showed us in my dorm room back in college doing things that caused Buddy to cover his eyes with his paws and Rick to say, "Pretty frisky back then, weren't you." The next picture showed us at our wedding reception, and the one after that on our honeymoon.

At some point in my daydream I must have fallen asleep, although it wasn't clear whether it was my real self or my daydream self that was snoozing. I recall someone telling Rick to wake me up, and Rick saying, "He's had a rough night; let him catnap."

Rick and I continued our journey through my private art gallery. At some point I realized that the pictures had changed. Instead of showing Aimee and me, they showed just one of us. There were several of Aimee at an art gallery, and several of me in a courtroom. And the paintings were no longer realistic. I found myself having to guess what each one was supposed to depict.

We worked our way around the room, eventually coming to the wall with two windows overlooking the circular driveway in front of the house. My Mustang was parked outside, and Mr. Goatee was admiring it. Stacey McCain was there as well, wearing a short skirt and peering into the engine compartment. Between the two windows was one last painting. Only this wasn't an actual painting, just a blank canvas.

Rick put his hand on my shoulder and handed me a paintbrush. "You have to paint this one," he said, nodding toward the blank canvas.

I blinked, and the paintbrush changed into a pen. The hand shaking my shoulder was Scott's, who was asking, "Did you have a nice nap?"

I looked around the conference room and saw that Avery had left. Rick's body was still seated across the table from me, but Rick himself was gone, replaced by his empty-eyed doppelganger.

28

"Do what he says and you'll walk."

After the meeting Rick was in no shape for that conversation he and I were going to have. So I went back to my office and began preparing for *State of New Jersey v Berkowitz,* which the state would no doubt pursue when the feds were finished with Harvey. The act that led to his "ultimate chutzpah" tax deduction could potentially put him behind bars for five, and perhaps ten, years under New Jersey law.

I was reviewing a site plan of the property at the heart of that case when my secretary buzzed me. "Stacey McCain from the *Star Ledger* is on line one, and Eddie Rizzo and another man are in the waiting room."

"Don't tell me, let me guess," I said, "Eddie has to see me right away; it's urgent"

"However did you know?"

Decisions, decisions. Cute little redhead destined to play a leading role in my dreams, and hopefully in my life, or a smelly client who drops by without an appointment.

I punched the button for line one and said, "Great article, Stacey"

"My editor didn't think so," Stacey replied. "He thought you were making the whole thing up, but I told him you wouldn't do that. I finally convinced him to run with it. You owe me one."

"You're right, I do. How about letting me pay off my debt by taking you to dinner tonight?"

"According to your firm brochure, you're married," Stacey said, pointing out a bothersome little detail. "I don't usually have dinner with married men."

"At the moment, that's technically correct," I conceded, "but things are in a state of flux at the moment." I wasn't quite sure what I meant by that, but it came out of my mouth before I could formulate a better reply.

There was a pause as Stacey processed that information. "Okay," she finally said. "I suppose I could consider this a business dinner, an opportunity to get additional information from you, just in case my editor decides he wants me to write a follow-up piece." We both knew that wasn't likely, but if that's what it took for her to rationalize having dinner with me, so be it. "Besides," she continued, "the way you attract trouble, you'll probably end up getting mugged again, and I can write an article about that." Her words, said in jest, proved to be prophetic, if not wholly accurate.

We arranged to meet that evening at the New Amsterdam Inn, a very nice restaurant owned by Martin von Beverwicjk. Ironically, Martin's restaurant is across the street from a Proctor billboard proclaiming Troy Forge as the friendliest town in the county.

No tuna sandwich for dinner tonight.

After hanging up with Stacey, I buzzed my secretary and told her to send in Eddie.

I had just put the site plan on the credenza behind my desk when Eddie and another man walked through the door. "Counselor," he said, "I gotta talk to you. My cousin here needs your help."

The man with Eddie was perhaps ten years older and fifty pounds heavier. He had a thick neck that was so short his head looked like it was attached directly to his shoulders. Atop that head sat what had to be the world's worst comb-over. Like Eddie, he struck me as the kind of guy you probably didn't want as a friend, but definitely didn't want as an enemy. "Gino Monti, meet Brendan O'Brian, best damn lawyer in New Jersey," Eddie said by way of introductions.

Eddie and Gino took seats across from me at my desk, and Eddie started the conversation with a confession. "Gino's got himself an attorney, so what we need from you is a second opinion. Like with a doctor, you know?"

"Who's your attorney?" I asked Gino.

"Rocco Gambardelli," Gino said somewhat defensively, making it clear that coming to see me was Eddie's idea, not his.

I knew of Gambardelli, but had never actually met him. He and his brother had a firm in Essex County that specialized in criminal defense work.

"He got Gino a deal," Eddie said, "but it don't smell right. That's why we come to you. Gino gets one year in Club Fed, but first he's gotta testify in two different courts."

"If he gets a year in a minimum security federal penitentiary, then I assume one of those courts is federal and the other is state," I said.

"See, what did I tell you," Eddie said to Gino. "Mr. O'Brian don't know nothing about your case and he's already figured out it's state and federal. You shoulda hired him instead of Gambardelli."

I was about to explain that requiring testimony in two different courts might not be typical, but it wasn't that unusual either. But before I could, Eddie said to his cousin, "Tell Mr. O'Brian what happened."

Gino began to tell me, in very general terms, about the crime he had been accused of committing. I pressed for details, and he slowly began to provide them. After about ten minutes, I realized who was sitting across from me at my desk. Either I was the luckiest attorney in the State of New Jersey or Eddie the Skunk was doing me another favor. Either way, this was a game changer.

"This incident you're telling me about, Gino, did it take place at a certain strip mall in Denville?" I asked.

Gino looked at Eddie and said, "How's he know that? You tell him?"

"Nah, I didn't tell him nothing," Eddie said. "Counselor O'Brian's a smart guy. You shoulda hired him instead of Gambardelli."

"So whadda you think?" Eddie asked me. "This deal a good one?"

Before I could answer, Gino said, "I can do a year. No problem."

Eddie looked at his cousin, then shook his head and rolled his eyes.

"Hey, better to spend a year in Club Fed than ten years in Rahway," Gino said defensively, referring to a state prison hell hole that's at the other end of the spectrum from the cushy prisons the federal government runs for non-violent offenders. "I do my year, then I'm finally going to go see the Grand Canyon."

"Grand Canyon, my ass," Eddie said. "You been talking about seeing the Grand Canyon your whole fuckin' life, but all you ever do is go to Atlantic City and play craps. Hell, you ain't never been outside New Jersey."

"Yeah, well this time I'm going," Gino said.

Eddie looked at his cousin and rolled his eyes again. Then he turned to me and repeated his question. "So whadda you think?" This a good deal or what?"

"Well, a year isn't bad," I said, pausing for effect before adding, "but no time at all is a whole lot better."

"How's that possible?" Gino asked. "They got me on video."

"I know," I said. "You forgot to disconnect one of the sur-veillance cameras. The one at the south end of the parking lot."

Gino was incredulous. "How's he know this stuff?" he asked Eddie.

"I told you he's a smart lawyer," Eddie said. "You shoulda hired him."

For the next half hour I explained to Gino what he had to do to avoid serving any jail time at all, concluding with the predic-tion, "You'll not only walk away a free man, if they prosecute you at all it, the worst that could happen is you'll have to pay a five hundred dollar fine."

Gino was relieved, but still not certain my plan would work. That's when Eddie sealed the deal. "O'Brian's a smart guy," he told his cousin. "He's always done right by me. Do what he says and you'll walk."

As Eddie and his cousin were leaving my office, Eddie told me to send him my bill. "No bill," I said. "This one's on me." *You should be sending me a bill.*

"Thanks, counselor," Eddie said, pausing at the door and watching as Gino made his way back to the waiting room. Then he asked, "How you doing with that other thing I told you about? You okay?"

"I'm working on it," I replied. "Not yet sure what to do."

"Well, as I see it, you got three options," Eddie said. "Option number one, you find the guy your old lady hired to whack you and you get him first. Of course, that might not be easy if he's any good."

"That assumes Aimee hired someone," I said. "I'm having trouble believing that."

"Believe it," Eddie shot back. "Carlos keeps his ear to the ground, and he's reliable."

I had no idea who Carlos was, and decided that was just as well. More to the point, I had no idea how I could find Aimee's purported hit man, assuming such a person even existed, so I asked Eddie, "What's my second option?"

"Option number two, you deal with your old lady. That's the easy way to handle this cause you know how to find her."

In retrospect, I should have asked Eddie to explain what he meant by "deal with," but instead I asked, "What's option number three?"

"Option number three is you do nothing and end up dead." It might just have been my imagination, but I thought he sounded genuinely concerned.

29

"You have no idea."

Stacey was waiting for me when I arrived at the New Amsterdam Inn, one of three area restaurants owned by Martin von Beverwicjk. "You look mahvelous," I said when I saw her standing in the lobby.

"You do a crummy Fernando impression," she replied with a laugh. "Don't quit your day job."

"Unfortunately, my Obi-Wan Kenobi impression isn't much better." In response to her quizzical expression, I added, "I'll explain over dinner."

The hostess, who I think was one of Martin's daughters, showed us to a table in the back corner, next to one occupied by an obnoxious middle aged couple who, judging from their accents, had driven from New York (to the "hinterlands" as the wife put it) to dine in Martin's upscale eatery, only to be disappointed that the décor featured photographs of New York City through the years instead of windmills, tulips, and wooden shoes. "We could have stayed home and seen this," was her comment at one point.

As we settled into our seats, Stacey said, "I don't usually have dinner with married men, unless it's business related. But, since you're a source, I guess this is business related." Before I could suggest that business and pleasure weren't mutually exclusive, she asked the question I knew would come up at some point during the evening. "On the phone this afternoon you said you were technically married. How is being technically married different than being married married?"

Even though I was anticipating her question, I had trouble coming up with an answer. Stacey was still a stranger, though I hoped that would change with time, preferably sooner rather than later, and there are some things you just don't discuss with strangers. So I resorted to a variation of the explanation I had given Rick that morning in the office. "There's her, there's me, but there's no us."

"Interesting," she said, before abruptly changing topics. "So what does a fictional Jedi knight have to do with tax fraud?"

It took me a moment to realize she was referring to my earlier comment about my Obi-Wan Kenobi impersonation. "Actually, it has nothing to do with tax fraud. It's connected to another case I'm working on for the owner of this restaurant." I told her in general terms about Martin von Beverwicjk's troubles with Troy Forge, being careful not to divulge anything confidential. "So we filed a lawsuit against the town, and all hell broke loose." I detailed my run-ins with the Troy Forge police department, explaining how I had used the line from *Star Wars* when the tail light smashing cops had stopped me. I also told her about Scott's slashed tires. She seemed to find that even more disturbing, perhaps because it had happened in Scott's own garage. I was about to tell her about Machias Phelps and his mysterious death, but decided that was information best kept confidential until I had a better idea what was really going on.

"So the two guys you told me about in Newark, the ones who were following you, had nothing to do with the tax case?

They were following you because of the lawsuit you filed for the owner of this restaurant." Stacey seemed mildly annoyed, apparently believing that I had deliberately deceived her.

"No, they showed up before we filed that lawsuit. The local cops came into the picture after we sued Troy Forge." I debated telling her about Eddie the Skunk's warning, but decided that would make my confusing story even more confusing ... and even more unbelievable. I could feel my credibility with Stacey slipping away. No point in making things worse. Little did I know that events were about to buttress my credibility.

I decided I needed to steer the conversation to a safer topic. "But enough about me. Let's talk about something much more interesting. Tell me about yourself." During the salad course, Stacy gave me the *Reader's Digest* version of her life story. I discovered that she was an only child, and that her father died when she was young, causing her mother to resume a nursing career. I learned that Stacey grew up in Hanover, the next town over from Troy Forge, attended a state college on a full tuition scholarship and always wanted to be a journalist.

From that point on, the conversation flowed more smoothly, perhaps because we were no longer talking about tax fraud and rogue cops, or perhaps because we were becoming more comfortable with each other. We were almost finished with our entrees when the conversation turned to politics, a dangerous topic considering neither of us knew the other very well. But we quickly discovered that we had remarkably similar views on a wide range of issues.

We both reviled Richard Nixon, not so much for his role in Watergate, but because he took the country off the gold standard. We both believed that the so-called immigration reform bill that President Reagan had signed a couple years ago was long on promises, but short on enforcement, and that it would encourage more people to break the law, eventually flooding the country with millions of illegal aliens. And we both agreed that Jimmy Carter's refusal to retaliate forcefully against Iran's assault on our embassy in Tehran would make that country's religious nuts even more dangerous in the years ahead.

I was in the process of perusing the dessert menu, trying to decide which of the delicacies listed would do the least damage to my waistline when there was a disturbance near the entrance. A dozen men rushed into the restaurant, each carrying an assault rifle or a shotgun. They were dressed completely in black, wearing helmets and body armor, their faces obscured by black hoods resembling ski masks. My first thought was that we were about to be robbed, but then I realized a police SWAT team was in the process of raiding Martin's restaurant.

Three of the men in black rounded up restaurant employees and herded them into the kitchen. The remainder of the raiding party dispersed throughout the restaurant, yelling at diners to remain seated and keep their hands in view. There was pandemonium, caused in no small part by the fact that many of the diners apparently believed, as I initially had, that a gang of criminals was attacking us.

It took a few minutes for everyone to realize what was happening, at which point the room became unnaturally quiet. When the SWAT team decided they had the situation under control, one of its members went to the restaurant entrance, opened the door and shouted "clear" to whomever was waiting outside. A moment later, a man in a black suit, who reminded me of the Gestapo officer from *Raiders of the Lost Ark,* entered the restaurant and went directly to the kitchen. He was accompanied by three uniformed Troy Forge cops, as heavily armed as their SWAT counterparts, but without the helmets and body armor. A man in a fire department dress uniform then appeared at the restaurant's entrance, had a brief conversation with a member of the SWAT Team, and joined the first group in the kitchen.

Everyone remained calm for about five minutes, or at least as calm as it's possible to be while being held at gunpoint by a band of masked men. But then one of the diners yelled to the cops, "Are we going to get to finish our dinner, or what?"

"Just remain seated with your hands in view," came the response.

"Are we under arrest?" another patron yelled.

"What's going on here?" another wanted to know.

Each question brought the same response: "Just remain seated with your hands in view."

A man with a crew cut, who looked like he had recently spent time in the military, finally dared to stand up. "I demand an explanation for what's happening here."

"Sit down and keep your hands where we can see them," the cop closest to him said.

Mr. Crew Cut had other plans. He threw his napkin on the table and headed for the exit. "Unless I'm under arrest, I'm leaving." Two cops blocked his path and he tried to shoulder his way through them. They pushed him back, then pointed their weapons at him. "What are you going to do, shoot me?" he asked.

Without a word, one of the cops removed what looked like a black transistor radio from an oversized pocket. "Last chance to sit down and be quiet," he said, walking toward Mr. Crew Cut, who defiantly took a step forward. Standing nose to nose, the cop put his finger on Mr. Crew Cut's chest. "Sit down." The order was delivered as two separate words, slowly and in a menacing tone worthy of a Hollywood tough guy.

The order was met with a defiant response. "Make me."

Without another word, the cop touched the black box to Mr. Crew Cut's chest. There was a buzzing sound and Mr. Crew Cut froze, his eyes wide with a mix of fear and confusion. Then he did a macabre little dance and fell to the floor.

"What the hell was that?" Stacey whispered.

"I'm not sure, but I think it's some type of electroshock weapon. I've read about them, but I've never actually seen one before."

"Oh, my gawd!" the obnoxious woman from New York wailed. "They're going to kill us all."

"Stay seated with your hands in view and nobody will get hurt," the cop closest to her said. He probably thought he sounded reassuring. He didn't.

The volume in the room increased as diners reacted to seeing what looked like a cop killing an unarmed man. One of the SWAT team members, apparently realizing what was happening, yelled, "He's just stunned. He'll be fine in a couple minutes. Everyone sit down and be quiet. You'll all be free to go shortly."

But "shortly" wasn't fast enough for the elderly woman sitting by herself at a table to our right. She slowly rose to her feet, gathered up her cane, and with great difficulty began to shuffle toward the exit.

"Ma'am, you need to sit down," one of the cops said.

She ignored him and kept going.

"Lady, you need to sit down," one of the other cops said more forcefully.

She ignored him too.

A third cop stepped in front of her. Ever so slowly she straightened her frail, hunched over frame so she could look him in the eye. "Son," she said, "I'm eighty-six years old. I've lived through the Great Depression and more wars than I care to count. I've seen men walk on the moon and other things I never would have dreamed possible. But I never thought I'd live to see the day my hometown police department would dress up like a gang of criminals and hold innocent people hostage."

"Ma'am, you need to sit down," the cop blocking her path said. It was still a command issued by a man holding a weapon, but he softened it a bit by adding, "please."

But the old woman wasn't about to be deterred. "No, I'm going home. If you want to stop me, you'll have to shoot me with one of those zapper thingies you used on that poor fellow," she said, pointing with her cane to Mr. Crew Cut who was still on the floor, but had managed to sit up. "With my bad heart, you'll probably kill me, but maybe that's just as well. I'm not sure I want to live in a country that's come to this." She walked around the cop who was blocking her path and continued her slow shuffle toward the exit. None of the masked "peace officers" made an effort to stop her.

Emboldened by the woman's refusal to be cowed, but also ashamed that it had taken an arthritic octogenarian to prod me into action, I stood up and in a loud voice announced, "I'm the attorney for this establishment. I want to speak to whomever is in charge of this SWAT team."

"Sit down," the storm trooper closest to me yelled in response.

"Who's in charge?" I demanded to know.

"You don't listen very well," his colleague said as he moved closer.

The masked bully who was keeping a watchful eye on the four senior citizens at a nearby table slithered over to join his buddy. Both of them were half a foot taller than me, with a physique made more threatening by their body armor. Either one could have mopped up the floor with me without working up a sweat. Discretion being the better part of valor, I should have sat down. But I didn't. "What, it takes two armed tough guys to deal with me? You're a couple of pathetic bullies."

"One more word and you'll discover just how tough I can be," the first cop said.

"I'll deal with these two," the second cop told his comrade. At least that's what I think he said. He was speaking softly, and the black hood muffled his words. He pointed first to Stacey and then to me. Then he crooked the same finger, the universal gesture that means "come here." I considered defying him, but was afraid that would make a bad situation worse. And, besides, maybe he was planning to take us to see the Gestapo in charge of this little invasion.

I nodded to Stacey, who looked both angry and scared, and the two of us got up from the table. We walked toward the cop, who stepped behind us, and holding his assault rifle horizontally across both our backs, used it to push us toward the entrance. "Keep moving," he barked as we passed three of his comrades in the lobby. The next thing I knew we were outside, alone with a heavily armed, masked cop. Not a good place to be. I turned around to face him so at least I'd be able to see what he had in store for us. As soon as I did, he started to remove the black hood hiding his face, apparently no longer caring if we recognized him. I considered rushing him, thinking he would never expect such a move. I wouldn't win the ensuring fight, but perhaps I could buy time for Stacey to get away. But before I could act, the cop removed the hood completely, and the two wall sconces on either side of the restaurant's doors illuminated his face.

It was Sean McDermott.

"Get the hell out of here," he said. "Now. Before things get worse."

"Worse?" How much worse could they get than that?" I asked, pointing to the building we had just left.

"You have no idea."

30

"What you don't eat for breakfast becomes dinner."

I spent Saturday morning working around the house before heading out to find a new source of firewood, a mindless distraction from all the craziness that was going on in my life. I briefly considered cutting my own wood from the two-acre lot behind our property, which fronts on Pin Oak Lane, the street running parallel to ours. I bought that parcel, despite Aimee's insistence that it was overpriced, to ensure we'd have a view of trees filled with squirrels instead of a mega-mansion filled with rug rats. Every few months a builder offers to buy that supposedly overpriced lot for two or three times what we paid for it, but I'd never consider selling. No amount of money could replace the pleasure I derive from watching the trees change with the seasons, from the pale green of spring to the vibrant yellows and reds of autumn.

But even though several of the trees in my personal forest were prime candidates for conversion to firewood, I discarded the idea of cutting my own supply, for a number of reasons. For starters, anything I cut now wouldn't be dried out and ready to burn until next winter. An even bigger impediment to a do-it-yourself solution to my firewood problem was the fact that I have absolutely no desire to operate a chain saw, in my opinion the deadliest weapon ever invented. But without question, the biggest obstacle was the hassle of securing the necessary permit from the Borough of Mountain Springs.

One of my neighbors learned the hard way that you don't chop down trees in Mountain Springs, even if they're on your own property, without first filling out forms, paying fees, obtaining a permit, and arranging for inspections from someone called a certified arborist. He lopped a dead branch off one of his oak trees and ended up with a five hundred dollar fine instead of a stack of firewood.

I started my search for firewood at the local garden center, where an earnest young lady quoted a price that prompted me to ask if their firewood was gold plated. After a similar experience at other nearby establishments, I ventured farther afield and eventually found myself at the western edge of the county where there are still as many farms as shopping centers. I finally found someone who would be delighted to deliver all the firewood I could burn for about half what the local places were charging.

By the time I got back to Mountain Springs, the sun had almost set and the wind had picked up, signaling that the TV weatherman who had called for snow that evening might have gotten his forecast right for a change. However, there was still enough light filtering through the thickening clouds for me to recognize Jorge behind the wheel of the white pickup truck pulling out of my driveway as I approached. When he saw me, he hit the accelerator and flew by me, heading back to the main boulevard that leads to the highway.

I had no idea what Jorge was doing at my house, but assumed whatever it was wasn't good. After parking my Mustang in the circular driveway, I got out and checked the front door. It was still locked. Then I made a slow circuit around the house, checking windows for signs of a break-in. They were all closed, locked, and intact. By the time I worked my way around to the back porch by the kitchen, I was starting to feel a little silly. There was no damage, no graffiti, no dead skunks hanging from the gutters. I checked the cap to the underground tank that feeds the oil burner, but it was still in place and locked. There was nothing out of the ordinary that I could see. I concluded that Jorge had most likely come by to present his bill for the last load of firewood he had delivered. Finding no one home, he probably tucked it into the stack of logs on the back porch.

But before going to check, I decided to look in the garage out back, just to be sure everything there was okay. Instead of fighting with the heavy overhead door, I went in through the side door, which is never locked. I flipped on the fluorescent light, walked to the middle of the empty garage and looked around. Everything seemed fine. All my tools were hanging where I had left them, nothing was moved, missing, or disturbed. Gardening supplies were neatly lined up on the shelf in the back of the garage. My workbench was still covered with sawdust from my last disastrous home improvement project.

I went back outside, making sure the door was closed securely so a gust of wind wouldn't fling it open. As I was walking back to the house, I saw movement out of the corner of my eye and whirled around in time to see a deer leap through the underbrush at the back of the property. Relieved that my stalker was more interested in eating my shrubs than fulfilling Aimee's supposed contract to have me "whacked," I headed to the back porch to retrieve Jorge's final bill, which I had decided to pay, primarily to avoid the embarrassment of having to defend myself against the small claims action I was pretty certain he'd file if I didn't pay him.

Jorge's bill, which I assumed would be tucked into the stack of firewood, wasn't there. I searched the porch, but there wasn't any other place he could have left it. Aside from the stacked logs, the only things on the porch were a small table and two chairs, and Buddy's two bowls, one for water and one for his food. I noticed that both were still almost full. Apparently he hadn't eaten his breakfast, which was unusual for him. Unlike some cats, Buddy wasn't a grazer, nibbling away at his food throughout the day. Ordinarily, he and I ate breakfast and dinner at the same time, keeping each other company. This morning, however, wanting to get an early start, I had skipped breakfast and picked up coffee at the diner near the local garden center. Perhaps Buddy had also skipped breakfast when he realized he had no dining companion, or maybe his ordeal at the hands of Jorge had affected his appetite.

I tried the kitchen door and found that it was still locked, the final proof that whatever Jorge had wanted, it didn't include some nefarious action inside my home. I was in the process of unlocking the door when I felt something brush against my ankles. It was Buddy, poking his head through the swinging cat door that, at Aimee's insistence, had been installed exactly six inches above the floor, supposedly making it impossible for wild animals to enter our kitchen. I don't know where Aimee came up with the six-inch rule, probably something she read, but I do know that I've never seen raccoons, squirrels, or skunks use a tape measure to decide what opening they can or can't enter. But to avoid an argument, I had the royal carpenters follow Queen Aimee's edict.

Buddy strolled over to his food dish, sniffed at it, and looked up at me with an expression that I interpreted to mean, *This isn't dinner food, it's breakfast food.*

"What you don't eat for breakfast becomes dinner," I said.

He seemed to think about that for a second, and then began to eat.

I walked through the house to ensure everything was as it should be before returning to the kitchen where I made bacon and eggs for dinner. I must have been hungrier than I thought because I finished eating before Buddy, a rare occurrence.

My furry friend was still dining on the back porch when I settled into my favorite chair in front of the television, a glass of Jameson's in hand. I flipped through the channels and eventually found an old black and white movie featuring an actor I had seen before, but whose name I couldn't recall. He and a very pretty young lady were driving along a highway. It was a monotonous stretch of road, the kind that can lull you to sleep before you realize it. Ahead in the distance was a building that looked suspiciously like Martin von Beverwicjk's restaurant, its parking lot overflowing with police cruisers and fire trucks. As they passed the restaurant, I saw the familiar sign with *The New Amsterdam Inn* in fancy script. The car, which I now realized was a Mustang, continued on its westward journey, passing shopping centers, office buildings, and apartment complexes. Color began to suffuse the black and white landscape, beginning with green trees and yellow traffic signs. But the sky remained a cold, hard gray.

At some point I was no longer watching an unnamed actor drive the car, but had become the driver myself. I looked to my right and saw Stacey McCain in the passenger's seat, intently reading a romance novel. Looking in the rear view mirror, I spotted Buddy perched on the back seat. But this dream version of my feline friend was shimmering and translucent. He was there, but he wasn't there.

We drove in silence for miles. There was no conversation, no familiar hum of the tires on pavement, not even the musical soundtrack that seems to accompany all my dreams. The shopping centers and residential developments eventually gave way to farms and fields, and the level terrain to rolling hills. As we crested one of them, I saw a billboard with a giant smiling Bob Proctor. But instead of proclaiming the wonders of the kingdom he ruled, Billboard Bob was advertising Buddy's favorite brand of cat food.

"Check it out, Buddy," I said, looking in the mirror to see his reaction. But the shimmering Buddy had completely disappeared.

31

"Save me a spot in the afterlife."

I awoke to a test pattern on the television instead of a movie. It was dark and the wind was howling. Checking my watch by the light of the television screen, I saw that it was just before six in the morning. I was groggy and disoriented, and more than a little stiff from spending the night sitting in a chair, but instinctively knew that something was wrong.

Unsure of what was causing my unease, I began to inspect the house, looking for a broken window or open door that would signal the presence of an uninvited guest. Would I find Mr. Goatee sitting at the kitchen table or Reynaldo poking around my desk? Perhaps Jorge had let himself in, not to stack firewood or deliver flowers to an absent Aimee, but to get even with me for firing him. Or maybe Eddie the Skunk had been right after all, and Aimee's hired assassin was lying in wait somewhere in the darkened house.

"It's probably just Colonel Mustard in the library with a candle stick," I said aloud to fill the silence and calm my jittery nerves.

I checked upstairs first, starting with the master bedroom, which turned out to be empty, as were the adjoining bathroom and walk-in closet. As I was leaving the room, I had a thought and walked to the window overlooking the circular driveway in front of the house. We had received several inches of snow during the night, just as the weatherman had predicted, providing an ideal way to determine if someone had visited the house while I slept. My Mustang was where I had parked it the day before, its front end obscured by the snow-covered shrubbery. There were tire tracks leading from the road to a spot just behind the Mustang, most likely made by the guy who delivers the weekend paper. I scanned the ground for footprints, but didn't see any. Moving to the window on the north side of the house, which overlooks the driveway leading back to the garage, I repeated the process. No footprints, no disturbance of any kind.

I entered what I now thought of as Aimee's bedroom on the other side of the hallway. It was also empty. Looking out the windows on the south side of the house, all I could see was an unbroken field of snow.

My search of the second floor ended in Aimee's office at the back of the house. Everything there looked just as it had the last time I had been in that room. There were two particularly ugly paintings leaning against one wall, a cluttered desk with a typing extension holding Aimee's red IBM Selectric under the back window, a file cabinet and a desk chair. Leaning on Aimee's typewriter, I peered through the window overlooking the back of the house, and then repeated the process with the one on the north side. In both cases there were no human footprints, only tracks made by an animal, most likely a deer.

I realized the lack of footprints didn't prove I hadn't had a visitor during the night. Someone could have come and gone early in the evening, his or her presence masked by the snow that accumulated later. But I felt some measure of relief as I headed back downstairs to continue my inspection.

By the time I reached the kitchen, the last room I checked, it was obvious that I was alone in the house. That's when I realized what the problem was. I was alone. I had searched the entire house and hadn't seen Buddy anywhere. By this time, he would have normally made his presence known, rubbing against my ankles and begging me to fill his food dish. According to Buddy's inner clock, breakfast should be served within five minutes of me waking up, regardless of the actual time.

I found Buddy when I opened the door to the back porch, the only part of the house I hadn't checked. He was lying on his side, motionless. At first I thought he was asleep, which was odd since I had never known him to sleep on the back porch, even on a hot summer night. I knelt down and stroked his fur. It was cold and stiff. I scratched behind his ears, which is guaranteed to put his purring machine into high gear. There was no purring, no response of any kind. Only silence.

Buddy was dead.

That's when I saw the empty food and water bowls and realized that Jorge had exacted his revenge. Sadness gave way to anger, and then anger to guilt. "What you don't eat for breakfast becomes dinner," I said, my words a self-inflicted wound to the heart.

I decided the clearing in the center of the wooded lot behind the house would be Buddy's final resting place. The wild flowers would keep him company in the spring, along with the birds that visited the feeder hanging from the dogwood tree I had planted two years ago. But I couldn't just drop his body in a hole. I needed a suitable container, a kitty sarcophagus, if you will. So I spent the next hour searching every room in the house, this time not for an imagined intruder, but for a box in which to bury my feline friend. The shoeboxes in Aimee's closest were too small, and the cardboard box I found in the basement was too big. So I decided to wrap Buddy's body in the purple silk dress with pearl buttons that Aimee wore to her Art Alliance fund raising dinners. She'd throw a fit when she found out (assuming she ever came home again), but it seemed a fitting way to grant Buddy his final revenge.

After retrieving a shovel from the garage, I trudged through the unbroken field of snow to the clearing behind the house. I scrapped away several inches of snow and then attacked the frozen ground. It was difficult work, and despite the cold, sweat was pouring down my back, chilling my body. I had managed to dig a hole about two feet deep when I heard a sound and saw movement out of the corner of my eye. As I spun to my left, I raised the shovel, intending to use it to defend myself. My attacker turned out to be a deer leaping through the underbrush. I returned to my digging, eventually creating a hole sufficiently deep to ensure Buddy's body wouldn't become a meal for wild animals. Then I held him one last time, gently lowered him into the ground, and refilled his grave with dirt.

"Save me a spot in the afterlife," I said as I threw the last shovelful onto his final resting place.

I returned to the house, showered, and changed my clothes. Then I made a fire in the fireplace and, sick at heart over the loss of Buddy, just sat watching the flames. "He was just a cat," I said to the empty room at one point, repeating Jorge's line. But I knew that wasn't really how I felt. I remained there until midday when hunger got the better of me, and I went to the kitchen to make myself a tuna sandwich. I was tempted to wash it down with a glass of Jameson's, but it was too early in the day. Instead, I decided to read the comics in the Sunday papers, hoping they would cheer me up. I retrieved the *Record* and the *Ledger* from the front porch, threw another log on the fire and settled into my chair by the fireplace.

Both papers had a front-page story about the Friday evening raid on Martin von Beverwicjk's restaurant. If I hadn't known better, I would have thought each paper was reporting on a different event. The story in the *Record* was based on information provided by Troy Forge authorities. In that version of events, the restaurant had been shut down for health code and fire code violations that were discovered when the police, acting on a tip, entered the establishment and busted one of the employees for operating a drug ring from the premises.

The story in the *Ledger*, written by Stacey, who was actually there, disclosed that over a dozen heavily armed men stormed the premises with the Health Inspector and Fire Inspector in tow, apparently with the intention of finding a pretext to shut down a restaurant operated by someone who had recently filed a lawsuit against the town. While they were terrorizing the frightened customers, who initially didn't realize the masked men in black were a police SWAT unit, the cops came upon a kitchen employee who was smoking a marijuana joint behind the building. Accompanying Stacey's article was a sidebar with the headline: Your Tax Dollars At Work. It explained how local police departments were using federal grant money to become what amounted to para-military units, complete with the type of armaments ordinarily only found on the battlefield. It concluded by mentioning Stacey's earlier article about the Berkowitz case and the list of ill-advised government expenditures that piece detailed.

Stacey's article cheered me up temporarily, but the effect was short lived. I accomplished only two things the rest of the day. I telephoned Professor Clay to ensure he was ready to testify, and I left a message for my secretary to call Eddie the Skunk and ask him to meet me at the office at the end of the day on Monday. Aimee's alleged contract to have me killed had weighed on my mind for too long. It was time to get some answers. The remainder of my time was spent in front of the television, clicking from channel to channel in a futile attempt to find something that would cheer me up.

The sun remained hidden behind somber gray clouds for the rest of the afternoon, and snow flurries buffeted by the wind occasionally filled the sky. By six o'clock my rumbling stomach was reminding me that it was time to eat. So I fixed myself another tuna sandwich, this time accompanied by a generous glass of Jameson's, and settled into my favorite chair by the fireplace.

Five minutes later the doorbell rang.

32

"The '80' is the route number, not the speed limit."

I opened the front door to find Reynaldo standing on the porch with his hands in his pockets. "Good evening, Mr. O'Brian," he said. "Mind if I come in?"

Without waiting for a response, he brushed past me and came inside. I followed him into the living room. "Nice place you've got here," Reynaldo said, looking around, seemingly admiring the furnishings, but more likely checking for whatever guys like Reynaldo look for when they enter a room. "Very comfy."

"Thanks, decorated it myself," I said as I casually picked up a book from an end table and crossed to the bookcase on the far side of the room. It was a lie, of course. I don't know the first thing about decorating. That's Aimee's area of expertise. But I was hoping my attempt at idle conversation would serve as a distraction. I was going to the bookcase not to return the book to its shelf, but to retrieve a gun I had hidden there years ago. It wasn't loaded, but Reynaldo wouldn't know that.

But apparently he did, because before I had made it halfway across the room, Reynaldo said, "Don't waste your time with the gun. It's not loaded. Which is pretty dumb when you think about it. What's the point having a gun if it's not ready when you need it?"

I stopped in mid-stride and turned to face him. He gave me the *just sayin'* palms up gesture. Then, pointing to the chair positioned across from the sofa, he said, "Sit down. I think we need to talk." He took a seat on the sofa, leaned back, and crossed his legs, waiting for me to sit down. When I had, he said, "For starters, I'm a former Navy Seal. With my training, I could break your back without working up a sweat. But I wasn't hired to break your back, I was hired to watch your back."

I was stunned and relieved at the same time. And I had so many questions I didn't know which one to ask first.

Reynaldo made the decision for me. "You're probably going to ask who hired me," he said. "I'll save you the trouble and tell you I'm not at liberty to reveal that, and even if I was, it wouldn't do you any good. The person who hired me did it for someone else, who did it for someone he knows. That's the way these things are done so it's nearly impossible to ever find the person who's actually behind the assignment. You could try to follow the money, but that'd be tough to do. These people have all kinds of ways to move money around so you can never tell whose it is."

His answer reminded me of Eddie the Skunk's convoluted explanation of how he learned about Aimee's supposed contract to have me killed.

"And who, exactly, are 'these people'?"

"Everyone from international drug cartels to government agencies you never heard of."

I was relieved that I wouldn't have to worry the next time I saw Reynaldo, assuming he was telling the truth, of course. But I still had a bunch of questions.

"But why would anyone hire you to protect me?" I asked.

"They obviously think you're in danger," he said. He didn't begin his answer with "Duh," but he didn't have to. His tone of voice did it for him.

"Have you done this kind of thing before?" I asked.

I wasn't questioning Reynaldo's abilities, but apparently he thought I was because he said, "Don't worry, I know what I'm doing. I've done this sort of work for years."

"Ever kill anyone in the process?" I wasn't sure why I asked that. It just came out.

He hesitated momentarily, presumably searching for a way to answer my question without actually answering it. He succeeded. "I'm hired to keep people safe, not to kill people."

"Well, if you had killed that kid in the alley the other night, it would have been okay with me," I said. "And by the way, thanks."

"I'm hired to keep people safe, not to kill people," he repeated. "And by the way, you're welcome."

There was one other thing I needed to know. Reynaldo's answer could put my mind at ease or signal that his appearance this evening hadn't resolved my problems. "Do you work with a partner? Tall, bald guy with a goatee?"

"I work alone," Reynaldo said. "The person who retained my services didn't mention hiring anyone else, but then again I didn't ask." He thought for a moment, then added, "Tell me about this guy with the goatee."

I told him the story of Mr. Goatee following me home from the courthouse in Newark, and then showing up at the scene of my abruptly halted mugging in Morristown. I gave Reynaldo as many details as I could remember, assuming the information would help him keep me safe. I was beginning to think he really had been hired to protect me. If he wanted to harm me, I reasoned, he would have already done it instead of sitting on the sofa in my living room conversing.

"I'll look into this," he promised.

I was trying to think of what to ask next when Reynaldo delivered the message I realized later was the real reason for his visit. "Stop talking to the press about me. It makes my job more difficult. In order to stay close enough to protect you, I have to blend in. That's tougher to do when people are looking for me. And for God's sake, slow down when you drive. I followed you on I-80 yesterday and had a tough time keeping up with you. The '80' is the route number, not the speed limit. If I get pulled over by a cop, it doesn't do either of us any good."

"One more question," I said as Reynaldo got up from the sofa.

"Shoot," he said.

I thought that was an ironic word to use, given the question I asked. "How did you get a gun into the courthouse?"

"These days it's tough to get a gun into a courthouse, or any government building, for that matter," he replied.

"Then how did you do it?"

"I didn't. I got the gun out of my car after I left the building. I might have been able to get it through security, but why take the risk?" he said as he shrugged his shoulders and walked toward the front door. "Besides, the courthouse is filled with armed federal marshals who could protect you if necessary, not that I think anyone would be foolish enough to come after you there."

He stopped to retrieve his coat from the chair by the telephone table in the hall where he had left it, opened the door and stepped onto the front porch. I followed him, closing the door behind me. "One last thing," he said, as we stood on the porch watching the snowfall. "From now on, I'd suggest putting your car in the garage." He pointed to a giant "FU" scratched into the front fender of my Mustang that had been hidden by the shrubbery when I looked out the upstairs window that morning. I assumed I was looking at Jorge's final bill. "That's just cosmetic, but next time it could be something more serious, like a severed brake line."

Reynaldo surveyed the front yard the same way he had scrutinized my living room earlier. "Sorry about the car," he said. "I'm around more often than you realize, but I have to sleep some time." Then he turned up his collar and disappeared into the swirling snow flurries.

33

"For a dead guy, he's pretty good with a gun."

The impact of Stacey McCain's article was obvious the minute I stepped off the courthouse elevator Monday morning. The elevator lobby, which at this hour would ordinarily have perhaps a dozen individuals rushing to the courtrooms on that floor, was packed with people milling around, many holding signs that read: *Tax Politicians, Not Patriots.*

As I made my way to the double doors leading into Judge Abrams' courtroom, a man fell into step beside me. "Mr. O'Brian," he said, "Steven Scott, the *Morris Record*. What do you think your prospects are in court?"

It was the typically silly question reporters always seem to ask, and I was tempted to give him the silly answer his question deserved: *My client is a jerk, his case is a turkey, and I fully anticipate having my ass whipped. That's why I took the case in the first place.* But that wouldn't help Harvey. So, suppressing a smile, I said, "Even someone as principled as Harvey Berkowitz has a difficult time taking on the federal government, which has virtually unlimited resources. It's not a fair fight, but we intend to win anyway." *There you go, buddy, a nice succinct quote for your opening paragraph.*

The courtroom's public gallery was packed. Every seat was taken, and people were standing along the wall in the back and in both of the side aisles. Many of the spectators were carrying signs with the slogan Harvey's daughter had come up with, and I wondered how long Judge Abrams would permit those signs in her courtroom. She couldn't bar the protestors from the public gallery as long as they weren't disruptive, but she could limit their numbers and their signs. It was going to be an interesting day at the circus.

Harvey was already seated at the defense counsel table when I arrived. "Did you arrange all this?" he asked, waving toward the public gallery?

I hadn't of course, at least not directly, but I wasn't about to tell him that. "I'll share the credit with Leah. After all, she's the one who came up with the slogan."

I surveyed the public gallery for Professor Clay and spotted him in the third row. We made eye contact and he smiled and shook his head, apparently relishing the spectacle that was about to unfold.

Judge Abrams took the bench a moment later. She had obviously been told what was going on in her courtroom because as soon as she sat down, she made an announcement. "I want to make it clear that spectators are expected to remain silent throughout these proceedings. This is a court of law, and any person engaging in behavior that I deem disruptive will be removed from the courtroom."

Next, Abrams turned to face the jurors. "I want to emphasize what I told the jury at the beginning of this trial. You are to base your verdict only on the evidence that is properly admitted in this courtroom. You are not to rely on anything you read, see, or hear in the media or obtain from any other outside source. You must not let your personal opinions or the opinions of others enter into your decision about the innocence or guilt of the defendant. The only thing on which you can base your verdict is the evidence that is properly admitted in this court." Then she instructed Newton, "Call your next witness."

But instead of calling a witness, Newton said, "Your Honor, I'd like to move for a continuance."

Abrams' response was immediate. "Absolutely not. During jury selection I refused to excuse people who had made airline reservations and other arrangements for Thanksgiving because I said the trial would be over by then. I'm not going to let you prolong it."

"In that case," Newton said, "I'd like to reserve the right to call one final witness after the defense puts on its case."

What Newton was proposing wasn't the way a criminal trial is supposed to be conducted. Ordinarily, the prosecution presents its entire case first. The defense then puts on its case, each side makes closing arguments, and the jury deliberates.

"Why can't you put your witness on now?" Judge Abrams asked.

"He's not available at the moment," Newton replied.

"Why not?" the judge wanted to know.

"He's traveling at the moment, Your Honor."

"Traveling where?"

Newton clearly didn't want to answer that question, but eventually said, "My witness went to the Grand Canyon, judge."

I couldn't help myself. I burst out laughing, recalling my recent conversation with Eddie and Gino. The public gallery followed my cue and exploded in laughter as well.

"You find this amusing, Mr. O'Brian?" Abrams asked after banging her gavel for silence. Obviously she didn't. But then again, she didn't know what I knew.

"Sorry, Your Honor." I quickly came up with a plausible reason for my laughter. "I thought I had heard every prosecutorial excuse in the book, but the my-witness-can't-testify-because-he-went-to-the-Grand-Canyon excuse is a new one on me."

My logical move was to insist that Newton either produce his witness now or rest his case, but since I knew who he planned to call, I took advantage of the situation and said, "Since I think it's becoming increasingly obvious that the government's case is completely without merit, I'm amenable to giving Mr. Newton an additional opportunity to embarrass himself."

My snide remark elicited snickers from the public gallery and made Newton mad as hell, but before he could reply, Abrams said, "I'll interpret that to mean you have no objection to the prosecution calling an additional witness at the conclusion of your case."

That cooled Newton off, and he sat down, thinking he had won the round. If only he had known.

"Are you ready to proceed with your case, Mr. O'Brian?" the judge asked.

Although Professor Clay was in court and ready to testify, I said, "I had no idea the government's case was so weak its witness would flee the jurisdiction to avoid testifying. Consequently, I didn't arrange for my witnesses to be in court today."

There was more laughter from the public gallery, and Newton was on his feet again. "Your Honor, I would ask the court to sanction Mr. O'Brian for his outrageous conduct."

"What outrageous conduct?" I asked before Abrams had a chance to respond. "You're the one who put together such a flimsy case that your witnesses are embarrassed to appear in court."

"Your Honor," Newton whined again.

"That's enough, both of you," Abrams said. "We'll recess until tomorrow morning at which time Mr. O'Brian will put on his first witness." She banged her gavel and added, "I'll see counsel in my chambers."

As I was packing up my briefcase, Harvey asked, "Why did you agree to let the government call another witness?"

"Because that witness isn't going to say what Newton thinks he's going to say."

"You know who the witness is?"

"Yup."

"How? I though you said we couldn't get their witness list?"

"We can't, but there are other ways of getting the information I need to defend you. They're not necessarily cheap," I added, setting Harvey up for some additional charges when we rendered our final bill, "but they're effective."

"Why didn't you call our witness?" Harvey wanted to know. "You said he was here today."

I wasn't about to tell him that saddened by the death of Buddy, exhausted from dealing with rogue cops, and tired of wondering where things were going with my wife, I needed some downtime. So I simply said, "Tactics."

I could see that Harvey was about to ask what I meant by that, but I never gave him the chance. "Do me a favor and call my office on that fancy portable phone of yours and give my secretary a message."

"Sure," Harvey said. If he was unhappy that I didn't elaborate on my answer to his question, he didn't show it.

"Ask her to see if she can move up my late afternoon appointment to around two o'clock. Then ask her to see if Scott can schedule a meeting with the subdivision client for the end of the day." Carolyn would know who the subdivision client was, but Harvey didn't need to know the name of our client. "See you tomorrow morning," I said as I set off for Judge Abram's inner sanctum.

Newton was already there when I arrived, seated in his usual spot at the right hand of the Almighty Abrams. I briefly considered sitting on his lap, but took the empty chair to her left instead. "My contacts in Washington have gotten back to me," Abrams began. "The man who assisted Mr. O'Brian and me last Monday is this person," she said, putting two photos on her desk. The first was the blurry photo from the lobby surveillance camera. The second was a sharp, clear, black and white photo of Reynaldo. He was looking straight into the camera, and there was no question it was him.

"Who is he?" Newton asked.

I held my breath, waiting to see if her explanation matched what Reynaldo had told me the previous evening.

"According to people in Washington, he's a former Navy Seal by the name of Reynaldo Renoir. He's now a freelance security specialist who's hired to protect people. At least that's the official description of what he does. Unofficially, he's a hired gun."

My ears perked up when I heard the term "hired gun." I recalled Reynaldo telling me he was hired to protect people, not kill them. Apparently he had been somewhat less than forthright, or perhaps the killing part had just slipped his mind.

"Here's where things get interesting," Abrams said. "According to my sources, Mr. Renoir died three years ago."

"For a dead guy, he's pretty good with a gun," I said.

Abrams ignored my wisecrack and looked right at Lionel Newton. "Despite being dead, he's worked for a number of government agencies, including the State Department, the Department of Justice, and the IRS."

"I don't know anything about him," Newton said. "I made some calls like you asked, but nobody I spoke with knows anything about him."

Pointing at me, Abrams said, "I've learned to expect him to play fast and loose with the truth, but you're a DOJ employee. I expect better from you."

Newton protested mightily that he was telling the truth, that he knew nothing about Reynaldo, and that nobody at IRS or DOJ knew anything about Reynaldo. I almost felt sorry for poor Lionel. He probably knew less about Reynaldo than I did. The list of supposedly dead, former Navy Seals secretly working for the Justice Department was probably above his pay grade.

"You apparently have some good contacts in D.C.," I said. "I don't suppose they could do something about getting the new parking garage open, could they? The lot next to the courthouse is still a skating rink, and you know as well as I do how dangerous it can be to walk to one of the other lots. Mr. Renoir might not be there next time." I couldn't help myself; I had to add, "After all, he is dead."

"There's not going to be a next time. The parking garage should be open tomorrow," Abrams said, quickly adding, "not that I had anything to do with that." Then she leaned back in her chair and looked first at Newton and then at me. It was clear that she had more on her mind, and was trying to decide what to say next. The silence continued for perhaps another thirty seconds before Abrams leaned forward, planted her arms on the desk and continued. "I don't like the way this trial has proceeded. I'm tired of the theatrics and I'm disappointed in the way both of you have performed in my courtroom. I have half a mind to declare a mistrial and start all over after the holidays." Before I could decide whether to object or agree to that surprising suggestion, the judge said, "But that's not going to happen. It wouldn't be fair to the jurors."

She reached into the top drawer of her desk, pulled out a copy of Stacey's *Ledger* article about the trial and slammed it on the desktop. "I'll tell you something else that's not fair to the jurors: polluting their minds with this collection of outright lies, half truths, and misleading innuendos. This is obviously your handiwork, Mr. O'Brian." As she was speaking, she shook her finger at me like an outraged schoolmarm.

"I didn't write that," I protested.

"No, but you arranged to have it written."

"Not true." *Well, not completely true.* "The reporter approached me, not the other way around."

"And you supplied her with the information, or I should say misinformation, she needed to write it, as well as the photographs."

"The photos were introduced into evidence in a public trial in an open courtroom," I reminded her. I didn't say anything about the information. Or the misinformation.

Newton got into the act. "This article is highly incendiary and prejudicial to the prosecution's case. I think the court needs to give a more robust instruction to the jury than the one you gave this morning."

I started to laugh. "More robust? Seriously?"

"All right. Enough from both of you," Judge Abrams said. "The jury instruction I gave this morning is sufficient. Going forward I'm putting both of you on a short leash. Now get out of here. You're giving me a splitting headache."

I assume she meant Lionel Newton the Eighth was giving her a headache. She couldn't possibly have meant me.

34

"You know where I live?"

Assuming the Troy Forge cops would be waiting for me when I got off Interstate 280, I decided to take a different route to the office. Instead of heading west out of Newark, I went north, swung west through Montville, and came into town from the north, bypassing all the major roads where Proctor's palace guard would likely be lying in wait for me. The circuitous route I had taken got me to the office later than I had expected, but it did allow me to see a billboard I hadn't seen before. On this one, His Most Glorious Eminence was reminding his loyal subjects that *Troy Forge has the lowest crime rate in the county.* I assume that's due to having the county's most aggressive police force.

When I got to the office, Elaine, our receptionist, informed me that Eddie the Skunk had arrived and was waiting for me in Rick's office.

"What's he doing in there?" I asked.

"Rick came into the waiting room," she said. "You know how he walks around the office like he's not quite sure where he is. Breaks my heart to see him like that."

I nodded in agreement. Rick's condition wasn't getting any better.

"Well, Rick wandered into the waiting room, saw your client sitting there, and told him he could wait for you in his office."

When I got to Rick's office, I found him sitting behind his desk and staring out the window. Eddie was on the sofa thumbing through a magazine. "Thanks for being so hospitable to Mr. Rizzo," I said to Rick. If he heard me he didn't acknowledge it, just kept looking out the window.

As Eddie and I walked to my office I asked, "Did you and Rick have a good conversation?" There are some things our clients don't need to know. And these days, who knew what Rick would say.

"Not sure you could call it a conversation," Eddie answered. "He thanked me for being a client, then he started talking about some guy named Joshua. Used to play golf with him or something. Then he says something like 'time flies' and starts to look out the window. No disrespect, but I think your partner's losing it."

"Actually, there are days when we think he's already lost it," I replied. "But he's the founder of this firm and we owe him."

"I respect that," Eddie replied. "If you owe someone, you gotta be loyal to him." It was a casual comment, but coming from someone like Eddie, I assumed there was an understood "or else" at the end of the sentence.

When we got to my office, I took my seat behind the desk and Eddie settled into the chair across from me. I got right to business. "Eddie, tell me exactly how you heard about this contract my wife put out to have me killed."

"Well, it's like this," Eddie began. "Guy I know says his buddy was in a bar the Mexicans go to and he overhears this beaner talking about whacking someone who lives in a big house in Mountain Springs. Describes the place, right down to the little squirrel on the mailbox. I knew right away he was talking about your place."

"You know where I live?" I asked, unable to hide my surprise.

Eddie laughed. "Counselor, in your business sometimes it's best not to know things. But in my business I gotta know as much as I can about everyone and everything."

"Oh," was all I could say, wondering just how much Eddie knew about me.

As if reading my mind, Eddie said, "Don't worry, counselor. It's not like I got cameras hidden in your bedroom. Nothin' like that. It's just that you're important to me, and I like to make sure people who are important to me stay safe."

"Oh," I said again, unable to decide if Eddie's revelation obligated me to thank him. I'd have to consult Emily Post. Hopefully she had a chapter on the proper protocol for thanking thugs.

I decided to move the conversation in a different direction. "Do you know a guy named Reynaldo?"

Eddie thought for a moment. "No," he finally said. "Name don't ring a bell. Why? He a problem for you? I can have Tony take care of him for you, if you want."

I had a feeling Tony, whoever he was, would have a tough time finding Reynaldo, much less taking care of him, but I was careful not to say that to Eddie. Instead, I asked, "Who's Tony?"

"Works for me," Eddie said. "Tall, bald guy with one of them funny chin spinach beards. After I found out your old lady wanted you dead, I asked Tony to watch your back. You wasn't supposed to know he was there, but the dummy lets you see him when he brings you lunch at the courthouse." Despite using the word "dummy," Eddie didn't seem particularly angry. He confirmed that by adding, "Tony can kill a man with one punch, but he's a big teddy bear. Brought you lunch cause he felt sorry for you."

"Is Tony still watching my back?" I asked.

"Nah. I had to send him to Jersey City to do something that needed doing right away." I was curious what Eddie needed done in Jersey City, but didn't ask. He was right that sometimes it's better for lawyers not to know too much about their clients' affairs. "Besides," he continued, "big, bald guy with a funny beard is too easy to spot."

I was about to steer the conversation back to Reynaldo when Eddie looked at his watch and got up. "I gotta go," he said, "but I'll see what I can find out about this Reynaldo."

35

"Switcheroo!"

Scott, Avery, and Rick, were already in the conference room with Martin von Beverwicjk when I got there. I took the empty seat next to Rick just as he said to Martin, "I haven't seen your father lately. How is he these days?"

Martin looked around the table at the rest of us, understandably confused at being asked the same question he had answered at our last meeting. If he was annoyed, he did a good job of hiding it. "My father is in the hospice wing in Morristown Memorial. He probably doesn't have much longer."

"Oh, I'm sorry to hear that," Rick said. "If I had known, I would have gone over to visit him. Joshua was one of my first clients when I opened the firm. He and I played golf every Wednesday until he hurt his back."

"Yes, I had heard that," Martin said. From the way he said it, it was obvious that he realized his father wasn't the only one with a medical problem.

There was an uncomfortable silence that Scott finally broke. "Martin, I asked you to come by because we want to bring you up to speed on what's happened since we filed suit against Troy Forge. You obviously know about the SWAT team raid at your restaurant Friday night, but there are a few other things that have happened that you don't know about, but should." He then proceeded to tell the client about my run-ins with the local constabulary and the break-in at his garage.

"Proctor apparently wants to play hardball," Martin said. "The question is why. Is it some sort of personal vendetta against me or my family, or is it because of what I'm trying to do with the old fairgrounds property?"

"According to one of our sources in town hall, Proctor is no fan of you or your family," I said. "But this person also says all this has to do with the property, not you personally. His Highness apparently wants to encourage you to sell the property to one of his cronies. And we have a second informant who confirmed that. At least we had a second informant. Unfortunately, he turned up dead under somewhat suspicious circumstances."

Martin seemed genuinely stunned by that revelation. "Good Lord, you're not seriously suggesting..."

Avery, cautious as always, jumped into the conversation. "We're not suggesting anything. At this point, all we know for sure is that one of our contacts in town hall is dead. We have no proof that foul play was involved, much less that Proctor had anything to do with it.

"But given all that's happened," Scott said, "it wouldn't be a bad idea to take some extra precautions. We prefer our clients to be alive and kicking."

It was a poor choice of words in view of Joshua von Beverwicjk's impending journey into the great beyond, but before Scott had a chance to say anything more, Rick slapped the table with his hand and shouted, "Switcheroo!" He pushed back his chair and stood up. "Switcheroo," he said again, looking around the room at each of us, apparently surprised that we had no idea what he was talking about. He held up his right hand and said, "Martin," then held up his left hand and said "Joshua." Then he pointed to the left with his right hand, and to the right with his left hand. "Switcheroo, that's what we'll do."

The client was understandably beginning to get a bit agitated at this point, so I leaned toward him and whispered, "I realize he's a bit eccentric, but he usually has a point," hoping to buy time until one of my partners could come up with a way to salvage the situation.

As it turned out, no salvage operation was needed.

Rick walked to the bookcase on the far wall, muttering "forty, forty, forty" as he scanned the volumes holding the New Jersey Statutes, the collection of laws enacted by the Legislature. He reached up and took down one of the dark green volumes and carried it back to the table. Taking his seat, he began to thumb through the book. None of us had any idea what he was doing, but there was nothing to be gained by stopping him at this point, so we watched as he flipped page after page, finally stopping in the middle of the book. He held the volume up so I could see that he was holding Title 40, the state laws dealing with land use. Then he laid it on the conference table, slid it in front of me and pointed to the bottom of the page on the left.

He was pointing to section 55D-7, which contained a bunch of definitions. It's standard practice for laws to define commonly used words in uncommon ways. That's because the politicians who write our laws speak a different version of English than the rest of us. I scanned the section that Rick was pointing to and discovered that for purposes of the New Jersey land use laws, a street isn't just something you drive on, it's a complicated monstrosity that requires an entire paragraph to define. I worked my way down the list of words until I came to "subdivision," the one that seemed most pertinent to Martin von Beverwicjk's property. I read the definition, and then re-read it while everyone in the room waited.

Avery broke the silence. "What did you find?"

"I didn't find anything, but it looks like Rick did." I leaned back in my chair, put the statute book in my lap and began to read. "Subdivision means the division of a lot, tract or parcel of land into two or more lots, tracts, parcels or other divisions of land for sale or development."

"Now tell us something we don't know," the client snapped. He was apparently getting annoyed.

"Okay. Here's something you probably don't know. According to this, as long as no new streets are created, a subdivision doesn't include, and I quote, divisions of property by testamentary or intestate provisions."

"Switcheroo," Rick said with a satisfied smile. "Switcheroo."

"What in blazes is he talking about?" Martin von Beverwicjk demanded. "What does 'switcheroo' mean?"

Rick answered the question by repeating the gesture he had made earlier. He held up his right hand and said, "Martin," then held up his left hand and said "Joshua." Then he pointed to the left with his right hand, and to the right with his left hand. "Switcheroo."

Scott started to laugh. "Won't that piss off Proctor."

"I'm all for pissing off Proctor," the client said, "but I have no idea what the hell you guys are talking about."

"Let me explain what Rick's proposing," Scott began. "You deed the fairgrounds property to your father in exchange for one of the properties he owns. Then Avery drafts a new Will for your father that divides that property into individual lots leaving each lot to you or one of your corporations. When your father dies, we probate the Will and the land is divided according to his instructions in the Will without us ever having to deal with the planning board. It's called a testamentary subdivision, a holdover from the days when the Garden State had more farms than office parks. It was intended as an easy way for farmers to divide their farmland among their children. Many attorneys don't even know it exists, and even those who handle a lot of subdivision work seldom use it because it only applies in situations where no new roads need to be created. It works in your case because you have a road that runs around the property, providing access to all the lots created."

"It sounds a bit ghoulish," Martin said. "And too good to be true."

"It's not foolproof," Scott said. "The town could file suit to block it, claiming that your conveyance of the land to your father was fraudulent."

Avery, our tax expert joined the discussion. "That's why you can't just deed the property to your father for a dollar. It has to be a legitimate arms length transaction. The town could also claim that this was a fraudulent conveyance because it had no economic purpose other than to do an end run around the land use laws, but the fact that the law provides for a testamentary subdivision in the first place makes it more difficult for the town to make that argument."

"There's a good chance you'll end up in court," I said, "but it will be the town suing you instead of the other way around. The burden of proof will be on them, not you."

"That's if they sue," Scott said. "If they don't, you've got your subdivision. Of course, all this depends on your father's cooperation."

"He'll cooperate," Martin said. "He'll die a happy man if he knows the last thing he did was to stick it to Bob Proctor."

As Scott and Avery discussed the details with Martin, I looked over at Rick, who was staring at the painting of the Ford Mansion hanging on the far wall. His lips were moving, but I couldn't hear what he was saying. I leaned in closer and heard him whisper, "Joshua was one of my first clients when I opened the firm. Time flies by so fast." His eyes had that far-away look that had become much too common, and a single tear was running down his cheek.

36

"In that case, I might as well pack up and go home."

When I got to the courthouse the following morning, there were more armed deputy marshals than usual, apparently called in to deal with the growing number of people showing up with signs reading *Tax Politicians, Not Patriots*. Six of the marshals stood by the bank of elevators, scrutinizing everyone going up to the courtrooms. As I waited for an elevator, the marshals stopped a man neatly dressed in a suit and tie and asked him if he had business in one of the courtrooms. "Yes, public business, in a public courtroom in a public building," was his answer. That was apparently the wrong answer because one of the marshals promptly escorted him to a non-public room where the two of them presumably had a decidedly non-public conversation.

Harvey Berkowitz was waiting for me as I stepped off the elevator. "Big turnout."

"The bigger, the better."

The courtroom itself was even more packed than on Monday. It was a diverse group, young and old, black and white, some well dressed and others less so. There was no apparent leader, and no coordination that I could see, other than the fact that most members of the crowd wore clothing with various combinations of red, white, and blue. There were no signs bearing the slogan that Harvey's daughter had dreamed up, all of them having been confiscated by a trio of unsmiling federal marshals at the door who greeted the public with a continuous chant of "no signs in the courtroom."

Judge Abrams took the bench and immediately gave a variation on her speech of the previous morning, this time admonishing spectators that she "wouldn't stand for any nonsense" in her courtroom. I was making a mental note that her admonition had only been directed to the public when she instructed me to call my first witness.

"Defense calls Cassius Marcellus Clay."

A man in his early sixties, no more than five feet tall and slightly stooped with age, with wild gray hair that looked like it hadn't been combed in a decade, got up from his seat in the public gallery and shuffled down the aisle to the witness stand. He was an older version of the firebrand professor I remembered from my law school days. As usual, he was dressed in baggy brown pants with wide cuffs that might have been considered stylish back in the 1940s, an unbuttoned plaid sports jacket that looked like a Goodwill reject, a shirt that refused to stay tucked in, and a tie with a prominent stain right in the middle. Mismatched socks, one black and one blue, completed the outfit, making C.M. Clay look more like one of the city's sidewalk denizens than one of the country's foremost experts on the U.S. Constitution.

"That's our expert witness?" Harvey whispered nervously.

"Just wait," I replied. "Remember the old Irish saying: don't judge a book by its cover."

Professor Clay answered a handful of preliminary questions, after which I offered him as an expert on constitutional law. The judge asked Newton if he had an objection to the professor testifying as an expert witness, a routine question that should have elicited the routine response, "no objection." But just to give me a hard time, or perhaps because he had attended law school on another planet and had actually never heard of C.M. Clay, Newton insisted on inquiring about the professor's qualifications before accepting him as an expert. Judge Abrams, who, like me, had studied constitutional law with Clay, gave Newton a look that could only be interpreted to mean, *Are you out of your mind?* Newton showed no sign of changing his mind, so with an almost imperceptible shrug of her shoulders, she told him, "You may inquire."

Newton began by asking Professor Clay to provide details about his academic credentials. With characteristic understatement, Clay answered by saying that he had an undergraduate degree in history and a law degree. Newton pushed for more detail, and the professor was obliged to elaborate by explaining that both degrees had been awarded with highest honors from Harvard, where he had served as Editor-in-Chief of the law review and graduated at the top of his class. Newton asked if Clay had ever practiced law. That question elicited a one-word answer: "yes." Newton followed up by asking if Professor Clay had ever argued a case involving constitutional principles. The professor replied that, yes, he had made a "handful" of court appearances in Washington. "State or D.C.?" Newton wanted to know. "D.C.," Professor Clay answered, adding almost as an afterthought, "before the U.S. Supreme Court." When Newton asked if the professor had ever written anything about constitutional law, the professor answered, "A couple dozen law review articles and ten books, including the one you most likely used in law school." After five minutes, two things became obvious: Clay was indeed one of the country's foremost experts on the Constitution, and Newton was a fool for questioning that fact.

When Newton finished, he tucked his tail between his legs and sat down. Then I began my direct examination by asking, "Is the Internal Revenue Code constitutional?"

"No," the good professor replied, as we had agreed.

Newton objected, as I assumed he would. "Harvey Berkowitz is on trial, not the Internal Revenue Code."

"Good grief," I said, mustering as much mock outrage as I could. "Mr. Newton has spent the last couple weeks putting on a parade of witnesses, many of whom were blackmailed into testifying, and he objects when the country's foremost expert on the Constitution, one of only two witnesses I plan to call, says exactly one word!" The two senior DOJ attorneys at the prosecution's table that morning exchanged glances. One rolled his eyes and the other shook his head. Their newbie colleague had not yet learned the importance of timing.

"Mr. Newton," Judge Abrams said, "what do you say we allow Professor Clay a little more latitude?" It was phrased as a suggestion, but it clearly was anything but. "Continue, Mr. O'Brian."

"Why, in your expert opinion, is the Internal Revenue Code unconstitutional?"

"For starters, our tax laws violate the Fourth Amendment prohibition against unreasonable search and seizure. Section 7602 of the Tax Code allows the IRS to seize virtually all of a taxpayer's financial records without showing probable cause and without a court order."

Newton objected. "Your Honor, the IRS didn't seize 'virtually all' of Mr. Berkowitz's records. The IRS has strict guidelines controlling how it goes about collecting the information needed to enforce our laws."

"That might well be true," I countered, "but those are internal IRS guidelines, written by IRS employees, interpreted by IRS employees, and acted on by IRS employees. There's no judicial overview until after the fact. In this case, the IRS has done everything from stalk my client's family members and browbeat his accountant, to have a local cop stop a completely innocent delivery van driver so they could interrogate him at the side of a busy highway as traffic whizzed by at sixty miles an hour. So much for IRS guidelines."

"Enough." Judge Abrams was even more steamed than usual. "Remember what I told both of you in chambers yester-day. Mr. Newton, your objection is overruled. Now sit down. Mr. O'Brian, you will confine yourself to asking questions of the witness. You will not address Mr. Newton or make speeches for the benefit of the jury. Do both of you understand?" We both told her we understood completely. Of course, understanding her instructions didn't necessarily mean we'd follow them.

I continued by asking if the Tax Code violated any other provisions of the Constitution.

"Oh, yes indeed," Professor Clay said. "The Tax Code also violates the Fifth Amendment's protection against self-incrimination. It's the classic damned if you do, damned if you don't situation. If you file a tax return, the government can use that information to prosecute you. But if you don't file a tax return, the government can prosecute you for failing to file a return."

Newton objected again. "That argument has been rejected by the courts numerous times."

"Which courts?" Clay wanted to know. "Cite a case to support that contention, Mr. Newton." It was a line I had heard Professor Clay use many times in law school. He was treating the DOJ attorney like one of his students.

Newton either couldn't or didn't want to answer the question, so he appealed to Judge Abrams for help. "I would ask the court to instruct the witness not to address counsel directly. He's here to provide testimony, not to engage in a debate with me."

"Very well," Professor Clay said before Abrams could respond to Newton. "Perhaps Mr. Newton is referring to *U.S. v. Schiff*, which came out of the Second Circuit in 1979, or *U.S. v. Brown*, a Tenth Circuit case the same year. Or perhaps Mr. Newton is going all the way back to the 1929 Supreme Court case, *U.S. v. Sullivan*. I have a fundamental, conceptual problem with those cases, but that's a discussion best left for another day. For the moment, I think it's sufficient to remind my earnest young colleague that courts, even those presided over by one of my former students, have been known to make mistakes." Turning to face the jury, and making eye contact with the black electrician in the back row, he continued, "Never forget that in the infamous *Dred Scott* decision the United States Supreme Court ruled that Negros were property, not people."

Newton was on his feet so fast his chair went flying. "Objection," he bellowed. "This is another one of Mr. O'Brian's outrageous stunts."

"Outrageous stunts?" I countered. "Like taking naked pictures of a sixteen year old girl in the privacy of her bathroom or having the local cops tail me and harass my firm's clients?"

The mention of the cops tailing me got Judge Abram's attention. "Sidebar," she demanded, and Lionel Newton and I walked to the bench. "What's this about the police tailing you?" she asked.

I told her about my recent run-ins with the Troy Forge cops, Scott's tire slashing troubles, and the ticketing of clients leaving the firm's parking lot. Everything I said was detailed and factually correct, although I did forget to mention Bob Proctor or the von Beverwicjk matter. When I finished, Abrams asked Newton, "What do you know about all this?"

"Absolutely nothing," came his indignant response.

Judge Abrams was clearly troubled by my revelations, perhaps because of her own recent encounter with an urban thug and the appearance of the mysterious Reynaldo Renoir. She put her elbows on the bench, rested her head in her hands, and kneaded her temples. Lionel Newton the Eighth was most likely giving her another headache. "Step back," she finally said.

I returned to the lectern and I picked up where I had left off by asking the professor if, in his opinion, there were any other constitutional provisions that the Tax Code violated.

"Yes, indeed," came his answer. "It violates the Equal Protection Clause in a couple different ways. For starters, two different taxpayers can have the same amount of income yet end up paying vastly different amounts of tax. And secondly, taxpayers with higher incomes end up paying both a greater dollar amount and a greater percentage of their income than taxpayers with a lower income. This is what's commonly referred to as a progressive taxation scheme. Its proponents claim that this is fair." As he said "fair," he used two fingers on each hand to make the gesture for quotation marks. "Whether or not it's fair is a matter of opinion. What's indisputable fact is that different taxpayers pay different percentages of their income to the government."

"Your Honor," I renew my objection," Newton whined. "None of this is relevant."

"Of course it is," I said. "A law that's unconstitutional is unenforceable."

"It's enforceable until it's declared unconstitutional," Newton countered. "No court has declared the Internal Revenue Code unconstitutional, and there's no reason to think this court will either."

"Oh, so you and the judge have already gotten together and decided the outcome of this case?" I shrugged my shoulders and headed back to my seat. "In that case, I might as well pack up and go home. Heck, the jury might as well go home too. Who needs a jury when government employees can decide everything."

"Enough!" Judge Abrams shouted. "From both of you." She started kneading her temples again. Lionel Newton was obviously giving her a monster headache. "We'll recess early for lunch. Court will reconvene at one thirty."

37

"Dean Wormer must be running the IRS."

Judge Abrams was her old self when court reconvened, beginning the afternoon session by reiterating her earlier instructions to the public gallery, and then instructing me to "get on with it."

Professor Clay took his seat on the witness stand, and I began by reminding the jury of the professor's earlier testimony. "This morning you testified that the Tax Code is unconstitutional because it violates the Constitution's Equal Protection Clause and protection against self-incrimination."

Before I could continue, Newton was on his feet. "Your Honor, Mr. O'Brian is attempting to mislead the jury by saying the Tax Code is unconstitutional. It's not. No court has ever ruled..."

I cut him off before he could continue. "I'm not attempting to mislead anyone. In fact, it's Mr. Newton who's attempting to mislead both the court and the jury by making that statement. I never said the Tax Code was unconstitutional. Professor Clay is offering his expert opinion that the Code is unconstitutional."

"That's just it," Newton replied. "It's his opinion, it's not the ruling of a court."

The professor jumped into the fray. "Of course it's my opinion, young man. That's what expert witnesses do. We give opinions about matters within our area of expertise." His rebuke caught both Newton and Abrams off guard. Harvey's unofficial supporters in the public gallery started to laugh.

Judge Abrams banged her gavel and demanded silence. "The witness will answer questions, not address opposing counsel. Mr. Newton is correct that no court has ruled on the constitutionality of the Internal Revenue Code. However, the witness is free to offer his opinion as an expert on constitutional law that the Code is unconstitutional. But his opinion is just that, his opinion. Continue, Mr. O'Brian."

"Professor Clay, are there any other provisions of the Constitution that the Tax Code violates?"

"Oh, yes indeed. The Tax Code is unconstitutional because it violates the Due Process Clause." He looked directly at Newton before adding, "in my considered opinion."

"And would you please explain to the jury what due process is."

Professor Clay turned to face the jury. "Due process may well be the most important legal concept in the Constitution. It's incredibly complex and yet remarkably simple at the same time. Due process has been the subject of more law review articles than you can count, including several that I've written for *The Harvard Law Review* and *The Rutgers Law Review*. Legal scholars use thousands of words to describe the concept of due process, but it boils down to this: the government has to play fair with its citizens."

Clay had a gift for explaining complex ideas in a way that made them understandable. And that's what he proceeded to do. "I tell my students that the starting point for understanding due process is to recall the scene from the movie *Animal House* in which Dean Wormer tells the fraternity members they've unknowingly been on double secret probation." There was laughter from the jury box as well as the public gallery. Judge Abrams actually smiled. The professor continued. "It's a funny scene, but it demonstrates a serious concept, namely that it's inherently unfair to make people obey rules they don't know about. In 1926, the U.S. Supreme Court held that it's also unfair to make people obey rules they can't understand. The court said, and this is a pretty accurate quote: 'a statute that forbids or requires the doing of an act in terms so vague that men of common intelligence must necessarily guess at its meaning and differ as to its application violates the first essential of due process of law.' This has come to be known as the 'void for vagueness' doctrine."

Lionel Newton was busily writing on his legal pad as Professor Clay testified, most likely making notes in preparation for cross-examination, so the professor looked right at the DOJ newbie and said, "For those students diligently taking notes, the case I'm referring to is *Connally v. General Construction Company*. The courtroom once again erupted in laughter. The two other attorneys with Newton that day tried to suppress a smile, but failed. As Newton looked up from his note taking, the professor added, "The court's opinion was written by Justice Sutherland, who to the best of my knowledge was no relation to Donald Sutherland, the actor who played the bored English professor in *Animal House*." Even Judge Abrams laughed at that.

"And is it your expert opinion that the Tax Code is unconstitutional because of the 'void for vagueness' doctrine?" I asked.

"Absolutely," Professor Clay replied. "But it's not just the Internal Revenue Code, or Tax Code, if you will, that we're talking about. In addition to the Tax Code, taxpayers have to contend with Treasury regulations, which are the Treasury Department's official interpretations of the Code, and revenue rulings, IRS decisions about how the Tax Code is applied to a specific set of facts. On top of all that, there are revenue procedures that explain how taxpayers are supposed to apply the revenue rulings. All together, there's something like forty thousand pages of constantly changing laws, rules, and regulations."

Newton objected again. "Your Honor, this testimony is clearly inappropriate. None of this is relevant."

Before Abrams could rule, I said, "Judge, Mr. Newton seems intent on objecting every few seconds in a blatant attempt to disrupt the witness' testimony. I'd like to remind the court that the professor is one of only two witnesses I plan to call. I didn't constantly object when the government's witnesses testified, and I would ask the court to direct Mr. Newton to afford my witness the same courtesy." Before Abrams could respond, I added, "I should also point out that when Mr. Newton was unable to produce a witness at the conclusion of his case in chief, I was well within my rights to insist that his witness either testify at the appropriate time or not at all. But I didn't do that." That little reminder caused Newton to withdraw his objection.

The judge looked from Newton to me and back to Newton, massaged her temples, took a deep breath, and said, "Get on with it, Mr. O'Brian." Newton had apparently given her yet another headache.

"So to summarize, Professor Clay, it's your contention that our tax laws violate the Constitution's due process requirements because they're so voluminous that taxpayers of ordinary intelligence can't understand them, is that correct?"

"That's partially correct," the professor replied. "But it's not just the volume of laws, rules, and regulations, it's the fact that those thousands of pages are written in a way that even the experts can't understand them, much less the men of common intelligence that Justice Sutherland referred to in the *Connally* case. Every year one of the popular finance magazines – I don't remember which one – asks half a dozen tax professionals to prepare a tax return for a hypothetical taxpayer using the same data. If the tax experts are using the same data to prepare the return, all the returns should be the same. Yet every year, these experts come up with different results. And we're not talking about returns that differ by a few dollars. Sometimes the returns are radically different."

"How could that be?" I asked.

"It's because the tax laws are so complicated they can be interpreted so many different ways. As Justice Sutherland wrote in the *Connally* case, a law is void for vagueness if people differ as to its application. Our tax laws are a perfect example of what he was talking about."

"I'll save Mr. Newton the trouble of objecting," I said, "by pointing out that you're only talking about half a dozen tax experts hand picked by one magazine. Perhaps the magazine's editors find the six dumbest tax preparers in America so they have raw material for the story they want to write."

"Oh, but it's not just these tax preparers who are confused by our tax laws. Virtually everyone is. In fact, our tax laws are so complicated that even the IRS doesn't understand them. Studies done by the Treasury Department's Inspector General have found that when taxpayers call the IRS for help with a tax problem, they get incorrect guidance more than forty percent of the time." Professor Clay looked right at the jurors before continuing. "Now here's the thing that, more than anything else, shows how unfair the system is. If you act on the information the IRS gives you, and it turns out that what they told you is wrong, you're still on the hook for interest and penalties. They make the mistake, but you have to pay for it. Remember what I said earlier: due process basically means that the government has to play fair with people. I don't think any reasonable person would regard that as fair. Dean Wormer must be running the IRS."

The courtroom filled with laughter yet again. When it subsided, I asked Professor Clay, "Can you give us an example of a tax law that's so complicated people can't understand it?"

"Certainly. Section 509(a) of the Tax Code is typical of many sections that drive people crazy. I defy anyone in this courtroom, and that includes all the government lawyers as well as Judge Abrams, to tell me what section 509(a) means." Demonstrating his remarkable memory, the professor recited the Code section verbatim. "For purposes of paragraph (3), an organization described in paragraph (2) shall be deemed to include an organization described in section 501(c)(4), (5), or (6) which would be described in paragraph (2) if it were an organization described in section 501(c)(3)."

An exasperated Lionel Newton shot to his feet. "Your Honor, this is another one of Mr. O'Brian's outrageous..."

Before the DOJ attorney could finish his sentence, Professor Clay pointed at him and said, "Thank you for volunteering, Mr. Newton. Please tell the class what section 509(a) says."

The courtroom erupted in laughter and Newton turned a bright red. Then he went ballistic. "This is outrageous," he thundered. "From the very beginning of this trial, Mr. O'Brian has behaved like a Philadelphia lawyer, making a mockery of these proceedings and turning the courtroom into a three ring circus."

A sly smile appeared on Professor Clay's face, and I realized he was about to go off script and use Newton's Philadelphia lawyer reference to do an end run around *Dougherty* and argue for jury nullification.

It was a risky move, as we discovered moments later.

38

"My job is to interpret the law, not make the law."

Professor Clay's smile turned into outright laughter, which made Judge Abrams somewhat less than happy. She leaned toward the witness stand, a scowl on her face. "I see nothing humorous in this," she said in a tone of voice that made it clear her patience was wearing thin, not only with me, but with her former teacher as well.

"I'm sorry, Your Honor," the professor responded. "It's just that although Mr. O'Brian was one of my best students, he's no Andrew Hamilton."

Demonstrating why she'd never join me on the professor's 'best students' list, Abrams asked, "What does Alexander Hamilton have to do with this trial?"

"Not Alexander Hamilton, Andrew Hamilton. Two different people." Professor Clay said. "The term 'Philadelphia lawyer' was first applied to Andrew Hamilton, one of the most renowned attorneys of his day."

Lionel Newton was still on his feet. "That has nothing to do with this trial. It's not even remotely connected."

I wasn't sure I wanted the professor to upset my trial strategy by taking his testimony in the direction he apparently had in mind, but agreeing with Newton would undermine my own witness. Before I could come up with a way to get the professor's testimony back under control, he turned in his seat and told Abrams, "Actually it is connected, and in a fascinating way." That must have piqued her curiosity because she waved at Newton and me to sit down while nodding for the professor to continue.

"Mr. Berkowitz operates several businesses in Morris County," Clay began, "which is named in honor of Lewis Morris, who served as Chief Justice of New York before becoming the first governor of New Jersey. As Chief Justice he issued a ruling against the colonial governor of New York, a man named Cosby. Morris published the rationale for his ruling in a newspaper called the *New York Weekly Journal*. As it turns out, that publication had printed a number of articles critical of Cosby who, by all accounts, was a thoroughly despicable man."

Clay paused and looked directly at the jury before continuing. "I suspect the only people who liked Cosby were his wife and children, and I'm not even sure they were all that fond of him, truth be told." That comment got a laugh from several of the jurors, as well as a large segment of the public gallery.

Newton was once again on his feet to object, and Abrams once again waved him down. Perhaps she was enjoying the story as much as the jurors, most of whom had leaned forward in their seats and were hanging on the professor's every word. I again considered trying to take control of the situation, but decided that would do more harm than good. At this point my best option was to let Clay proceed, and hope his gambit wouldn't backfire.

"Now, here's where Andrew Hamilton comes into the story," Professor Clay said. "Cosby charged the publisher of the *New York Weekly Journal* with seditious libel, a crime that carried a life sentence." The professor had cannily refrained from using the publisher's name, which Abrams would almost certainly have recognized, alerting her to what Clay was up to. "In those days, seditious libel was printing anything derogatory about the government, even if it was true. Mr. Hamilton came to New York from Philadelphia to represent the publisher of the *Weekly Journal* after his original lawyers were disbarred for disrespecting the court."

The mention of disrespecting the court must have triggered something in Abrams. "Professor, I've given you a lot of latitude, but I think you've gone about as far with this line of testimony as I can permit. None of this is really germane to the case at bar."

"Oh, but it is," Clay insisted. "In colonial times, a tyrannical government wielded enormous power over our ancestors, silencing them when they dared to speak truth to power. And although the publisher of the *Weekly Journal* was technically guilty of libel as that crime was defined at the time, the jury used that trial to send a message to the government by deliberating for just ten minutes before returning a not guilty verdict for the publisher, John Peter Zenger."

It remained to be seen what effect the professor's impromptu testimony would have on the jurors, but its impact on Abrams and Harvey's supporters in the public gallery was immediate. Abrams was stunned, perhaps by Clay's testimony itself, but more likely by her inability to have realized what he was up to in time to stop him. Harvey's informal, anti-tax army, on the other hand, was quite pleased, demonstrating their appreciation of the professor's performance with nodding heads and polite applause.

The applause prompted Abrams to bang her gavel and demand silence in her courtroom, which caused the polite applause to become somewhat less polite. The increased volume made Abrams slam her gavel more furiously and raise her voice in an effort to be heard. The spectators' response was to add cheering to the applause, which made the judge even more determined to regain control of her courtroom.

"Clear the courtroom," she finally instructed when it became apparent that the public gallery wasn't going to be tamed by mere words.

In response, two armed marshals grabbed one of the spectators and manhandled him toward the exit. He fought back, and several other spectators went to his aid. The two marshals were quickly overwhelmed, and instead of removing the spectator from the courtroom, they found themselves being pushed through the doors into the hallway beyond. Moments later the marshals returned with reinforcements, and the confrontations escalated.

As the applause gave way to shouts and screams, Judge Abrams decided the jury had seen enough, and ordered them to return to the jury room until things settled down. A marshal touched the elbow of the impeccably dressed black woman who had risen from her seat in the front row of the jury box to watch the mayhem playing out in the back of the courtroom. It was an innocent gesture meant to direct her toward the side exit leading to the jury room. But instead of following his lead, she indignantly pulled her arm away and said something I couldn't make out, but which the marshal clearly didn't appreciate.

The juror seated next to the woman, an older man with thinning hair and wire rimmed glasses that constantly slid down his nose, said something to the deputy, and the two got into a heated discussion. Another marshal, an older man who reminded me of the one who had let me out of the holding cell to use the phone, took charge of the situation, and the jury left without further incident.

It took a good fifteen minutes for the marshals to empty the courtroom, at which point Judge Abrams asked Professor Clay, who had remained on the witness stand throughout the chaos, to step down and leave the room. I assumed that after more verbal skirmishing, the professor would return and the trial would continue. My assumption was proven incorrect a moment later when Abrams said, "Professor Clay's testimony is clearly irrelevant, and I'm going to order it stricken from the record."

"What part of his testimony are you referring to?" I asked.

"All of it," came her immediate reply. "Every last word of it." From her tone of voice I deduced that it was payback time. And what she said next confirmed that. "That little stunt you pulled, arguing for jury nullification, was the last straw."

"I never said a word about jury nullification," I countered.

"No, you had your witness do it for you."

"At no point in preparing for trial did Professor Clay and I ever plan to raise the issue of jury nullification," I said. "It never would have come up at all if Mr. Newton hadn't referred to me as a Philadelphia lawyer." That statement was completely truthful, but at this point in the trial I couldn't blame Abrams if she didn't believe me.

And she didn't. "That may or may not be true, but you've blown your credibility with me. In criminal trials I always give defense counsel a lot of leeway so nobody can ever say I didn't afford defendants every opportunity to put on a vigorous defense. But there are limits, Mr. O'Brian, and you've clearly exceeded them many times throughout this trial."

"I'm sorry you feel that way," I responded, "but I'm telling you the truth when I say that Professor Clay and I never even discussed jury nullification when preparing for trial."

"I'm not buying it" was her response.

"Okay, strike the testimony about the Zenger trial, but the rest of the professor's testimony should stand. Professor Clay is one of the country's leading experts on the Constitution, and there's no reason why the jury shouldn't be allowed to consider the rest of his testimony."

"No," Abrams said, "it's all out. Our tax laws may not be perfect, but they are the law until Congress changes them or a court rules they're unconstitutional." She leaned forward and waved a finger in my direction before adding, "and I'm not about to do that." She sat back and drew a deep breath before continuing. "My job is to interpret the law, not make the law. If your client and his supporters want a different tax law, they can elect people to Congress to do that. This trial isn't about whether or not our tax laws could be better. It's about whether or not your client obeyed the law as it's written."

Lionel Newton was sitting back in his chair with his arms crossed, a very satisfied smile plastered across his face. The two other attorneys with him that day, a man in his late fifties with white hair and a blonde woman in her thirties, didn't seem quite as happy. The woman whispered something to her colleague, causing him to nod and shrug his shoulders. I couldn't hear what they were saying, but I suspected they were discussing whether or not the judge had committed a reversible error by throwing out all of Clay's testimony.

"If you have a different line of inquiry," the judge told me, "you can continue. Otherwise, Professor Clay is finished testifying."

I thought about it for a moment before responding. "I have nothing further for this witness." That wasn't really true, but I reasoned that it was my best move at this point. Harvey frantically scribbled something on the legal pad in front of him, then pushed it in my direction. He had written a single word, "what," followed by more exclamation points and question marks than I could count. I leaned toward him and whispered, "tactics."

"Very well, then," the judge said. "We'll take a ten-minute recess, after which we'll bring the jury in, I'll announce my ruling on Professor Clay's testimony, and Mr. O'Brian will call his next witness."

I got up to protest, but Newton beat me to it. "Judge, I'd like an opportunity to cross-examine this witness before Mr. O'Brian calls his next witness."

"Oh, no," I said. "Cross-examination is limited to matters raised on direct examination. If the court strikes the witness' entire testimony, it's as though he never testified, meaning there's nobody for Mr. Newton to cross-examine."

That prompted Newton's female colleague to stand up. "Your Honor," she said, "may I respectfully remind the court that Rule 611 of the *Federal Rules of Evidence* gives the court discretion to permit inquiry into additional matters as if on direct examination."

"Quite true," Abrams replied, "but Rule 611 also states that the court should exercise reasonable control over the presentation of evidence to avoid wasting time. And I can't see where allowing the prosecution to cross-examine a witness whose testimony has been stricken from the record would be a good use of anyone's time. Thursday is Thanksgiving, and I promised the jurors that this trial wouldn't interfere with their holiday plans. I intend to keep that promise. That leaves the rest of today and tomorrow for each side to put on its final witness. We'll take a ten-minute recess, and when we return, Mr. O'Brian will call his next witness."

"I can't do that," I said, rising to my feet. "My final witness will testify about matters referred to in the third court of the indictment. That testimony will be meaningless and without foundation until Mr. Newton finishes presenting whatever evidence he has pertaining to that count. Of course, if his witness is still hiding out at the Grand Canyon to avoid testifying, then there's no need for my witness to testify at all."

That may not have been what Abrams wanted to hear, but she had to concede that I had a point. "Is your final witness in court today?" she asked Newton. When he told her the witness wasn't present, she decided to recess for the day, but not before making it clear that tomorrow morning we were to be "on time and ready to proceed."

Abrams left the bench, and Team Newton packed up and hurried out of the courtroom. I took my time filling my brief-case, waiting until Harvey and I were alone so I could explain why I hadn't continued my direct examination of Professor Clay. But before I could say anything, Harvey asked, "Why in heaven's name did you say you were finished with Clay's testimony? You told me that you and he had spent days preparing for trial, and he only testifies for a couple hours?"

"Calm down," I said. "Professor Clay could have walked into the courtroom and testified the way he did, right off the top of his head, without any preparation at all. The guy's a certifiable genius when it comes to the Constitution. Most of our prep time was spent fashioning responses to all the things Newton could come up with on cross-examination. And believe me, there are a million ways Newton could have shot holes in the professor's testimony. But now Newton never gets that chance. Now, the only thing the jury gets to hear is what we want them to hear."

"Yes, but the judge is going to tell them to ignore all that," Harvey insisted.

"Harvey," I said, "once a jury hears something, they don't ignore it just because the judge tells them to." That ended the conversation and, more importantly, seemed to satisfy Harvey.

We left the courtroom and walked to the elevators, where to my surprise (and delight) Stacey McCain was waiting with Professor Clay.

"We're done for the day," I told the professor. "Harvey will fill you in." Harvey got the hint and, with a wink in my direction, steered the professor to a waiting elevator. The two of them got on, the door closed and they disappeared, leaving me alone with Stacey.

"I didn't see you in the courtroom," I said.

"Oh, I was there," she replied. "The Berkowitz and O'Brian circus is the best show in town. It's filled with lion tamers and clowns, and admission is free. How can you pass up a free day at the circus?" I laughed. Stacey's oddball sense of humor was irresistible. So was Stacey.

"Free for dinner?" I asked.

"Only if you take me someplace that doesn't feature a SWAT team with dessert."

We agreed to meet at a restaurant conveniently located near her apartment. With any luck, I could have dessert at her place.

Stacey headed off to another part of the courthouse to charm information out of one of her sources, and I made my way to the newly opened parking garage across the street.

39

"I don't want to be a part of that."

A stiff wind greeted me as I exited the courthouse and crossed the street to the new parking garage. I rode the elevator to the top level where I had parked my Mustang, now with a tail light customized by Bob Proctor's private police force and "FU" scratched into its front fender, presumably by my ex-gardener, Jorge. I had taken the long way to Newark that morning to avoid another encounter with the Troy Forge cops, causing me to arrive later than usual, at which point the only remaining parking spaces were in the garage's uppermost reaches.

I stepped off the elevator into the half-empty parking level and immediately surveyed my surroundings, looking for signs of trouble. Perhaps it had been the attempted muggings or the run-ins with Proctor's people, or perhaps I was just becoming paranoid, but whatever the reason, I was far more cautious these days. It was no way to live, but what choice did I have?

When I was about halfway down the aisle where I had parked my Mustang, a woman appeared from between two cars. Reynaldo materialized from the shadows behind her. He had a hand on her shoulder and was gently easing her forward, using just enough force to make it clear he was issuing an order, not giving a suggestion. I didn't recognize her at first, but when she stopped directly under one of the light fixtures, I realized she was one of the DOJ attorneys with Newton in court that morning.

"I caught her lurking around your car," Reynaldo said.

"I wasn't lurking," the woman said indignantly. "I was waiting for you."

"It's okay," I told Reynaldo. "I know her."

Reynaldo nodded, turned on his heel, and melted into the shadows. In seconds there was no trace of him. I assumed he was still there, keeping an eye on things, but I couldn't see him. I wished I knew how he managed to become invisible like that. It was neat trick that could come in handy, in the unlikely event I mastered it.

When we were alone, or as alone as we were going to be, I said to the woman standing in front of me, "I know you. You're part of Newton's team."

"No," she corrected me. "Newton and I both work for the Department of Justice, and we're both assigned to prosecute your client, but that's it. The name's Evelyn Kruidlow." Was there dissension in the prosecutorial ranks or was Ms. Kruidlow just not a team player? I got the answer a moment later when she said, "One year out of law school and Newton thinks he knows everything about everything."

"Speaking of knowing things, how did you know which car was mine?" I asked.

"You mentioned driving a Mustang during the sidebar conference this morning when you told the judge about being stopped by local cops." Newton had apparently relayed the details of that conference to his colleagues.

While she was talking, Kruidlow reached into her coat pocket, withdrew an audiocassette and handed it to me. "You asked Agent Rollins how we knew about your client's trip to Hawaii. Here's your answer."

"What's on the tape?" I asked.

"Listen to it and find out."

"Why are you doing this?"

She had an immediate answer. "Well, it's certainly not because I think your client is innocent. Berkowitz is guilty as hell and everyone in the courtroom knows it, including you." I started to protest, but she held up her hand to stop me. "I don't expect you to admit that, but we both know it's true."

She looked into the distance, apparently gathering her thoughts before continuing. "You offended people when you compared the IRS to the KGB and the Gestapo, but you're closer to the truth than you realize. The IRS is one of the most powerful government agencies on the planet, far more powerful than most people realize. It has access to personal information about virtually everyone in the country." That was no doubt true, but it didn't really answer my question. I was about to point that out when she continued. "It starts small with things like illegal phone taps on ordinary people like your client. But who knows where it goes from there. I don't want to be a part of that."

"So you're telling me the IRS tapped my client's phone without a warrant?"

"I'm not telling you anything," Ms. Kruidlow said. "I'm just giving you a cassette tape I thought you might enjoy." She gave me a conspiratorial smile, then turned and walked away. She had taken about half a dozen steps when she stopped and turned back to face me. "You owe me one." Then she continued toward the stairs.

Kruidlow had just disappeared from view when I heard a noise behind me and wheeled around to find Reynaldo standing there with arms crossed. "You were over there a minute ago," I said, pointing to the far wall where I had last seen him. "How did you get behind me?

He laughed. "If I told you, I'd have to shoot you, and then I wouldn't get paid."

40

"Things aren't always what they seem."

Mindful of Judge Abram's command to be on time for Wednesday's court session, I left Stacey's apartment well before dawn, went to my place in Mountain Springs to shower and change, and arrived in Newark with an entire minute to spare. There were at least a dozen marshals on hand to prevent a repeat of yesterday's chaos, but they weren't needed. The summer soldiers and sunshine patriots of Harvey' unofficial anti-tax army had apparently found a better way to spend the day before Thanksgiving, leaving the public gallery virtually empty. A single individual occupied the back row, someone I would never expect to voluntarily appear in a courtroom: Eddie the Skunk.

Newton was seated in his usual place, with Kruidlow, my parking garage informant, on his left. A distinguished man with graying hair, who I judged to be in his late fifties, sat to Newton's right. It was a different attorney than the one who had occupied that chair yesterday. This guy had been in the courtroom on and off throughout the trial, but had never said anything. I got the impression he was there to observe, not to actively participate.

The rest of Team Newton was either hovering around the counsel table or sitting in the first row of the public gallery.

Harvey was seated at our counsel table, nervously drumming his fingers on its polished surface. The stress of the trial was clearly getting to him, so I gave him my standard pep talk, pointing out that jury trials were as much about charming the jurors as they were about laws and facts, and that the jurors seemed pretty disenchanted with Lionel Newton. Before I could tell him about the cassette tape I had gotten during my parking garage rendezvous the previous afternoon, Judge Abrams entered the courtroom, directed a marshal to bring the jury in, and gaveled the proceedings to order.

She began by addressing the jurors. "The testimony you heard from Professor Clay yesterday has been stricken from the record as being irrelevant to this case. You are to accord it no weight when arriving at your determination of the defendant's guilt or innocence. As far as you're concerned, that testimony doesn't exist. Am I clear on that?" She surveyed the jurors to ensure they understood her instructions. Team Newton and I did as well in an effort to guess the impact those instructions would have on specific jurors. The electrician and plumber in the back row, who I considered my best bet for getting a hung jury, showed no reaction, but the well-dressed, older, black woman in the front row didn't seem at all pleased by what the judge had said.

Satisfied that the jury had understood her instructions, Abrams told Newton to call his next witness. He called Gino Monti, who strode confidently to the witness stand. He was decked out in a charcoal gray suit, a collared shirt that concealed his almost non-existent neck, a conservative stripped tie, and a pair of black wing tips that looked as though a Marine platoon had spent an entire day spit polishing them. He looked like a respectable businessman, the antithesis of the shady character who had appeared at my office with Eddie the Skunk on Friday.

After Gino had taken the stand and been sworn in, Lionel Newton asked the usual preliminary questions and then said, "I'm showing you a document taken from the defendant's office that's been entered into evidence as prosecution exhibit 244." He handed the document to Gino. "Please tell the jury what that document is."

"It appears to be an insurance claim form," Gino said.

"Relating to a building and its contents," Newton prompted.

"So it seems," Gino answered.

"And does that claim form contain an address of the property in question?"

"Yes."

"And is that address the same one shown here?" Newton asked, pointing to an oversized page of Harvey's tax return displayed on the bulletin board that a member of Team Newton had moved to the center of the courtroom.

Gino looked at the document in his hand and then at the one on the bulletin board before answering. "Yes, it's the same address."

Newton turned to Abrams and said, "Let the record show the witness is referring to the address on a Schedule E of the defendant's tax return that was used to deduct expenses incurred in connection with rental real estate." Abrams nodded, and Newton turned back to the witness stand. "The third count of the indictment alleges that the defendant, Harvey Berkowitz, hired an arsonist to burn down the commercial building at the address you've just identified, and then deducted the fee he paid the arsonist on his tax return. You are the arsonist in question, are you not?"

Having helped Gino prepare the testimony he would deliver in exchange for a reduced sentence, Newton knew exactly what

Gino's answer would be. Or at least he thought he did. But instead of providing the testimony he was supposed to, Gino answered, "Yes and no."

Newton tried unsuccessfully to conceal his surprise. He looked directly at Gino for what seemed an eternity, either sizing up the situation or hoping the staring contest would result in Gino changing his answer.

Gino said nothing, so eventually Newton asked, "What exactly do you mean by that?"

"Yes, I was hired by Mr. Berkowitz to burn down that building. But no, I'm not an arsonist. And until I saw that," he continued, pointing to the document on the bulletin board, "I had no idea whether or not he deducted my fee on his tax return. My clients' tax returns are their business, not mine."

Newton turned to look at his team. Boutwell, the lead investigator on the case, gave the universal shoulder shrug that means, *I have no idea what's going on.*

"Mr. Monti," Newton pressed, "isn't it true that you're known in some circles as Gino the Torch?"

"Some people call me that," Gino replied.

"And isn't it true that you're an arsonist?"

"Absolutely not," Gino answered. "I'm a pyro-demolition specialist."

Newton had apparently never heard the term before. How could he? To the best of my knowledge, it didn't exist until I made it up the afternoon Gino and Eddie came to my office seeking a second opinion about Gino's plea bargain.

Gino took advantage of the ensuring silence to deliver the explanation I had helped him prepare. "I specialize in using fire to demolish buildings in situations where conventional techniques would take too much time or cost too much money." On its face, it sounded plausible, but it was a complete lie. Newton knew it, and he set about attempting to destroy his turncoat witness. He was forceful and relentless, causing me to object several times on the grounds that he was harassing the witness. Each time, I concluded my objection with "and it's his own witness, Your Honor" to suggest to the jury that the government's case was so weak, even their own witness didn't support it.

About twenty minutes into his examination of Gino, Newton posed the question that Eddie the Skunk had predicted he'd ask. "Other than Harvey Berkowitz, who else hired you to burn down a building?"

During our meeting at my office, Eddie had said his cousin would have an appropriate answer for that question. When I asked what he meant by that, Eddie had said, "This is one of those things you're better off not knowing."

Based on that conversation, I assumed Gino would name some obscure company owned by one of Eddie's untraceable associates. But he surprised me by saying, "My client list is a trade secret. If I answer the question, my competitors will know who I work for." This wasn't a particularly good answer, but it wasn't half bad for something that Gino had apparently made up on the spot.

Newton asked the judge to instruct Gino to answer the question, and Abrams thought for a few seconds before ruling. "I'm not sure a client list is a trade secret. The witness will answer the question."

But Gino wasn't giving in, at least not yet. "My contract with clients has a confidentiality clause. If I answer that question, my clients could sue me for breach of contract."

Gino's argument probably seemed reasonable to the jury, making it difficult for Abrams to force him to answer Newton's question without appearing to favor the prosecution or expose the witness to litigation. So the prosecutor-turned-judge helped the government out in a way that wouldn't be too obvious. "I'll allow the question," she said, "but I'm going to limit the scope of inquiry. Mr. Monti, I'm only going to require you to name one client, other than Mr. Berkowitz, for whom you did a pyro-demolition project. You can select any client you'd like, but I suggest you choose one with whom you have a long-standing relationship, and who would be unlikely to sue you." Abrams was playing to the jury by being so seemingly accommodating, but she was really providing Gino with the rope with which she assumed he would hang himself.

Gino appeared to run through a client list in his head before answering. "I demolished a warehouse in Jersey City." In response to Newton's questions, Gino provided details about the supposed warehouse demolition job. After he mentioned the name of the client and the address of the warehouse, a member of Team Newton scurried out of the courtroom, apparently to check his story and provide Lionel Newton with the ammunition needed to destroy Gino on re-direct. That never happened. The antiquated warehouse in question, which I later discovered was owned by someone who owed a favor to Eddie the Skunk, had indeed recently been destroyed by fire. Whether or not Gino had a hand in its supposed demolition was another matter.

Newton spent another half hour attempting to discredit Gino. I made numerous objections, each time reminding the jury that Lionel Newton was attempting to discredit his own witness. Newton's sole victory was getting Gino to admit that he had disconnected the video surveillance system before burning down Harvey's building, but had overlooked one camera, which recorded the entire event.

His victory was short lived.

I began my cross-examination by asking Gino why he had disconnected the video system, and he delivered the answer I had suggested in my office. "Trade secrets." He went on to explain, "I can demolish a building faster than any other pyro-demolition specialist on the East Coast because of the techniques I use. I disconnected the cameras because I didn't want a video record of my techniques that might wind up in the hands of a competitor." If the Gino who had appeared unannounced at my office had said that, the jury would have been howling with laughter. But coming from the mouth of the very polished, very professional-looking Gino Monti sitting on the witness stand, it sounded entirely plausible.

"The prosecution has made much of the fact that you demolished my client's building at three o'clock in the morning," I continued. "Mr. Newton contends that you choose that early hour so you wouldn't be seen."

It wasn't actually a question, but it gave Gino the opportunity to tell the jury, "I always do this type of demolition around three in the morning because studies show that's when almost everyone is home in bed. My goal is to bring down a building without anyone getting hurt. You do this kind of work during the day and it's just a matter of time before someone gets injured, or worse. Even if you close off an area, there's always that one person who ignores the signs and takes a shortcut across a parking lot and ends up where he shouldn't be." Gino's testimony was more polished than I expected. He must have rehearsed it over and over during his trip to the Grand Canyon or, more likely, his favorite Atlantic City casino. It was so good, in fact, that I almost believed it myself.

"Have you ever been convicted of arson?" I asked next.

"Absolutely not," Gino said, right on cue. "I've never been convicted of arson. I've never been indicted for arson. I've never even been accused of arson." All those statements were true. Of course, half a dozen police departments in northern New Jersey suspected him of being an arsonist, but had never been able to catch him in the act, until the incident at Harvey's strip mall in Denville. But if he had done it at Harvey's request, then it wasn't arson, unless it was part of a scheme to defraud an insurance company, as suggested by the prosecution's exhibit 244, the claim form seized from Harvey's office.

But things aren't always what they seem, as Lionel Newton was about to learn the hard way.

41

"You got your ways, I got mine."

I concluded my cross-examination of Gino, and Newton declined the opportunity for re-direct. Apparently, his colleagues, who had returned to the courtroom, hadn't been able to dig up anything that would help the government's case. Judge Abrams called an early, shortened, lunch recess, announcing that we would conclude the day's proceedings earlier than usual to avoid interfering with jurors' Thanksgiving travel plans.

Harvey and I joined the exodus out of the courtroom and took an elevator to the ground floor. We were standing in line at the lunch counter when Mr. Goatee, aka Tony, appeared out of the crowd. "Mr. Rizzo would like a word with you," he said.

I looked around for Eddie the Skunk, but didn't see him. Come to think of it, I hadn't seen him as we'd left the courtroom.

"Outside," Tony said, motioning with his head toward the four massive glass doors at the building's main entrance.

"Get me a tuna on rye, would you," I said to Harvey, handing him a twenty dollar bill. "I'll be back in a few minutes," I added, making a mental note to tack twenty-five dollars onto the list of disbursements that would appear on Harvey's final bill.

I followed Tony outside and found Eddie leaning against the wall to my left, well away from the stream of people coming and going.

"You don't gotta worry about that Reynaldo guy you asked me about the other day," Eddie said as I approached. "He's got your back."

"You know Reynaldo Renoir?" I asked.

"Renoir," Eddie said, surprising me by adding, "like the painter?" You have to have the proverbial poker face to be an effective litigator, but apparently I was off my game because Eddie said, "You're surprised because I know about art? Maybe I didn't go to law school, but it's not like I don't know nothing."

I was afraid that I might have offended him, but then he laughed and said, "Never met the guy. But after I sent Tony to Jersey City, I put the word out to people who owe me a favor, and one of them had Reynaldo keep an eye on things. Let's face it, if your old lady has someone whack you, what am I gonna do when I need a lawyer? Hire Gambardelli? If Gino had listened to that schmuck, he woulda ended up doing a year. But Gino done what you told him, and now he's off to see the Grand Canyon. For real this time."

Eddie turned and walked away, but stopped after a few steps. "By the way, how did you find out Reynaldo's last name?"

I hesitated, not sure how much I wanted to reveal. Sensing my reluctance, Eddie said, "Never mind, it don't matter. You got your ways, I got mine." Then he shoved his hands into the pockets of his navy pea jacket, leaned into the stiff breeze that had picked up during the morning, and vanished into the mid-day crowd.

42

"This is a question for the jury."

When I finished my conversation with Eddie, I went back inside the courthouse, expecting to find Harvey hovering near the lunch counter with my tuna on rye, but he was nowhere to be seen. Having skipped breakfast, I was hungry and looking forward to the sandwich I had asked him to get me. I went searching and finally found him in one of the phone booths. In response to my tapping, he opened the door wide enough to hand me my sandwich before going back to his conversation, something to do with an order for his furniture store.

I ate while Harvey talked. When I was finished, I walked over to the lunch counter and got a cup of coffee. I stood in the lobby sipping my coffee, watching the comings and goings of the attorneys, litigants, and members of the public. It was a smaller crowd than usual, being the last day before a four-day holiday weekend. I had drained half the cup when I saw Harvey heading in my direction. He was pointing to his watch and motioning with his head toward the elevators, signaling that it was time to head back upstairs for the afternoon session.

I fell into step beside him as we made our way through the lobby, and when no one was within earshot, I leaned toward him and said, "I had an interesting meeting after I left you yesterday.

I now know why Newton didn't call your buddy, Aaron Gertz, as a witness."

"I told you Aaron wouldn't testify," Harvey said. "My friends are loyal to me."

"That might well be, but it's not why Aaron didn't testify."

"Okay, why?"

Before I could answer, we were overtaken by a group of people heading toward the elevators. "I'll explain later. Too many ears here."

When we got back to the courtroom, Newton, Kruidlow, and the third attorney were already seated at the prosecution's counsel table, but the rest of Team Newton was gone, apparently given leave to begin their holiday weekend. Newton and the older attorney were having an animated, hushed conversation that didn't appear to be all that friendly. Kruidlow was swiveled around in her seat, looking toward the back of the courtroom, presumably waiting for Harvey and me to return, or perhaps trying not to get involved in the discussion her colleagues were having.

Judge Abrams must have left word to let her know as soon as everyone was back because she appeared on the bench the second Harvey and I sat down. The jurors filed back into the courtroom, and the session began with Newton resting the government's case, not having called Aaron Gertz to testify. Then I called my final witness, Steve Decker, Harvey's insurance agent.

Wearing his trademark red suspenders, Steve calmly walked to the witness stand, was sworn in, and took a seat. He seemed remarkably relaxed, an odd condition for a man who I was reasonably certain was about to commit perjury. I had gone over his testimony several times before trial, and each time I became more convinced that the jury wouldn't believe a word of it. Steve, however, stuck to his version of events, adamantly insisting that however improbable his story might seem, it was, in fact, the truth. Every time I questioned his story, his response was always the same: "The IRS jumped to conclusions."

I began by showing him the prosecution's exhibit 244. Like Gino Monti, Steve testified that the document was an insurance claim form, and that the address shown matched the address of Harvey's property that Gino had burned down. Steve also identified the signature at the end of the form as Harvey's. He was remarkably nonchalant as he answered my questions.

"When did you first see this document?" I asked.

"I don't remember the exact date," he said. "Harvey, that is, Mr. Berkowitz, and I filled that out a couple weeks before he had the building demolished."

Steve's answer caused some of the jurors to stir in their seat. So I asked the question they were obviously thinking. "How could you and he fill out a form to claim a loss for a building that was still standing at the time?"

"It's a claim form," Steve answered, "but we didn't fill it out so Harvey could file an insurance claim." That answer caused several jurors to lean forward.

"Why did you fill it out?"

"Mr. Berkowitz was planning to demolish that old strip mall and replace it with a new, bigger building. We were in his office one day, putting together numbers to get insurance quotes for the new building. I didn't have any application forms with me, so we used a claim form I had in my briefcase to collect the necessary information, intending to use it to fill out the application forms later."

"And did you ever complete and submit those application forms?" I asked.

"No."

"Why not?"

"Harvey told me not to. He said financing for the project fell through."

"Objection," Newton said. "Hearsay."

"It's not hearsay, Your Honor," I said to Abrams, "because the statement isn't being offered for its truth, but just to explain the witness' action, or in this case, inaction."

She thought about that for a moment and finally said, "I'll allow it."

Then I asked the question that I knew I had to ask or risk having Newton ask it on cross-examination. "If you were using a claim form just to collect information, why did Mr. Berkowitz sign it?"

I held my breath, waiting to see if Steve could answer the question with a straight face. He did better than I expected. "When we finished filling out the form, I told Harvey I'd have to come back to get his signature on the actual application forms, but he misunderstood me and thought I meant that I wanted him to sign the claim form."

Newton objected. "There's no way the witness could know what the defendant was thinking."

"I'll rephrase the question," I said, before Abrams could rule on the objection. "After you told Mr. Berkowitz that he'd have to sign the applications for a new policy, what did he do?"

"He signed the claim form we used to collect the information for the new policy."

I was about to ask the next question when Steve added, "I guess he misunderstood what I said."

Newton was halfway out of his seat to object when the older attorney grabbed his arm and pulled him back down, apparently realizing there was no point in fighting a battle that was already over.

I had one more topic to cover with the witness, but decided to leave it for Newton to stumble over on cross-examination.

And he did with his very first question. "Do you have even a shred of proof to back up your preposterous story?" the newbie government attorney asked indignantly.

"Yeah," Steve said defiantly. "The form itself, which the IRS apparently never took the time to look at very closely."

The answer, and the manner in which it was delivered, caught Newton by surprise. Decker was turning out to be a better witness than I had anticipated. "If you guys had looked at the form more closely instead of jumping to conclusions," he continued, "you would have realized the square footage shown is much greater than the square footage of the building that was demolished. And the personal property listed couldn't have physically fit inside the old building. The IRS saw what it wanted to see instead of what was actually there. This wasn't a claim for the loss of the old building, it was an outline of coverage needed for the new, bigger building." Steve's delivery was perfect. He made what I considered a completely implausible story sound downright believable.

Knowing Harvey, he and his pal had padded that claim to soak the insurance company for more money, but Decker's testimony made it possible for the jury to think the IRS had fouled up. Combined with Gino's testimony, which did more harm than good for the government's case, it might be enough to convince one or two jurors. And one or two was all I needed.

Before Newton had a chance to ask another question, I got to my feet and said, "Your Honor, in light of this evidence, the defense moves for a dismissal of the third count of the indictment. The prosecution has failed to make a prima facie case." I didn't actually expect Abrams to grant my motion, but I wanted the jury to hear me make it.

Unfortunately, that's all they heard because instead of responding to my motion, Abrams looked at her watch, then turned to the jurors and said, "Ladies and gentlemen of the jury, at the outset of this trial I promised that I wouldn't let it interfere with your holiday plans. That's a promise I intend to keep. You're dismissed until next week. Have a happy Thanksgiving."

I started to speak, but Abrams held up her hand to stop me. She waited until the last juror had left the courtroom before asking, "Mr. O'Brian, what's the basis for your motion?"

"The third count of the indictment alleges that my client filed a fraudulent tax return by taking an impermissible deduction for the cost of demolishing a building he owned. The government's theory seems to be that the deduction was impermissible because it represents payment for a criminal act rather than a legitimate business expense. But it's not a crime to pay someone to demolish your building, whether by fire or a wrecking ball, unless it's done to defraud an insurance company. The government's own witness testified that he demolished the building to clear the land for a new structure, not to enable my client to defraud an insurance company. And the mere existence of an insurance claim form, the government's exhibit 244, doesn't prove that my client committed fraud. The government has never produced any evidence to show that my client submitted a claim to his insurance carrier. In fact, the only witness who had firsthand information about that document has just testified that not only was there never any intention to make an insurance claim, but that the document was intended to secure insurance on a new building, thus supporting the testimony of Mr. Monti."

Newton started to stand up to respond, but the older attorney sitting next to him rose instead. He had never said a word before this, but it now appeared that he was taking charge. "Darren Liebenthal, Your Honor, supervising attorney on this case."

"Mr. Liebenthal," the judge said, acknowledging him and giving him permission to proceed.

"Your Honor, the IRS seized that claim form before the defendant could submit it to the insurance company. The existence of the document is proof of the defendant's intention to commit a crime, rendering the amount in question an impermissible deduction under our tax laws. The situation is analogous to one in which the authorities arrest a man with the floor plans of a shopping mall and a bomb before he has a chance to detonate it."

Abrams looked to me for a response. "There's a big difference between a bomb and an insurance claim form," I pointed out. "The prosecution has failed to provide any proof at all that my client intended to submit that claim form to his insurance company. The only evidence we have, Mr. Decker's testimony, shows just the opposite. Mr. Liebenthal's conjecture isn't evidence. My client has a right to be tried based on evidence, not conjecture." It was a terribly disingenuous statement since my trial strategy was based on getting one or two jurors to ignore the evidence, but I wanted a statement on the record that I could use for an appeal if one became necessary.

Liebenthal wasn't about to give up. "The issue isn't my conjecture, to use Mr. O'Brian's colorful language, it's the credibility of the witness. The jury could well decide that Mr. Decker's wildly improbable version of events is nothing more than a fanciful story cooked up by the defense. This is a question for the jury. I would respectfully request that Mr. O'Brian's motion be denied."

Abrams looked at her watch again. Perhaps she had travel plans of her own. "I've heard enough," she said. "I'll take his under advisement and render a decision on Monday. We're in recess until then."

Liebenthal seemed disappointed by the judge's decision, but he didn't say anything. He apparently considered Steve Decker's story as improbable as I had, and assumed the judge would deny my motion on the spot.

Harvey and I packed up and headed for the exit, but Newton and his colleagues remained where they were, huddled together in whispered conversation. I couldn't hear much, but I did manage to overhear Liebenthal say "a bird in the hand," which I interpreted to mean a plea bargain discussion would be our first order of business on Monday morning.

I was wrong.

43

"Everyone hates the IRS."

The few members of the public who had attended the day's court session had already descended to the ground floor, leaving Harvey and me alone in the elevator lobby.

"I had an interesting meeting yesterday afternoon in the parking garage," I began. "Now I know why your buddy Gertz wasn't called as a witness for the prosecution."

"He wouldn't have testified against me," Harvey said. "I'm loyal to my friends, and my friends are loyal to me."

"A bunch of contractors you trusted showed up to testify against you," I reminded him.

"That's different. They're acquaintances, not friends."

I had just started to tell him about my meeting with Ms. Kruidlow when Liebenthal came out of the courtroom. "Oh good, you're still here," he said. "Come back in and let's see if we can wrap this up so we can enjoy the holiday weekend."

I wasn't sure the government would make a proposal that would allow Harvey to enjoy the weekend, but we had nothing to lose by listening. So Harvey and I followed Liebenthal back into the courtroom, which was now completely empty except for Newton and Kruidlow, who were still seated at the prosecution's counsel table. Liebenthal took the empty seat to Newton's right, while Harvey and I pulled over chairs and sat across from the three DOJ attorneys.

Liebenthal extended an outstretched palm in my direction, signaling that I had the floor, but I wasn't about to fall for that negotiating trick. "You're the one who wanted to meet. We're perfectly happy to take our chances with the jury."

"You'd be doing your client a disservice," Liebenthal said. "We have a lot of evidence against Mr. Berkowitz."

"A good deal of which is inadmissible."

"What's that supposed to mean?"

"Fruit of the poisonous tree," I responded, using a phrase from a 1920 Supreme Court decision that means evidence obtained by illegal means can't be used in court.

Newton jumped into the conversation. "What are you talking about?" he demanded, apparently taking my statement as an accusation aimed at him personally.

I reached into my briefcase, withdrew a cassette player, and placed it on the table in front of me. To her credit, Kruidlow's only reaction was a slightly raised eyebrow. The movement was so minor that I doubt anyone but me saw it, and I would have missed it if I hadn't been looking for it.

"What's that?" Newton asked.

"Looks like a cassette player," I said.

"We know it's a cassette player," Liebenthal said. "What's it for?"

"To play the cassette tape that's in it."

"You're trying my patience, Mr. O'Brian," Liebenthal said. "What's on the tape?"

"Oh, come on," I replied. "You know damn well what's on the tape." I could have just played the tape, but dragging things out raised the tension in the room, and that worked in my favor.

"I have no idea what's on the tape," Liebenthal said.

"Okay, I'll give you a hint. It's a recording of a phone conversation."

Liebenthal sighed, leaned back in his chair, and folded his arms across his chest. It's a posture that makes a person look relaxed, but psychologists who study body language contend that crossed arms are a defensive gesture. I tend to discount most of the psychobabble spouted by shrinks, but they may have gotten the crossed arms thing right. Liebenthal had to have known what was on the tape. Of course, if he didn't, it meant he had a bigger problem than the one I was about to expose.

"Okay," I said, "I'll give you another hint. It's a telephone conversation between my client and another person."

Nobody on the other side of the table spoke.

"Fine, one last clue. It's a phone conversation between my client and another person that the IRS recorded using a phone tap obtained without getting a warrant." Instead of waiting for a response, I pushed the "play" button on the cassette player and everyone at the table heard Harvey arranging his family's trip to Hawaii with Aaron Gertz, his college buddy and travel agent.

"Where did you get that?" Liebenthal demanded.

I turned off the cassette player, sat back, slung my arms over the back of the chair and smiled. "Wouldn't you like to know."

Liebenthal looked at his colleagues then back to me with a mixture of annoyance and confusion. Perhaps he wasn't expecting me to know about the tape, much less have a copy of it. Or perhaps he didn't know about the tape and was hearing it for the first time. He was much harder to read than Newton.

"And wouldn't you like to know what else I know that you don't realize I know," I added, seemingly as an afterthought. I didn't actually have any additional information, but nobody in the room knew that.

Liebenthal stood up, put both hands on the table and leaned forward. "I want to know where you got that recording." He said it slowly, articulating each word.

I had an ethical duty to Harvey to tell the truth, thereby calling into question all of the evidence the government used to prove the second count of the indictment. But I also had a moral obligation to Kruidlow, who had jeopardized her career, and perhaps even her freedom, by giving me the tape. As she pointed out in the parking garage the previous day, I owed her one.

I decided the best way to deal with my ethical conundrum was to tell a lie. "I got the recording from my client's answering machine. He routinely records conversations when he makes travel arrangements in case there's a problem later."

Out of the corner of my eye I saw Kruidlow exhale and her whole body relax. To his credit, Harvey didn't react at all.

I stood up, put both hands of the table and leaned forward until I was nose to nose with Liebenthal. "Of course, your reaction tells me that in addition to my client's recording, the IRS has one just like it. And that one was obtained illegally."

Liebenthal sat down and smiled his best crocodile smile. "Even if what you say is true, and I'm not saying it is, that doesn't mean the evidence would be excluded."

"Perhaps," I agreed. "But then again, perhaps not. I guess we'll have to wait for an appellate court to make the call."

"Even without that evidence, we have enough to win this case," Newton said.

"Let me explain something they don't teach you in law school," I replied as I sat back down and casually slung my arm across the back of the chair. "It's the jury that determines the outcome of a trial, not the evidence, not the law, not the facts. Not even the judge. And you clearly don't have the jury on your side, Lionel." I pointed to the now empty jury box. "Everyone hates the IRS, including four of those jurors who can hardly wait to stick it to the tax man." I had no idea if there was a single juror we could rely on to do that, much less four, but Team Newton didn't know either.

"Nobody knows for certain how this trial is going to play out, which is why we're all here instead of on our way home," Liebenthal said. "So let's just see if we can come up with a resolution to the case that everyone can live with." He wrote something on the legal pad in front of him and slid it across the table in my direction.

I picked up the pad and saw that it contained two numbers. The one on top was a six-digit number with a dollar sign in front of it. The one on the bottom was a two-digit number with "months" after it. I showed the pad to Harvey who, to his credit, displayed no reaction. I tore off that page and on a clean sheet wrote two numbers of my own, each of which was preceded by a dollar sign. Then I slide the pad back across the table to Liebenthal.

"I don't understand what this means," he said, looking at what I had written before passing the pad to Newton, who in turn passed it to Kruidlow.

"The top number," I explained, "is the most the IRS could reasonably expect to get from my client. The bottom number is what Uncle Sam owes my client for tapping his phone illegally, harassing his employees, interfering with his business, stalking his family in Hawaii, and taking naked photos of his teenage daughter. If my calculations are correct, the government owes Mr. Berkowitz fifty thousand dollars."

Newton shot to his feet. "Your client's a tax cheat and you want the government to pay him? This is the sort of nonsense you've pulled right from the first day of trial."

I shrugged my shoulders and got up. Harvey followed my lead. "Suit yourself," I said. "Have a nice Thanksgiving. See you in court next week." I know from years of experience that you can't win a negotiation if you're not willing to walk away.

I had taken only two steps when Kruidlow said, "Hold on. Walking out won't accomplish anything. Let's see if we can make this work."

Harvey and I sat down, and Liebenthal went through the legal pad routine again. This time there were two different numbers, each smaller than the ones he had originally written. I put a line through the number with a dollar sign in front of it, and replaced it with a figure half the original amount. I put a big "X" through the second number with "months" written after it, and slid the pad back to Liebenthal.

"No can do," he said. "Your client has to do some time."

"Then we have nothing to discuss," I said, once again getting up from my seat. "The best I can do is to have my client agree not to sue the government for the things your people did to him and his family."

"Come on, O'Brian," Liebenthal said. "Your client doesn't have a case, you know that.

"I wouldn't be too sure of that. I can see the headlines now: 'IRS Peeping Tom sued over porno pics' and 'IRS caught in illegal wiretap.' I'll have to give my friend at the *Ledger* a call. Her articles seem to resonate with readers."

After motioning to his colleagues to lean toward him, Liebenthal held the legal pad up in front of them. It wasn't exactly the Cone of Silence, but it afforded them a modicum of privacy. I could hear them whispering to each other, but could only make out the occasional word. The impromptu conference ended, and Liebenthal scribbled something on the legal pad, which once again made its way across the table. This time there was a more reasonable number with a dollar sign in front of it. It was still a hefty chunk of change, but an amount that Harvey could manage with little difficulty. Underneath that figure, Liebenthal had written "one month in minimum security."

"I need the one month to make this work," Liebenthal said. "And your client can serve it in a place that's more like a country club than a prison. No violent offenders, close enough that his family can visit. This place even allows conjugal visits."

Mission accomplished. Or so I thought.

But then Harvey opened his mouth and sunk the deal.

44

"There's always one more thing with you guys."

"I'd rather take my chances with the jury than agree to serve a day in prison," Harvey said, getting up from his seat.

"O'Brian, talk to your client," Kruidlow said. "This deal is a gift."

"Easy for you to say," Harvey shot back. "You'll be spending the holidays with your family. I'll be spending them in prison." He picked up his coat and headed for the door. "See you next week."

"Wait a minute." This time it was Liebenthal who stopped Harvey's exit. "Let's see just how much you think a month of your time is worth." He picked up the legal pad with his most recent offer and made some changes before sliding it across the table to me. He had upped the dollar amount by ten grand, scratched out the reference to one month in Club Fed and replaced it with "Payment in full within ten days."

I held the pad up so Harvey could see it.

"That I can live with," he said, and sat back down.

"Oh, one more thing," Liebenthal said. "This deal is contingent on your client waiving any claims he thinks he has against the government."

"There's always one more thing with you guys." I looked at Harvey and he nodded. "Okay, but I have one more thing of my own. We put this on the record now so my client can go home and enjoy Thanksgiving." *And so somebody higher up the DOJ food chain doesn't decide to renege on the deal.*

"Agreed," Liebenthal said. Then to Newton he said, "Go tell the judge we've resolved the case and we'd like to put it on the record."

Newton scampered off and returned a few minutes later, followed by Judge Abrams and the court stenographer. Abrams took the bench, and Harvey and I returned to the defense counsel table.

"Mr. Liebenthal," she began, "I understand that there's a plea bargain in this matter. Is that correct?"

"Yes, Your Honor," Liebenthal said.

"Let's hear it."

Before Liebenthal had a chance to respond, I stood up and began to spell out the terms of our plea agreement. I concluded with, "Mr. Berkowitz agrees to waive his right to sue the federal government or any agency thereof for any loss, claim, or demand of any kind arising out of this case, including, but not limited to any claims relating to actions taken by the Internal Revenue Service leading up to his indictment."

My language apparently sounded fine to Liebenthal, Newton, and Kruidlow, because when Abrams asked if it was acceptable to the prosecution, Liebenthal said it was. I think he may feel differently when he discovers that the seemingly ironclad, all-inclusive language I used might not prevent Harvey's daughter, Leah, from suing Uncle Sam.

"Very well," Judge Abrams said, "the court accepts the proposed plea agreement. Court is adjourned." Then, looking at me, she said, "Mr. O'Brian, please approach."

I walked up to the bench, and Judge Abrams leaned forward until we were eye to eye. "Don't ever appear in my courtroom again," she said, barely above a whisper.

I would have been happy to accommodate her, but my gut told me she and I were destined to cross paths in the future. So I simply said, "Have a nice Thanksgiving, judge."

45

"There was one detail I clearly saw, but didn't mention."

As I pulled into my quiet side street in Mountain Springs I silently counted my blessings, which seemed an appropriate thing to do the day before Thanksgiving. I had just won an important case, making Harvey Berkowitz a happy man in the process. I had gotten all the way home, driving right through the heart of Troy Forge instead of taking the circuitous route, without once encountering Bob Proctor's palace guard. And, best of all, I would be spending the holiday with a cute little redhead who hated modern art as much as I did, had a sense of humor as quirky as my own, and who thought my graying hair made me look distinguished.

The X-rated mental pictures I had been drawing of how Stacey and I would spend our holiday together vanished as I pulled into my driveway and saw the red Miata in the circle in front of the house. "Your timing is impeccable, Aimee," I muttered as I parked my Mustang behind my wife's car and went in through the front door.

The chair that had been next to the telephone table that morning was now in the middle of the entry hall, the spot where

Buddy always sat to await my return at the end of the day. It was a cruel reminder that my feline friend would be spending the night in the cold ground behind the house instead of curled up on my lap by the fireplace.

I took off my topcoat and draped it over the chair, then headed upstairs toward the familiar hum of Aimee's electric typewriter. There were no typing sounds, meaning she was no doubt gazing out the window overlooking the back yard, seeking inspiration for whatever she was writing, most likely something for her precious Art Alliance.

Her office door squeaked as I opened it. "So you're back" was all I said before freezing in the doorway.

Aimee wasn't sitting by her typewriter, gazing out the window. She was lying on her back just inside the door, her sightless eyes staring at the ceiling, the pool of blood around her head an unmistakable sign that she was dead.

Had the person Aimee hired to kill me, if indeed such a person existed, killed her by mistake or because of a dispute over their arrangement? Had Bob Proctor stepped up his war of intimidation? Or was this unconnected to any of the crazy things that had complicated my life the last few weeks?

Thinking perhaps Aimee had been killed after returning home and surprising a burglar, I looked around the room for signs of a robbery. But with the exception of Aimee's body lying on the floor and the piece of paper sticking out of her humming typewriter, the room looked the same as it had the last time I saw it.

I crossed the room, carefully avoiding the pool of blood, and removed what she had been typing before she died. It was the beginning of a note to me:

Dear Brendan,

I'm leaving this where I know you'll see it when you come home. After reading it, if you can find it in your heart to forgive me, I'm upstairs in my office. I know Buddy meant a lot to you, and I'm sorry about what happened. But you have to believe me that I never thought Jorge would take me seriously when I said that

Aimee had been killed before she could finish, but what she had written confirmed Jorge's role in Buddy's death, although I now realized I had been wrong about his motivation.

But who had killed Aimee?

That question was answered a moment later when motion outside the window caught my eye. A man was running through the wooded lot behind the house, leaving a trail of footprints in the snow. He crossed the clearing with the dogwood tree where Buddy was buried, picked his way through the underbrush and got into the passenger's seat of a car parked on the shoulder of Pin Oak Lane, the road on the far side of the wooded lot. As the vehicle sped away, I realized that I was an unwitting actor in a comedy of errors that had now been transformed into tragedy by one misunderstanding piled on top of another.

I hit the typewriter's power switch with my elbow before retracing my steps out of the room, once again being careful not to step in the pool of blood. After using the phone in the upstairs hallway to call the Mountain Springs police department, I tore Aimee's note into pieces and flushed them down the toilet in the master bathroom. Finding Aimee like that had been a shock, but

I had enough presence of mind to realize that her note could be interpreted to provide me with a motive for her death.

Then I walked downstairs, returned the chair to its proper place by the table in the entry foyer, and sat on the bottom step of the staircase to await the police. I desperately wanted to call Stacey, but didn't. In the course of their investigation, the police would no doubt pull a record of calls made to and from the house. A phone call to a single woman ten years my junior wouldn't look good. And besides, what would I say to her? *I came home and discovered my wife dead on the floor; are we still on for tomorrow?*

The first police car pulled into the driveway five minutes later. An ambulance, two additional police cruisers, and an unmarked car, all with flashing lights, followed in rapid succession. I met the emergency entourage at the front door. "Upstairs," I said. "The room at the end of the hallway." A uniformed cop and a paramedic sprinted up the staircase.

A second cop pointed to the living room. "Why don't we sit down?" It was phrased as a suggestion, but I knew it wasn't. I went into the living room and sat on the chair across from the sofa, the same place I had sat during my meeting with Reynaldo on Sunday. The cop remained standing.

Two detectives, named Andrews and Selkirk, joined us and took up positions on the sofa across from me. I spent the next hour relating a carefully crafted version of events that had occurred during the last couple weeks. I started by telling them about Mr. Goatee and Reynaldo following me. I knew they had nothing to do with Aimee's death and didn't want to involve them in the ensuing investigation, in the unlikely event the cops could locate them. But because they had been mentioned in Stacey's newspaper article, I reasoned that not talking about them would seem suspicious. Of course, I didn't say I knew who they worked for or why they were shadowing me.

Next, I told them about the attempted mugging in Morristown, describing my assailants only as "a big black guy and a guy about my size with a mustache." Selkirk asked how the incident ended, and I told them my would-be muggers ran when a car approached us. I moved on to the incident in Newark, mentioning that a federal judge was with me at the time, and repeating what her Washington sources had discovered about Reynaldo. They would get that information from Abrams when they interviewed her, as they surely would, so there was no point in withholding it.

My story moved on to the harassment that had occurred after our firm filed the von Beverwicjk lawsuit against Troy Forge. To my surprise, the uniformed cop who had remained standing throughout the interview said, "Sounds like something Proctor's private police force would do." Andrews asked what he meant by that, and the uniformed cop told him he had a friend in the Troy Forge department who said it was common knowledge part of the town's police force acted more like a private army than public servants. The two detectives didn't say anything in response to that remark, but Selkirk jotted something down on his pad.

When I got to Jorge, I said that Aimee and I had recently fired him, but I couldn't imagine him killing my wife. "Poison is more his style," I said at one point, causing Andrews to ask what I meant by that. I told him about my sadistic ex-gardener poisoning the wild animals on the property, his mistreatment of the neighbors' pets, and the recent demise of my pet cat. The more I insisted I couldn't imagine Jorge killing Aimee, the more interested Andrews and Selkirk seemed to get. That was fine with me. Even if Jorge weren't accused of killing Aimee, a little scrutiny by the cops would be a good down payment on what he had coming to him.

We finally got around to what I had seen upon my return from court that afternoon. Naturally, I didn't mention the unfinished note I had found in Aimee's typewriter or the chair in the hallway where she had planned to leave it. But I spent a good deal of time telling them about the man I had seen running through the wooded lot behind the house. Andrews asked me if I could describe the vehicle the mystery man had driven away in. I shaded the truth a bit by telling him it looked like a light colored pickup instead of a dark sedan, but added that I couldn't really be sure. "It was getting dark, and I was still rattled from finding my wife's body," I told the detectives, who seemed very understanding.

In response to Selkirk's request for a description of the man, I said he looked taller than me and was wearing what looked like blue jeans, but that I couldn't be certain because of the distance. However, I was positive that he was wearing a dark colored coat, "either blue or black." Because his back was to me, I couldn't describe what he looked like, other than the fact that he had dark hair. "Sorry I can't be more helpful," I said when I had finished with my description, "but he was too far away to really see any detail." That wasn't completely true, of course. There was one detail I clearly saw, but didn't mention: the streak of white hair running down the middle of his head.

Epilogue

The Wednesday after Thanksgiving, Martin von Beverwicjk conveyed the fairgrounds property to his father, whose newly drafted Last Will & Testament would create a testamentary subdivision when he died. It was part of a complicated transaction that Avery cooked up involving several members of the von Beverwicjk clan. In addition to subdividing the property without going before the planning board, the deal gave everyone involved tax benefits that Avery explained to me in excruciating detail. "Very clever," I said when he had finished his explanation, though I had no idea what he was talking about.

Once the elder von Beverwicjk's new Will was safely tucked away in the firm's safe, I called Marty Callahan, the attorney representing Troy Forge in the lawsuit we had filed against the town on Martin's behalf. "I'm about to make you a real hero," I said. "Call Mayor Proctor and tell him you got me to dismiss my client's suit against the town, and withdraw his subdivision application to boot." Marty seemed skeptical, but I promised him I was on the level, which I was. I ended the conversation by reminding Marty that he owed me one.

Bob Proctor's private palace guard did a disappearing act as soon as Martin's lawsuit was dismissed. According to Sean McDermott, the word around town hall was that Proctor was under the impression that his harassment tactics had worked.

The Mountain Springs cops were a different story. They were relentless. They talked to all my neighbors, called in a forensics team from the State Police to examine my home in detail, and left no stone unturned in their attempt to find the person who murdered Aimee. But they never succeeded.

Only I know who killed Aimee. At least I think I do.

In February of 1989, while defending Eddie the Skunk against a charge of vehicular manslaughter, I happened to mention that Jorge had killed Buddy. It was a casual comment in response to something Eddie had said. "The beaner whacked your cat?" was Eddie's reaction. He seemed both surprised and angry. "Fuckin' Carlos should have his ears examined."

Two weeks after that conversation with Eddie, Jorge was killed by a hit and run driver, who was apprehended the following day after the police received an anonymous phone tip. The driver was named Carlos.

I'm sure it was just a coincidence.

Ironically, Joshua von Beverwicjk, who everyone expected to shuffle off this mortal coil in the waning days of 1988, outlived Jorge, who was half a century younger and far healthier the last time I saw him. The patriarch of one of the oldest families in Troy Forge lived to celebrate another Thanksgiving and Christmas, but contracted pneumonia and died in September of 1990.

Avery probated Joshua's Will later that month, prompting Troy Forge to immediately file suit in Superior Court. The town's complaint was a laundry list of allegations, ranging from those that were factually incorrect, such as the existence of wetlands on the property, to several based on some extremely novel interpretations of the law. The town managed to convince the court to issue a restraining order preventing the testamentary subdivision pending the outcome of the case.

We went through the normal discovery process – interrogatories, depositions, pre-trial motions, requests for admissions – all standard procedure, all generating income for the firm and spiraling costs for Martin von Beverwicjk. It took over a year for the case to wind its way through the system and get on the trial calendar.

The day before the trial was scheduled to begin, an attorney from one of the big law firms in Morristown showed up at my office with a signed contract to purchase the fairgrounds property. I had never heard of the buyer, a company called Andalusia Holdings, and neither had Martin. But it was an all-cash deal with a purchase price that would net Martin almost double what he could make developing the property himself. As a sweetener, the contract called for a non-refundable, six-figure deposit and closing of title the following week. And to encourage us to support the deal, the contract also provided for payment of a six percent brokerage commission to our firm.

Martin jumped at the chance to unload what was now a problem property.

Shortly thereafter we discovered Andalusia was a front for an organization that had quietly secured Mayor Proctor's blessings to build a mosque on the property. That revelation triggered a firestorm of controversy, landed Stacey in court, and led to the discovery of the secret that had cost Machias Phelps his life.

The story continues in **A Stranger in My Own Hometown**, the sequel to **Slow Death in the Fast Lane**.

A Note from the Author

The characters in this book are figments of my over-active imagination. Any similarity to actual persons, living or dead, is purely a coincidence. The cases and court rules referred to, however, are quite real (though their application in real life might differ from how they were used in this book).

Ironically, elements of the story that some readers might consider the most improbable are firmly based in reality. For example, the $880,000 study of snail sex and the $386,000 study of rabbit massage mentioned in chapter 27 are, unfortunately, very real examples of ways in which the federal government spends our tax dollars. Likewise, the third count of the indictment against Harvey Berkowitz, charging him with taking a tax deduction for amounts paid to an arsonist, is based on an actual case.

A number of people have read early drafts of this work and provided invaluable feedback. Whatever errors or shortcomings remain in the finished version are a result of my refusal to listen to their sage advice. Ordinarily, I would thank these individuals by name. But given the subject matter of this book, doing so might result in unwarranted scrutiny by the Internal Revenue Service. Accordingly, I hereby thank them publically and sincerely, but anonymously.

J.W. Kerwin
November, 2013

Made in the USA
Coppell, TX
14 November 2020